"This is in...

"The last time I tossed a pass, it was in front of ninety thousand people."

Liz wouldn't have called it intimate, but at least everyone was finally seated, and the flight attendants were closing the door. "Mmm." She gave a thoughtful nod.

"You've never seen me operate in private," he pointed out. "I'm very persuasive."

Liz raised her eyebrows. "What a terrifying prospect! Remind me not to let you get me alone. I wouldn't want to run the risk of getting talked into anything."

"Good game plan. One-on-one, I'm unbeatable." He curled his fingers around the back of her neck and stroked the sensitive skin. "There's one problem, though. It won't work. I have every intention of getting you alone, and when I do, there's no limit to what I plan to talk you into."

Dear Reader:

Romance offers us all so much. It makes us "walk on sunshine." It gives us hope. It takes us out of our own lives, encouraging us to reach out to others. Janet Dailey is fond of saying that romance is a state of mind, that it could happen anywhere. Yet nowhere does romance seem to be as good as when it happens *here*.

Starting in February 1986, Silhouette Special Edition is featuring the AMERICAN TRIBUTE—a tribute to America, where romance has never been so wonderful. For six consecutive months, one out of every six Special Editions will be an episode in the AMERICAN TRIBUTE, a portrait of the lives of six women, all from Oklahoma. Look for the first book, *Love's Haunting Refrain* by Ada Steward, as well as stories by other favorites—Jeanne Stephens, Gena Dalton, Elaine Camp and Renee Roszel. You'll know the AMERICAN TRIBUTE by its patriotic stripe under the Silhouette Special Edition border.

AMERICAN TRIBUTE—six women, six stories, starting in February.

AMERICAN TRIBUTE—one of the reasons Silhouette Special Edition is just that—Special.

The Editors at Silhouette Books

BROOKE HASTINGS
Forward Pass

Silhouette Special Edition

Published by Silhouette Books New York
America's Publisher of Contemporary Romance

SILHOUETTE BOOKS
300 East 42nd St., New York, N.Y.   10017

ISBN: 0-373-09312-8

First Silhouette Books printing May 1986

Books by Brooke Hastings

Silhouette Romance

Playing for Keeps #13
Innocent Fire #26
Desert Fire #44
Island Conquest #67
Winner Take All #101

Silhouette Special Edition

Intimate Strangers #2
Rough Diamond #21
A Matter of Time #49
An Act of Love #79
Tell Me No Lies #156
Hard To Handle #250
As Time Goes By #294
Forward Pass #312

Silhouette Intimate Moments

Interested Parties #37
Reasonable Doubts #64

BROOKE HASTINGS

is a transplanted Easterner who now lives in California with her husband and two children. A full-time writer, she won the Romance Writers of America's Golden Medallion Award for her Silhouette Romance, *Winner Take All*. She especially enjoys doing the background research for her books, and finds it a challenge to come up with new plot twists and unique characters for her stories.

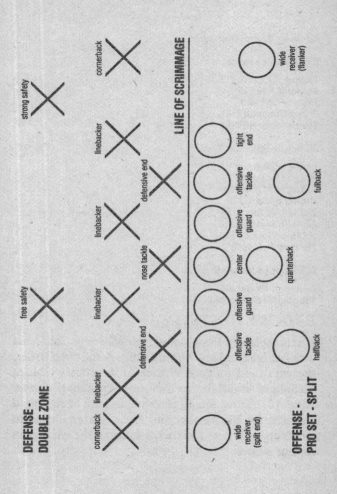

DEFENSE - DOUBLE ZONE

cornerback · linebacker · defensive end · linebacker · nose tackle · linebacker · defensive end · linebacker · cornerback

free safety · strong safety

LINE OF SCRIMMAGE

OFFENSE - PRO SET - SPLIT

wide receiver (split end) · offensive tackle · offensive guard · center · offensive guard · offensive tackle · tight end · wide receiver (flanker)

halfback · quarterback · fullback

Chapter One

Elizabeth Reynolds had been lying about who she was and what she did for so many years now that she could almost do it in her sleep. But that didn't mean she could do it on national television, with a studio audience watching her every move and a bunch of cameras taping her every word. There were times when she wondered how she'd ever allowed herself to get talked into appearing on *Main Attraction*, and this was definitely one of them.

The show, at least, was a first-class operation, so she was suffering in relative comfort. They'd shown her into a private dressing room, sent her down for a professional makeup job and informed her that there was a buffet lunch down in the greenroom if she wanted something to eat. Between her fear of messing up her makeup and the flock of butterflies playing tag in her stomach, she doubted she'd want even a single bite of the food, but it was nice to know it was there. She checked her watch, saw there was over half an hour till taping time and slipped off her spike-heeled sandals. They were new, and they were killing her feet.

Her cousin, Michelle Pittman, had flown down to Los Angeles with her to provide some much-appreciated moral support. Michelle was a great believer in the fortifying value of food and kept nagging Liz to eat something. "At least let me get you a few slices of bread," she coaxed. "If you don't put something in your stomach, it's going to start growling right in the middle of the program."

"Having my stomach growl is better than throwing up all over the set," Liz answered. "I could kill Gloria for getting me into this. I never thought I'd be this nervous." She lowered her voice a little. "It's even worse than facing down Higgins and his knife. At least I could take some action with Higgins. It's so frustrating to sit here doing nothing."

"You probably had some food in your stomach when you tackled Higgins." Michelle started toward the door. "Take my word for it, you'll feel a lot less nervous once you've had something to eat. I'll bring you a little wine, too—just enough to relax you."

Since Liz wasn't much of a drinker, she figured that tossing back a glass of wine was the worst move she could make, but she didn't argue the point. Michelle could bring her all the food and wine in the world, but she didn't have to eat or drink it.

Her cousin pulled open the door and stepped into the hall. Liz could make out a short stretch of the empty corridor from the couch where she was sitting, but it didn't stay empty for long. A tall, broad-shouldered man came striding into view, walking through the hallway as though he owned it. The impression of arrogant self-confidence quickly vanished though, as his face broke into a boyishly crooked smile. It was directed at somebody approaching from the opposite direction, out of Liz's line of vision.

Michelle stopped dead in her tracks, croaked out a soft but impassioned "Oh, my God!" and scurried back into the dressing room, closing the door behind her. Her cheeks were flushed, her eyes were glazed and you didn't need a stethoscope to know that her heart must be hammering away at about a hundred beats a minute.

"Did you see that?" she asked. "Did you see who was out in the hall?"

"I saw him," Liz said. Almost anyone in California would have recognized the man, even out of his blue and gold jersey or without a football in his right hand. By Super Bowl Sunday in January, he and his team had managed to whip a good part of the West Coast into a state of frenzied expectation. The fans' hopes had exploded into a raucous celebration as the clock ticked off the final minutes of the game. Undefeated seasons had a way of turning people on, as did blowout championship victories.

Michelle looked at Liz as if her lack of excitement was nothing short of blasphemous. "That's all you're going to say? You saw?" Her expression turned soft and dreamy. "He's got to be the cutest guy in the whole country. And he's even better-looking in person than he is on TV. I can't believe he's here."

Liz couldn't disagree. Zack Delaney *was* cute, very cute. It was an adjective she usually reserved for cooing babies and teenage heartthrobs—not for rangy six-foot quarterbacks with guts and style who regularly put themselves into the paths of two-hundred-eighty-pound linemen with mayhem on their minds—but it fit him perfectly. He wasn't the sophisticated lady-killer type, able to leave you breathless with the suaveness of his smile, or seduce you with a single stare out of his darkly intense eyes. He didn't daze you with his smoldering sexuality or dazzle you with his picture-perfect features. But still, Liz had never met a female between the ages of twelve and sixty who didn't think he was absolutely adorable.

His eyes were a beautiful azure blue and they twinkled when he smiled. The smile itself was sunny, infectious and a little bit shy. The women Liz knew inevitably melted a little when they saw it on television and smiled right back at the screen. His hair was light brown streaked with sun-bleached blond and naturally wavy. It always looked a little unruly, probably because it usually needed cutting or at least combing. Throw in a dimpled chin, tiny laugh lines at the corners of his eyes and a body that could have served as the model for a heroic statue, and the result was irresistible. Zack Delaney had star quality.

Liz was about to admit as much when Gloria Moyers turned up, letting herself into the dressing room without knocking. Gloria wasn't exactly Liz's favorite person at that moment, but the two women had survived four years as college roommates and would no doubt survive Liz's appearance on *Main Attraction*. Besides that, Gloria was practically family, and you couldn't stay mad at family. She'd been living with Michelle's older brother for years now.

Gloria took one look at Michelle's dazed expression and started to laugh. "Don't tell me," she said to Liz. "The Rushers' number-one fan just got an eyeful of Zack Delaney."

The mention of Delaney's name was enough to jerk Michelle out of her reverie. "Why didn't you tell me he'd be here?" she wailed. "I would have gone on a diet. I would have changed my hairdo. I would have worn something sexy."

"That's why I didn't tell you. Ever since you went up north to college I've had to listen to you go on about Zack Delaney and the San Francisco Gold Rushers, and it's gotten even worse now that they're holding their training camps on your campus. I don't know how you talked your way into getting a job up there this summer, but I do know that none of those poor men will be safe around you." Gloria sat down on the couch, temporarily ignoring the smitten Michelle. "We scheduled two tapings today, the first with Ben Caine and the second with Zack Delaney. I know I told you you'd go on with Ben, but we've had to make a change."

Liz didn't like the sound of that at all. If she'd been nervous before, now she was ready to panic. "You can't switch men on me at the last minute, Gloria! You told me Ben Caine so I prepared myself for Ben Caine. Dammit, suppose I *win* this stupid contest?"

"Then you'll go on an eight-day, all-expense-paid trip to Hawaii with Zack Delaney. You have to admit it's better than traipsing around the Rockies with Ben Caine. A lot of women would kill to be in your shoes."

"But I'm not 'a lot of women.' We're not all infatuated with the man the way Michelle is—" Liz cut herself off, struck by a bolt of inspiration. "Let Michelle do the show. Delaney is too young for me, anyway."

"Oh, right. You're an old hag of twenty-nine, he's a mere child of twenty-eight, and all of us know you have affairs with one distinguished older man after another." Gloria looked as if she wanted to say more—it upset her that Liz avoided men like the plague, no matter what age they were—but Michelle had chimed in with half a dozen reasons why *she* would be a perfect contestant. Openly exasperated by now, Gloria ordered both of them to display a little common sense. "In the first place, Michelle won't even be twenty-one till August, and all of our contestants are at least twenty-one. And in the second place..." She rolled her eyes. "Can you see her on stage with Zack? She'd be like a loose cannon out there."

Gloria, unfortunately, was right. Michelle was too unpredictable for *Main Attraction*, equally likely to flirt outrageously, lecture the audience on the highlights of Delaney's career or go totally catatonic. "But I can't possibly get away to Hawaii," Liz said weakly. "Not for at least a month."

"Neither can Zack," Gloria assured her. "You see? There's no problem at all."

"But why me?" There was an edge of desperation to Liz's voice. "Can't you switch somebody else between the two segments? And why are you switching anybody at all?"

"Because Caine couldn't make it. Something came up in the case he's trying down in San Diego so he arranged for a friend to take his place—Assemblyman Dan Richard of Orange County, otherwise known as California's answer to Mr. Clean. And Richard refuses to appear on the same show with a woman who hustles drinks in a Nevada casino."

"But I don't *really* hustle drinks…" Liz began, and then realized it was hopeless. It didn't matter what she really did or didn't do. All that mattered was that people would be told that she had taken a job as a cocktail waitress in South Lake Tahoe in order to spend all her spare time boating, hiking and skiing.

She had too good a sense of humor not to see the irony in that. Underneath the Tahoe hedonist she was just the type of woman Richard would have loved to be seen with. The feeling wasn't mutual, though. She had about as much use for self-righteous windbags as she did for crooks and con men—in other words, no use at all.

"It would serve you right if I developed a sudden and acute case of appendicitis right in the middle of the taping," she went on. "If I were you I'd play it safe and tell Delaney to pick one of the other contestants."

Gloria managed to look scandalized. "Are you suggesting that we fix the outcome? You, of all people, a woman sworn to uphold the law?"

"Me of all people. Tell him I'm gay. Tell him I have a communicable disease that will ruin his sex life forever. You can even tell him I have a history of filing paternity suits against NFL quarterbacks, but see that he steers clear of me. I mean it, Gloria. My only other choice is to be so obnoxious he'll never choose me."

Gloria's expression said she might just as well fret about a tidal wave swallowing up Los Angeles. Liz was much too straight an arrow to play the loudmouthed floozy or the prissy prima donna, not when it would reflect back on Gloria, who had suggested her for the show. *Main Attraction* was a Yuppie version of the old *Dating Game* program, and for no reason Liz could fathom it had wound up as a primetime hit. The premise was a tried-and-true one: it took a celebrity and presented him or her with three possible dates. The one new twist was that the celebrities conducted the interviews themselves, one-on-one and face-to-face in a homey setting that resembled somebody's living room.

In the beginning the contestants had all been models of success in their professions, and the show had done only passably well. The ratings had first started to climb after they'd added people who had dedicated themselves to serving society in some way. The final wrinkle, Gloria's brainstorm, had been to include a free-spirit type on each show, and the viewers had loved it. The only problem was that most free spirits seemed to be floating out near Mars somewhere and weren't reliable contestants. That was where Liz had come in.

Knowing her target well, Gloria merely shrugged. "If you want to embarrass yourself in front of millions of your fellow Americans, I don't suppose I can stop you. I've got to run now. There's an actress down the hall who'll probably strangle me when I tell her she's got to take her chances with Dan Richard instead of Zack Delaney." She breezed out of the room, perfectly well aware that she'd handed Liz a crushing defeat.

Looking back on it, Liz could see that her crucial mistake had been to stop saying a flat and final "no" and agree to check with her boss. She'd assumed O'Dwyer would look at her as if she was rolling on only three wheels and tell her to forget it, but he hadn't. To her absolute astonishment, he'd decided that a higher profile might be just what she needed. It might open doors that had previously been closed and get Liz in with the right crowd—Ben Caine's kind of crowd. Liz had seen his point and reluctantly agreed, but she'd never developed any enthusiasm about it.

It went without saying that she meant to lose. She had better things to do than go running off with some celebrity, and besides, she didn't want her face to get too much exposure. It was one thing to make a single, four- or five-minute appearance on TV and another to star in a slick little minidocumentary about life with the rich and famous. People had a way of remembering winners.

Ben Caine, a flamboyant attorney with a taste for sophisticated, foreign-born women, would have been easy to discourage. Liz wasn't his type at all. Still, she was attractive and she knew it. Her all-American good looks were an asset in her work and Delaney might like them. But what really worried her was that bit about loving sports. She didn't know much about him but was afraid that a fellow athlete might be right up his alley. Fortunately, though, they were taping the other segment first. There was plenty of time to learn, and Michelle was just the person to teach her.

"I think I'll have that food," she said to Michelle, "and also something to drink. Make it a soda, okay?"

"You've got it. If I see Zack Delaney I'll be sure to give him your warmest regards. I wouldn't think of competing against you." Michelle giggled and went off to the buffet, returning about five minutes later carrying a platter laden with cold cuts, cheese and rye bread. She was also holding two cans of Berry's Natural Soda, a product Delaney had endorsed.

Visibly disappointed that she hadn't run into him, she brightened as she opened a can of Mandarin Orange. "I'd forgotten that Berry's is the show's sponsor," she said as she handed Liz the can. "Did you know that after they started showing Zack's commercial, sales jumped twenty-six percent?"

Liz decided not to remind her that the commercial was only one part of a multimillion-dollar ad campaign. It featured star athletes and was built around the theme, "Berry's. It's a natural. It's a winner." If Michelle wanted to attribute the product's success solely to Zack Delaney's charisma, who was she to quibble?

She took a small sip, found it tartly refreshing and drank more deeply. Her case of nerves was practically gone now, because she finally had facts to learn and a strategy to develop. Waiting and doing nothing had always been the hardest things in the world for her.

"So tell me about Zack Delaney," she said. "And you can skip the part about how he's the most gifted quarterback to ever play the game."

"But that's just the point," Michelle said quickly. "What makes Zack great is that he's such a superb athlete. He isn't the most gifted, not if it's a cannonlike arm you're talking about. But he's incredibly quick, he has the ability to scramble out of trouble and he has a talent for making things happen. He has an instinct for knowing if and when his receivers will get open and whether he has to make on-the-spot adjustments in his plays. He can look at the field, with twenty-one other guys running around in every possible direction, and sense what they're going to do next. So he doesn't have to rely on long passes, even though he gets better at them all the time."

Michelle chattered on, telling Liz about Delaney's league-leading statistics, but she was listening with only half an ear. As a woman in a mostly male world, she'd had little choice but to start watching the Rushers' games. She knew Delaney was good at what he did. She'd even grimaced and cheered and held her breath in response to what was happening on the field. But knowing about his athletic ability wasn't going to get her off the hook. She needed more personal information.

When Michelle finally ran out of data, she remarked that it was his private life that interested her most. Had he ever been married? Did he have a regular girlfriend?

Michelle was making herself a sandwich, slapping ham and cheese between two slices of bread. "He did, but they broke up early in the season. They'd been together for years, but I guess he didn't want to marry her. He's never been married."

"And his ex-girlfriend? What did she do for a living?"

"Good deeds. She was an heiress, from one of those wealthy San Francisco families you always read about in the *Times*. I saw something last summer about her designing a line of exercise clothing—things like jogging suits, sweat clothes and tennis wear—but I guess nothing ever came of it."

"Is she pretty?" Liz asked.

"Beautiful." Michelle gave an envious sigh and took a bite of her sandwich. "She's tall and slim with the most gorgeous reddish blond hair I've ever seen. I wonder why only rich people ever look that good?"

"Because, unlike you and me, they have enough time for health spas, beauty salons and shopping sprees and enough money to pay the bills," Liz said with a smile. "What else do you know about her? Is she smart?"

"She went to Stanford, so I guess she must be. Zack seems to like women with brains. He's been playing the field since he broke up with Allison. He dated a banker for a while, then a TV newswoman, then some kind of computer whiz.''

There wasn't much more Michelle could tell her. Zack Delaney was civil to the press but not particularly talkative, especially about his private life. After breaking up with his heiress girlfriend he'd moved in with his best friend, Rushers wide receiver Paul Travers. Now that the season was over he was back in his own place again, in San Francisco's pricey Pacific Heights district.

Unfortunately for him, his success had turned him into such a major celebrity that he couldn't take a woman anywhere without being recognized and photographed. When reporters asked questions that were none of their business, he would flash the grin that had sold so many cans of Berry's and either chide them for being nosy or give them a quick, amusing quip to print. He'd apparently learned to handle the unceasing attention and still maintain some semblance of privacy, a difficult juggling act for somebody as much in the public eye as he was.

Gloria returned to Liz's dressing room ten minutes later, sending Michelle off to the greenroom to watch the show on closed-circuit TV and walking Liz downstairs to the studio. They were still taping the first segment, so the people backstage were keeping their voices down.

There was a television monitor mounted high on the wall in front of a row of empty chairs, with the host of *Main Attraction*, an Englishman named Dirk Denning, currently on camera. Liz sat down to watch and Gloria hurried away. Denning was interviewing a previous celebrity guest and her choice of date, asking them if they planned to keep seeing each other. The date said yes, the celebrity said no, and the audience laughed. A minute later Gloria was back, a pretty brunette by her side. The two contestants smiled at each other but didn't say anything. The third contestant was escorted into the room just as the final credits began to roll.

At that point Gloria made the introductions. Nobody ever seemed to use last names on these shows; it was just Liz the cocktail waitress, Nancy the teacher and Emily the attorney. Nancy was petite and dark-haired, Emily was tall and athletic-looking, and both were attractive and articulate. The three women started talking as soon as Gloria left, trading information on their backgrounds. Liz decided she had nothing to worry about. She planned on being everything Delaney disliked,. and with two other women to choose from, his only problem would be deciding which he preferred.

Their conversation was interrupted by a commotion to their right. Zack Delaney had arrived and every technician and staffer in sight was scurrying to get a look at him. As Gloria led him across the room, Dirk Denning came bounding down a short flight of stairs to their left. It led to the walled-off set.

Denning held out his hand. "Zack! I can't tell you what a pleasure it is to have you here." Liz noticed that his English accent was a lot less pronounced in real life than it was when the camera was running. "I knew we would get you on the show eventually, if only we were persistent enough."

He pumped Delaney's hand and then put an arm around his shoulders. Michelle, Liz decided, had been right. Zack Delaney *was* even cuter in person than he was on television. For one thing, he looked smaller on television than his six feet three inches, and for another, his shoulders looked a little less broad. A typical quarterback, he lacked the massive chest and thick neck of a lineman, but there was no doubting his strength and power. Liz felt herself respond to him on some primitive, intensely feminine level. Glancing at his blue shirt, tan slacks and tan V-neck sweater, she told herself it was a case of the man making the clothes rather than the other way around. He would probably look good in anything, from workout clothes to a dinner jacket to absolutely nothing at all.

He smiled at Denning, but it wasn't the two-hundred-watt dazzler Liz remembered from the Berry's commercial. "It's been a crazy four months," he said. "There were times when I was lucky to know what city I was in. I couldn't fit the show in earlier, but now that I'm here I'll do the best I can for you."

"Of course you will! You'll be splendid, I'm sure." Denning patted Delaney's shoulder and then dropped his arm. "It's time to do the honors, luv," he said to Gloria. "Who are these three enticing creatures and what can you tell us about them?"

Liz stood up as the three of them walked over, feeling her face get hot when Delaney looked her straight in the eye and hit her with a charmingly diffident smile. The smile said the situation was a bit overwhelming for him, too, but if they all pulled together they would manage to muddle through. She was just as glad he didn't speak to her, because she wasn't sure how coherent she would have been. No man had ever had such a dramatic physical effect on her, but then, she'd never met a celebrity of Delaney's magnitude before, nor anyone quite so handsome.

Before she had the wit to smile back, he was giving the other two women a taste of the same mesmerizing treatment. Like Liz, they had gotten to their feet, Nancy silently staring at him while Emily, the lawyer, said hello and offered her hand.

"Emily, meet Zack," Gloria said as the two shook hands. She glanced at each of the women in turn, then went on, "As all of you can see, we like to give our contestants a chance to meet our guest star for just a few minutes before the show actually begins. We find it takes away some of the stage fright without sacrificing any of the spontaneity. Emily practices corporate law here in Los Angeles, Zack. She's the youngest partner in her firm and one of only two women."

Zack asked her the name of her firm and what sorts of cases she handled, then moved down the line to Nancy. Not only was Nancy a teacher but she taught children with learning disabilities and had developed an innovative writing program based on the use of computers. That left Liz, whose life-style was beginning to look like the essence of self-indulgence.

She ignored the jolt of electricity that sizzled up her arm when Zack took her hand, and swung into her dumb-blonde routine. "Wow! Zack Delaney! It's just such a thrill to meet you. You have to promise to come upstairs and say hello to my cousin when the show is over. Next to me, she's your biggest fan in the whole world!"

"I'd be glad to," he said. "I take it she's the cute little redhead who was gaping at me from your dressing room door?"

Liz stared at him, dumbfounded. He'd never even turned his head, so how could he have known it was her dressing room?

"I saw you sitting on the couch," he prompted. "You didn't look too happy to be here."

"You've got sharp eyes," she murmured.

"Indeed he does!" Dirk Denning gave Delaney a clap on the seat of his pants, like the two of them were teammates on a football field. "Great peripheral vision, Liz. He's got great peripheral vision. It's been a pleasure, ladies, but we've really got to be going. We'll see you on the set."

Denning put his arm around Zack's shoulders and led him toward the stairs while Liz sat down to wait. She'd be the third and final contestant, giving her a chance to observe Delaney's reactions and adjust her strategy accordingly. She was almost sure he would choose the teacher, but she wasn't about to take any chances.

Chapter Two

Idiots like Dirk Denning were enough to make Zack Delaney wish he'd never done the Berry's commercial in the first place. The pay had been great and the stuff was okay to drink if there wasn't any beer around, but he could have done without *Main Attraction* and Denning's continual slaps on his back and butt. Zack had never been able to figure out why the men who were furthest from being jocks insisted on treating him as if they were in a locker room together. "Jock sniffers," they called them, and Denning was exhibiting all the classic signs.

"Now all you have to do," Denning told him, "is wait right here until I announce your name." His tone was subtly condescending, as though his instructions might strain Zack's powers of comprehension. "Then you come out on stage—wave to the audience if you want to—and shake my hand. Then sit down on the couch nearest the chairs. We'll chat a bit and then take a break before we bring out Emily. Fantastic-looking bird, isn't she?''

"Fantastic," Zack agreed without enthusiasm. Personally, though, he wouldn't have wanted to run into her in a courtroom. She was the type who could take ten milligrams of Valium and still be charged up enough to make ground round out of her opponents. Come to think of it, he wouldn't have wanted to run into her on a football field, either.

Denning put his arm around Zack's shoulders—*again*. It was all he could do not to shove it away. "You know, Zack, I'm a real student of your game. I've got a couple of plays I think you should try, especially a tricky little devil you could use on third-and-long." He paused to look at the monitor. The opening sequence had started to roll. "Ah, here we go. But don't worry, we'll get to that play of mine later."

Zack forced himself to smile, hoping that "later" wouldn't be on camera. Denning stood stock-still until the offstage announcer called out his name, and then burst through the center curtain, the picture of animation and enthusiasm. Without prelude, he asked the audience, "Is anybody out there from Florida?" There was a scattering of applause. "Such a pity! My condolences to you all, because the man who ruined your January is here. And how about San Francisco? Do we have any Gold Rushers fans in the audience?" The applause grew louder and an excited buzz filled the air. The names of celebrity guests were never announced in advance of tapings, but the audience had apparently guessed who was coming out.

Raising his voice so he could be heard above the din, Denning shouted out, "Meet the man who led the Rushers to the first undefeated season in NFL history—the Super Bowl's most valuable player—Number 14 himself, *Zack Delaney!* Come on out, Zack. We've got the Dolphins' fans outnumbered here, so I assure you it's safe."

Zack walked through the curtain and stared at the cheering audience. He was always a little amazed by receptions like this one. It was nice to win nineteen straight football games but it wasn't as though he'd solved the energy crisis or ended the threat of nuclear war. What kept all the attention in perspective was the knowledge that the same people who were cheering him so loudly now would be booing him even more loudly later, the next time he screwed up.

His dislike of Denning was just strong enough to make him ignore the prepared script and move to the front of the stage, right past the spot where Denning was standing and waiting to greet him. Despite the glare of the lights, he could still make out individual faces in the dark sea of people in front of him. The applause began to die down when the audience realized he was waiting to speak to them.

"First of all, let me give the '72 Dolphins a little credit. They were undefeated too, but that was a fourteen-game regular season, not the sixteen-game season we play now." He paused and scanned the audience again. "Is there anybody here from Pennsylvania? From Butler County?"

A teenager in the third row called out the name of his old high school, and Zack grinned. "No kidding! Catch me after the show, okay? There are some people I want to ask you about." He waited for the kid to agree before walking over to Denning. There was a flash of irritation in Denning's eyes as they shook hands. Obviously he hadn't liked standing there doing nothing while Zack took over. He'd probably liked being publicly corrected even less. None of that bothered Zack in the least.

The couches they sat down on were arranged in a wide V facing the audience, with a square end table between them. There was a round, steel-and-glass cocktail table in front of them, with a silver water carafe and a pair of ice-cube-filled glasses on it. "So tell us what your life has been like for the last couple of months," Denning said. "Has all the fuss died down a bit by now?"

"I've been traveling around the country, making personal appearances. It's a lot different from two years ago, which is the last time we played in the Super Bowl. People on the street didn't recognize me as often then. I guess I have winning to thank for that—and the Berry's commercial, of course."

Denning gave him a sympathetic, almost pitying look. "I suppose it must get to be tiresome—fans never leaving you alone and so on."

Zack had more brains than to step into the trap Denning had sprung. If you complained about being recognized, it always came off as whining. Besides, he understood he was a hero to a lot of people, especially kids, and that his position imposed certain responsibilities. It made a lot more sense to accept them and try to fulfill them than to constantly battle against them.

"It's not tiresome," he said, "but I have to admit it's easier when things stay peaceful." He smiled at the audience, then gave a laughing shake of his head. "Last March I was down in Miami with Paul Travers—" there was a burst of applause for the Rushers' star wide receiver "—doing a big sports banquet. I guess some of the fans there haven't forgiven us for beating the Dolphins yet, because when we got back to our car it was wrapped in toilet paper and sprayed with the Dolphins' colors. It looked like a giant helmet, with the windshield where your face would go and the glass painted with eyes, a nose and a mouth. A couple of the Dolphins who'd been at the banquet with us stood around laughing while we cleaned things up. Paul told them that a little toilet paper and paint was nothing compared to what our fans would do to *them* if they ever set foot in San Francisco!"

Denning laughed along with the audience, but a lot less sincerely. "And what about your personal life?" he asked. "Is it lonely being on your own again, or do you enjoy showing the delights of San Francisco to one delectable lady after another?"

Zack wasn't about to give him a straight answer about whether he was lonely or not, or comment on any of the women he'd taken out. His private life was nobody's business but his own. "It's the most amazing thing, Dirk, but every time I'm out with a woman the photographers seem to show up." The audience was solidly with him by now, and laughed at his show of puzzlement. "It's the truth," he insisted. "They never come around when I'm out with friends, and that's seventy-five percent of the time. I can't figure it out."

"And is there any special lady in your life right now?"

"If there was," Zack answered, "I wouldn't have come on the show. There's only one thing worse than a defensive tackle headed straight for your legs, and that's an angry woman."

"In that case, we'll have to introduce you to three women who are anything *but* angry with you." Denning looked into the camera and winked. "Stay with us, everyone. We'll be right back."

Zack helped himself to some water as soon as they were off the air. Denning told him he was doing very well, a new respect in his voice, and Zack nodded. After all the interviews he'd done, both on television and with print journalists, he'd become surprisingly adept at hiding the discomfort he felt whenever the questions got too personal. After a while he'd developed a supply of stock answers and anecdotes, and he relied on them the same way he might rely on a well-practiced play when he needed only a yard or two for a first down. The only thing different about *Main Attraction* was that *he'd* be asking the questions, and he couldn't say he looked forward to it. He'd memorized four or five of them for each woman and he hoped it would be enough. He didn't really want to improvise.

He was the type of man who took life as it came and tried to enjoy it, but there was something about *Main Attraction* that struck him as downright bizarre. The women he'd met backstage were all extremely attractive. They could hardly be desperate for dates and yet they'd been willing to come on the show and let him judge them. The two he didn't pick would have the delightful experience of being rejected in front of their friends, relatives and millions of viewers, while the third would have the dubious thrill of accompanying him to Hawaii and spending eight days being trailed around by a cameraman and a chaperon disguised as a tour guide. He couldn't imagine why any sane woman would volunteer for something like that.

As soon as they were back on the air, Denning brought out Emily, the hotshot lawyer. Zack asked her about her childhood and family, then turned to the subject of her work. Although she kept her answers short and to the point, they were more revealing than she realized.

It had obviously been naive of him, but he'd forgotten about star athletes and reflected glory. As a corporate lawyer who was also a woman, Emily was forever running into the prejudices of the old-boy network. She could never be "one of the guys," but after eight days in Hawaii with Zack she'd have a generous supply of what-Zack-Delaney-is-really-like stories to share with her clients. The only thing better would have been to produce Zack Delaney himself, and he didn't put it past her to try it.

Of course, she wouldn't have been the first if she had. Professional athletes dealt with that sort of thing all the time, and sometimes it reached absurd proportions. One of his teammates was an accountant during the off-season. When he went to do his clients' taxes every year, all they wanted to talk about was football. More often than not he had to schedule a second appointment to go through the actual numbers. The man had long ago stopped asking himself why his firm put up with such inefficiency, because it was obvious; accountants were a dime a dozen, but professional football players weren't.

Zack had run into similar reactions from women, but he'd never learned to accept them. He didn't like being a notch in some groupie's belt or the catch of the week for an ambitious woman on her way up. Paul kept telling him he was too touchy, that his fame was inseparable from who he was, but Paul had married his college sweetheart instead of wasting almost three years on the likes of Allison Chase. Allison had been a mistake Zack didn't intend to repeat.

Emily exited stage right and Nancy appeared through the center curtain. Zack's first question concerned her motivation for teaching handicapped children and he almost didn't get in a second. She went on and on about her students and her work, as though nothing else in the world could possibly matter. When she finally stopped talking, he decided to forget the memorized questions and ask her what she thought of professional football. She looked at him blankly at first, then answered, "It has its place. The world can be awfully hard on people and they need to escape at times. To be honest, I prefer to reread the classics, but I suppose some men get a vicarious thrill out of watching sports." Clearly she considered both Zack and *Main Attraction* essentially frivolous, but wasn't about to turn down free airtime to talk about her life's work.

That left Liz, who came out after the second commercial break. When Zack noticed her sitting in her dressing room looking so adorably out of sorts with the world, he immediately began to hope she was one of the contestants. When he took a better look backstage he told himself that interviewing the other two women would just be going through the motions. With Liz, it was a case of instant physical attraction, stronger than anything he'd felt in a long time. If he was a little disappointed when she opened her mouth to talk, the feeling didn't last. A lot of people got nervous when they met celebrities, and when people got nervous they tended to babble. As long as she was halfway intelligent she'd be fine. After all, he wasn't making a lifelong commitment here, just planning a week or so of casual fun.

He studied her appearance as she made her way to the couch. She was wearing a beaded silver dress with long sleeves, a V neck and a hemline that ended well above her knees. Short skirts were back in style that year, and Zack, who was very much a leg man, thought that was terrific. Liz's legs were slender and shapely, and between her spike heels and short skirt they seemed to go on forever. Her dress was cut just low enough to show a little cleavage, and for a moment Zack pictured himself on a Hawaiian beach, with the sun blazing, the surf pounding and Liz at his side in a bikini. God knew she had the shape for one.

She smiled at him as she sat down, tossing her head to get a strand of her long blond hair off her cheek. It was silky and straight, like a sixties folksinger's, and he would have liked to touch it. Her eyes were a smoky green, and when she met his gaze with an innocently curious stare he felt his blood pressure take an upward leap. She didn't have Allison's patrician beauty, but her face was mischievous, lively and open. It was also very pretty, despite enough makeup to coat the entire front row of the audience.

Denning's introduction mentioned everything Gloria had already told him—that Liz had given up her job as an assistant buyer for a San Francisco department store to move to the Lake Tahoe area, where she waitressed at night and enjoyed herself during the day. "There are probably a lot of people who fantasize about doing what you did," he began. "You had a regular paycheck and a promising career but you traded them for more freedom. Was it a tough decision to make such a total change in your life?"

She kicked off her shoes and crossed her legs. Zack caught a healthy expanse of smooth, bare thigh out of the corner of his eye and was hard pressed not to look down. "It was no big philosophical deal," she said with a shrug. "I mean, I didn't go up on a mountaintop and meditate for six months before I decided what to do. Retailing was a drag. The pay was lousy and the promotions took forever, and I'm not getting any younger. I wanted to have some fun for a change and my horoscope said 'Go for it!' so I did. You know what I mean?"

Zack had hoped for a more thoughtful answer, but at least she'd been honest. It struck him that something about her didn't add up, but he didn't have time to figure out what it was. Nodding, he said, "I think so. I wouldn't play football unless I enjoyed it, but a lot of people aren't lucky enough to do something they really like. But what about ten or fifteen years from now? Do you ever think about what you'll be doing in the future?"

She shrugged again. "Why should I? In ten or fifteen years the world could blow up. I could get hit by a truck or killed in an avalanche. I'm having a great time *now*, so why worry? You know what I mean?"

Zack *didn't* know, because the future was something he'd thought a lot about lately. He'd played six seasons in the NFL and probably had six or eight left, but that would be it. He'd had the best game of his life in the Super Bowl the previous January and sometimes he wondered if he'd ever top it. Every now and then he and Paul would have a marathon conversation on the topic, "Is There Life after Football, and if so, What Form Will It Take?" but they hadn't come up with the definitive answer. The most Zack could say was that he was laying the groundwork for a number of different alternatives.

He doubted Liz would understand any of that so he didn't bring it up. "I see your point," he said, and changed the subject. "You know, Liz, I always wonder how people wind up on this show. How about you? Did you send in your name and picture or did somebody from the program discover you at work?"

"One of the production assistants is an old friend of mine," she answered. "And who wouldn't want a chance to win a free vacation, you know what I mean? So when they finally got around to using some real people instead of all those dressed-for-success barracudas, well, I was right in there offering my services. Anything for a friend, that's my motto! You know?"

Zack leaned back on the couch. He was beginning to find Liz a little tedious, but he still would have loved to sleep with her—providing she kept her mouth shut until she was out of his house. "If the friend is old and close enough, sure. I take it yours is?"

She looked at him vacantly and blinked, as though the question had strained her limited mental faculties. Then she gushed, "Oh! I see what you mean. Of course she is. Gloria is my dearest friend in the whole, wide world! You know what I mean?"

The audience laughed, and suddenly Zack wasn't sure whether they were laughing at Liz or with her. It hadn't previously occurred to him that her answers might be a put-on, but he didn't put anything past the producers of a prime-time television series. If they thought bringing in an actress to pose as a free spirit with whipped cream for brains would liven up their show, they would undoubtedly do it. At that point he realized what had bothered him about her. Her dress was flashy, but it was also sophisticated and expensive. The dumb blondes he'd run across had all had a lot less style than she did.

Ordinarily he was a little shy with women, especially until the first date was over with and they weren't total strangers anymore. It had been a bit of a handicap when he was younger, but all of that had changed when he'd become a starting quarterback in college. Women had started chasing *him*, and he'd gradually gotten lazier and lazier about pursuing anyone who didn't show an interest in him first.

Still, he was more than capable of coming on to a woman when he really wanted to. Oddly enough, the fact that they were on television made it easier rather than harder. It was more like a performance than real life. When the laughter died down he gazed into Liz's eyes and smiled knowingly, as though he were perfectly happy to share in her little joke if that's what she wanted. At the same time he caught a lock of her hair and curled it around his finger. It felt like burnished satin.

Her own smile faltered for a second, then came back more dazzling than ever. "Lucky Gloria," he drawled. "Can I apply for the position as your *second* best friend in the whole wide world?"

She reddened slightly, the smile becoming distinctly strained. He allowed his fingers to graze her cheek, which was just as smooth and silky as her hair was. "Sure, why not?" she finally answered. "You can never have too many best friends, you know what I mean?"

Zack put his hand down. He was about to tell her that he didn't know but looked forward to finding out when Dirk Denning gave a boisterous laugh and boomed out, "I'm afraid our time is up, Zack, so this little discussion about friendship will have to be marked 'To be continued.' Stay with us, everyone. When we come back, we'll find out which of these three lovely ladies will share eight days in Hawaii with Zack Delaney."

As soon as they were off the air, Liz reached for her shoes and silently put them on. She wasn't smiling anymore, much less bubbling over with mindless good cheer. She hadn't taken more than six steps toward the stairs before she was turning around. A moment later she was back on the couch, giving Zack a beseeching look. "I hate Hawaii," she said. "I think football is the stupidest, most boring game on earth. I'd be *terrible* company. Please, Mr. Delaney, take Nancy or Emily. You'll have a much better time."

Denning answered before Zack had a chance to get a word out. "Now, now, Liz, we can't have you getting cold feet. I have it on good authority that Zack is entirely harmless until he gets a football in his hand. Get a grip on yourself and run along offstage now."

She looked at Denning as if she wanted to kill him, then rolled her eyes and shook her head. She walked off the set without another word, leaving Zack thoroughly bewildered about what to do. "Does this kind of thing happen often?" he asked Denning.

"All the time, all the time! It's nothing to concern yourself about, Zack. Just a case of last-minute nerves at the thought of going off with a celebrity."

Zack had his doubts about that. After the pass he'd just made, every viewer in the country would expect him to pick Liz, and they'd all tune in next fall when the film of their trip was shown. Denning obviously had his eye on the ratings and Zack couldn't blame him but how fair was it to choose a woman who didn't want to be chosen?

On the other hand, nobody had forced her to come on the show. It was true that there had been a last-minute switch, and that she'd expected to appear with some grandstanding lawyer, but Zack couldn't see what difference it made. He wasn't exactly a Neanderthal man, and she'd only have to suffer his presence for a week.

Both his opponents and his teammates would have recognized the look that came into his eyes. Zack Delaney liked challenges. When the defense outguessed him or outsmarted him, he couldn't wait till the next play to show them their luck would never hold. Every instinct told him that there was more to Liz than her blond hair and great legs. He wanted to know the specifics. He also wanted to change her mind about Hawaii, football and him—and not necessarily in that order.

Disaster. Liz was sitting offstage between Nancy and Emily, letting their conversation wash over her. The word kept crashing through her mind, blocking out every other thought. Disaster, disaster, disaster.

It was her own damn fault of course, and the minute she got herself alone she was going to give herself a well-deserved kick in the shins. Delaney wasn't stupid, for Pete's sake. She'd had him right where she wanted him, bored senseless, and what had she done? She'd aroused his curiosity. She'd piqued his competitive instincts. Lord, how in the world had she let herself get so carried away?

She waited in silent dread, watching the monitor, wishing the show would never come back on the air. When the camera moved in for a close-up of Dirk Denning's face it was all she could do not to throw a shoe at the screen. If only Denning had kept his fat mouth shut, Delaney might have listened. He seemed like a reasonable man.

The next thirty seconds had a horrible inevitability about them. Denning asked Zack whom he'd chosen and Zack flashed his eighteen-karat smile. Liz had no use whatsoever for that smile, since she blamed most of her troubles on it. Without it, she might have had a fighting chance to convince him she was just as dumb as she seemed, but when he'd turned it up full blast and touched her hair and cheek, her mind had gone totally blank for a crucial couple of moments. Zack Delaney was too darn sexy.

"It was a tough choice," he said. "I had to decide what I really wanted—no, needed—when I go to Hawaii. It was a long, hard season, Dirk. Sometimes I think what followed—all the speeches and publicity—was even harder. So I need to relax, have some fun and put football on the back burner for a while. And I think Liz is just the person to do that with."

Denning looked absolutely delighted with Zack's choice, but then, he always looked delighted with his guests' choices. "I couldn't agree more, Zack! Liz, come on back here and we'll tell you what we've got planned for you."

A staffer appeared at Liz's side and led her back to the stage. She plastered a smile on her face and climbed the steps, trying to look enthusiastic as she waved to the audience. The worst had happened and there was nothing she could do about it now. Zack met her halfway, put his arm around her shoulders and walked her over to the couch. She was keenly aware of the sheer size of the man; he probably outweighed her by a good eighty to ninety pounds and was five inches taller despite her spike heels. She'd labeled him "cute" and "adorable," but he suddenly seemed tough and a bit intimidating. She was relieved when he took his arm away.

The announcer described their vacation while a series of slides flashed on the monitor. They'd go to three islands in eight days, stay in the best hotels and dine in the finest restaurants, and see the sights with a tour guide named Gladys Tibbs who knew Hawaii like the back of her own hand. Afterward Denning told them to have a terrific time and hustled them off the set. It was a tightly timed show, and he still had a couple from an earlier program to bring out and a film of their vacation to run.

Gloria was waiting for them by the bottom of the stairs. Liz gave her a withering look, the kind she'd used in college after one of the disastrous blind dates Gloria was forever arranging. She paid no more attention now than she had then. "We need to schedule your trip," she said. "Zack, I know you've got commitments during the next few weeks and training camp in late July...."

"We're going to need a couple of minutes alone first," he said. "We seem to have a problem to resolve here."

Liz had about as much desire to be alone with Zack Delaney as to shut herself up in a roomful of tarantulas, but she kept her mouth firmly closed. It had gotten her into enough trouble already. She was going to dump the whole mess in O'Dwyer's lap and let *him* handle it. After all, he was the one who'd thought doing *Main Attraction* was such a great idea.

They'd just reached the upstairs hallway when Michelle came running toward them, grinning from ear to ear. "You were a stitch!" she called to Liz. "I had a feeling you were planning something like that, but I never thought you'd go through with it."

Her smile faded to an adoring stare when she came face to face with Zack. Gazing up at him, she said, "Did my cousin tell you I'm madly in love with you? If *she* doesn't want to go to Hawaii with you, I'd be glad to take her place."

"I'll keep it in mind," Zack said. "First, though, I'm going to do my best to talk her into it. Do you have any advice?"

"Well..." Michelle looked at Liz, then thought the better of whatever she'd planned to say. The girl could be flighty and she loved to tease, but she knew exactly how much she could say and never went beyond it. "I'm afraid not. I want to get back to Lake Tahoe in one piece."

Gloria took Michelle's arm and started to drag her away. "I'll wait for you in the greenroom. Have a nice chat with Zack, Lizzie." Liz glared at her.

She was still frowning when Zack let her into her dressing room. He closed the door and leaned back against it, then asked, "Do you really hate Hawaii?"

Liz retreated to the opposite side of the room. She decided to be honest with him, at least to a point. "The truth is that I've never even been there. But Gloria pushed me into doing this show when I really didn't want to, and then she changed celebrities on me. No offense, Mr. Delaney, but the last thing I wanted was to win."

He thought about that for a moment, then said, "But you would have gone away with Ben Caine because he doesn't do something as vapid as playing football?"

"He never would have picked me. I'm not his type at all." Liz felt a sharp pang of guilt. Her crack about football had been terribly nasty, and there was a niceness about Zack Delaney that made her want to apologize. "Look, I have nothing against football. I'm no expert, but I've watched you on TV and I know you're a great quarterback. I said what I said because I don't want to leave Lake Tahoe."

"And you figured that with Caine, you could do your friend a favor without any problem."

"Exactly. You're obviously a nice person, Zack . . ."

"Which means I honor my commitments. When I shot the commercial for Berry's I promised to do the show. Like it or not, the two of us have just won a trip to Hawaii together, and people expect to see how it all turns out. So unless you're too busy waitressing . . ." He let the sentence hang.

Liz had always been quick on her feet. When she realized her arguments were getting her nowhere, she decided to change tactics. "But I'm not really a waitress. I'm an undercover agent for the parent corporation. My job is to keep the other employees honest.''

Zack took a few steps forward, wondering if she could possibly be telling him the truth. The lady in front of him was a far cry from the bubble-brained blonde downstairs, but an undercover private cop? He already knew what a good actress she could be. ''Does Gloria know about that?'' he asked.

She nodded. ''Yes, but only because she's practically a member of the family. She lives with my cousin Josh—that's Michelle's older brother. We're not supposed to tell anyone but our families. Even the casino management doesn't know, just the corporate office. If they ever found out I'd told you I would be in real trouble.''

''Okay, so you're a private cop.'' Zack still wasn't so sure about that, but he was willing to accept it for the sake of argument. ''What's that got to do with going to Hawaii?''

She pursed her lips, obviously a little impatient with his questions. ''I don't want to go to Hawaii. All I care about is my work. I'm nothing like what I pretended to be.''

''But all work and no play . . .''

''Really, Mr. Delaney!''

''No, I mean it. Hawaii is exactly what you need. You're too uptight, Liz. You need to learn how to have a good time.''

''And I suppose you think you're just the one to teach me,'' she grumbled.

Zack smiled at her tone of voice and walked a little closer. With her back against the wall there was nowhere she could really go, but she straightened to her full height and tried to look forbidding. The more he thought about it, the more he liked the idea of going away with her. Loosen her up and she'd be a lot of fun. Her performance on the show had proved it.

"I think I might be, yes," he said. "It's fine to be serious about what you do, but everyone needs to have some fun now and then."

It was on the tip of Liz's tongue to ask him what a man who played football for a living knew about being serious, but that would have been unpardonably rude. "It doesn't strike me as very much fun to have a cameraman trailing after me all day long," she said instead. "I'd get cranky and complain. If you'd ever seen me in a bad mood, you'd know that I'm the worst possible person to go on vacation with. Besides, I'm a dead bore. Since I can't talk about my work, I won't talk at all. You'll wind up wanting to kill me."

It was such a screwy claim to make that Zack burst out laughing. He was beginning to enjoy Liz's protests, not to mention relishing the idea of trying to get her into bed. "Liz," he said, "you have before you a man who can scramble away from a pass rush better than anyone in the NFL. Believe me, the cameraman won't stand a chance."

Liz didn't know which was more captivating, Zack's laughter or his playful boast. He seemed to have such zest for life, and even better, he didn't take himself too seriously. When she stood there, momentarily enchanted, he closed the gap between them and reached out to draw her into his arms. Her guard went back up in no time flat and she took a quick couple of steps to the side.

"Lay a hand on me, buster, and you'll wish you were wearing your football pads," she snapped.

Startled, he stopped stalking her and slowly lowered his hands. A smile gradually spread over his face. "That was great. Really intimidating. I think I'll let *you* handle the cameraman."

"I keep telling you," Liz said irritably, "there's not going to be any cameraman. There's not going to be any trip, at least not with me."

"We'll see." He walked to the door and held it open for her. "Let's go talk to your friend Gloria."

Liz decided it was pointless to keep arguing with him. Maybe it was his sense of duty and maybe he considered her a challenge, but he seemed determined to go through with the trip. O'Dwyer could handle it; she'd had enough aggravation today to last her a month.

Chapter Three

Liz had been working at Diamond's Hotel and Casino since early March, just under three months now. She'd started with the only job she could get, as a waitress working the swing shift in the main coffee shop. Her boss, Jack O'Dwyer, hadn't been too crazy about the idea of sending her back in the field, but he'd known that physically she was perfect for it—blond and very pretty, with the kind of body men notice. None of the other available people had even come close.

O'Dwyer's reluctance to send her back undercover wasn't due to misguided chivalry or sexism; he treated women the same as men. It stemmed from the fact that Liz was recovering from a duty-related injury and probably should have kept her desk job in San Francisco for another couple of months. She'd been stabbed in the abdomen by a man named Spider Higgins while working a case in San Diego, and the wound had taken two hours of surgery and several

pints of blood to repair. During the first months of waitressing she'd been dead on her feet most of the time, but
she'd gritted her teeth and carried on. Between the aerobics
program she'd put herself on and the old-fashioned stubbornness that was so much a part of her nature, the fatigue
had gradually gone away. Now she felt as good as she ever
had. Her only mementos of the case were the low, straight
scar across the left side of her belly and an occasional bad
dream.

She'd been working in the coffee shop for almost nine
weeks before she got her first real break. A job opened up
in the Marquise Room, the hotel's posh, top-floor restaurant. With its San Francisco prices and continental cuisine,
the place attracted entertainers playing the local clubs and
tourists with plenty of money. Those were exactly the people Liz had been sent to the area to meet, and the job, as a
cocktail waitress, was absolutely perfect.

The restaurant manager, a male chauvinist named Ernie
Corelli, had looked her up and down and promptly hired
her. Liz didn't doubt that he'd mentally stripped her naked
and dressed her in the sexy, Parisian street-dancer's outfit
the waitresses wore, but that was why O'Dwyer had used
her. She looked great in a red beret, V-necked striped top
and side-slit black skirt, and her legs were sensational in
black fishnet stockings.

She flew back up to Tahoe the morning after the taping,
having spent the night in Los Angeles with Michelle's parents, the aunt and uncle who had taken her and her brother
in after their mother's death. As usual, she arrived in the
restaurant about four, already dressed for work. The dining room opened at five and the bar at four-fifteen, but
Corelli liked her to come in early, just in case any customers had shown up.

She hadn't been in the place more than five minutes before one the the bartenders asked her how *Main Attraction*

had gone. Corelli, who also served as the restaurant's maître d', was standing a few yards away. He walked over to listen.

"You know how I told you the guest star was supposed to be some lawyer?" she asked the bartender.

"Right. The guy who's always suing doctors for malpractice. You mean he didn't show up?"

Liz shook her head. "No. He got tied up at the last minute and they substituted some assemblyman from California who refused to appear on the same stage with somebody who worked in a casino."

Corelli grimaced in disgust. "You mean you never got to do the show? I gave you time off for nothing?"

"I did the show all right, but with Zack Delaney. The segment will air a week from Friday."

The two men looked at each other, instantly impressed. "That's great!" Corelli said. "You think he'd remember who you are if you wrote him a letter inviting him up here? Whittaker is always looking for jocks to play in his charity golf tournament."

"Whittaker" was Sy Whittaker, an extroverted teddy bear of a man whose official title was assistant manager of the hotel. His duties included booking the entertainment for the nightclub and lounge, running special events like the golf tournament and supervising what the hotel called "special services." The last involved wining and dining important guests, the same sorts of guests Liz wanted to meet. She'd served him drinks once and tried to attract his notice, but he'd been too busy with his table of VIP's to pay her any attention. She planned to keep trying.

"Actually," she said to Corelli, "I won a trip to Hawaii. I tried to tell them I couldn't possibly get away from my job until I'd accumulated more vacation time...."

"Can't get away? Of course you can get away." Corelli put his arm around her waist. "You think I'd stand in your way, honey?"

Liz could hardly believe this was the same man who carped and grumbled whenever any of his employees wanted a few hours off. "But my job..."

"It'll still be here when you get back. And if you can get Delaney or any of his pals to come to the hotel, all the better. That's the image Whittaker loves—winners who keep their noses clean."

"Tell Mr. Whittaker I'll do my best," Liz said, having no such intention. "I really should get over to the table...."

"Right, honey." Corelli patted her on the backside. "You're sensational. If I was Delaney, I would've picked you, too."

Liz thanked him and went over to a table near the bar. There were three men sitting there, one of whom eventually made a pass at her. She turned him down as politely as she could, saying her boyfriend expected to see her when she got off work. There would be times when she would accept a customer's invitation, but it hadn't happened yet. She hadn't received the right invitation yet. As for her boyfriend, he was actually a fellow agent named Bill Genaro. If anybody ever asked her, she told them Bill was a pilot who had followed her from San Francisco and now worked for a local air transport company. She always added that she wasn't about to get as serious as he wanted her to because he gambled too much for her liking.

Wednesday was a slow night, but business picked up sharply on Thursday with the arrival of a big-name comedian who would be appearing in the main showroom through Sunday. After one of the busiest first hours Liz could remember, she noticed Sy Whittaker walk into the bar. The table he sat down at belonged to one of the other

waitresses, but Corelli told Liz to go over and take care of
him anyway.

"But that's Nina's table..." she began.

"He doesn't want Nina, he wants you." Corelli winked at
her. "News travels fast, especially when I'm doing the
spreading. Take him some Perrier with a twist, and then
smile and agree to do whatever he wants."

Liz got the Perrier and walked over to Whittaker's table,
smiling as ordered. He thanked her for the drink, congrat-
ulated her on winning a trip to Hawaii and then started to
question her about her appearance on *Main Attraction*. She
wasn't surprised when he brought up the golf tournament,
but he'd been so friendly and charming that she felt comfortable about reminding him that it was held in late August, when the Rushers were winding up their training camp.

"I know, I know." He sipped his drink, looking nettled.
"I keep telling them we're only forty-five minutes away, an
hour tops, and asking for a single round of golf, or even just
a personal appearance by one of their star players, but Halliday is tough about sticking to his schedule. That's Ben
Halliday, their head coach."

Liz gave him another smile. "Yes, I know who he is. I'll
certainly do whatever I can, Mr. Whittaker." She paused,
then added teasingly, "I guess it all depends on how the vacation goes, doesn't it?"

"Then make sure it goes well." He drained his glass, then
dismissed her with a crisp, "Bring me a refill and tell Corelli I want to talk to him."

"Yes, Mr. Whittaker." Liz hurried off to do his bidding,
wondering if she'd underestimated him. He'd always struck
her as a harmless front man, but front men didn't bark out
orders that way. She'd have to find out more about him.

Her general assignment was relatively straightforward.
She was supposed to check out a tip the agency had received, saying that Diamond's was supplying drugs to im-

portant customers as an incentive to come and gamble. They suspected that large-scale dealing might also be going on, for several reasons. First, any time you could link up gambling and drugs you had to start thinking about organized crime. And second, there had been lots of rumors about the Diamond Hotel Corporation. Nobody had ever been able to prove anything, mostly because the company was owned by such a complicated tangle of interlocking firms that nobody could find out who really controlled it. Maybe Whittaker could provide them with a lead.

Michelle flew back from Los Angeles on Friday, and Liz picked her up at the airport. As the baby of the family and the only girl, Michelle was both overprotected and a little spoiled. She hadn't wanted to go home before starting her job in the Marshal College cafeteria and her parents hadn't wanted her on her own, so they had finally compromised. She would live and work at the lake and Liz would keep an eye on her. Given the nature of Liz's job, she wasn't about to have her young cousin stay with her, so Michelle had taken a room in the home of an elderly couple. Her part-time job would begin the following Monday.

As soon as they were alone in the car, Michelle grinned and teased, "I know the way your mind works. You only set a date to go to Hawaii because you expect O'Dwyer to get you off the hook. What did he say?"

Liz didn't attempt to deny it. For all Michelle's immaturity, she was as tight as a drum when it came to Liz's work and would have died rather than breathe a single word to anyone outside the family. "He's been in Washington all week, but he's flying back to San Francisco this Sunday. His secretary told me he'd be in Sacramento for a meeting first thing Monday, and I asked her to tell him I'd meet him there. I know Jack. He's a lot easier to persuade if you can talk to him in person."

Michelle sighed. "Personally, I think you're crazy. I keep telling you, half the women in America would give their right arm to go to Hawaii with Zack Delaney."

"And I keep telling *you* that I'm in the other half." Liz changed the topic to Michelle's brothers, and Michelle, who knew when she was licked, cheerfully went along.

Friday was even busier than Thursday, and Saturday was the most hectic of all. Everyone had heard about Liz's victory by then, so she'd become something of a minor celebrity. Corelli had even taken to telling likely looking groups of customers about her as he led them into the cocktail lounge to wait until their tables were ready. People usually ordered more drinks if the waitresses could get them to talking, and her celebrity status encouraged conversation.

At about nine o'clock, Corelli approached Liz as she was waiting for an order of drinks and pointed to a pair of middle-aged men. "You see the guy with the crew-cut red hair? That's Cal Johnson." Liz, who had no idea who Cal Johnson might be, looked at him blankly, and he explained, "He's the Rushers' defensive line coach. I mentioned you work here, and he told me he'd heard all about the show. The guy with him is a Las Vegas businessman named Johnny Hoag. Give them as many free rounds as they want."

Whenever Corelli ordered free drinks for people, Liz immediately took a special interest in them. The interest had never been reciprocated, but that was only a matter of time and luck. "You're more of a Rushers fan than I realized," she remarked.

Corelli just laughed at that. "It isn't Johnson, honey, it's his pal. He does business with the hotel. He also happens to have dropped ten grand the last time he was in here."

"In that case, I'll get to them right away." Liz picked up her tray of drinks, hustled them over to the proper table and continued on to a table by the front window. There wasn't

much of a view other than the casinos across the street and
the motels that lined the road into California, but at least it
was nineteen stories up.

She gave Johnson a big smile and greeted him with an
enthusiastic, "Coach Johnson! It's our pleasure to have you
and Mr. Hoag here in the Marquise Room. The manager
says the drinks are on the house. What can I get you?"

She could tell Johnson liked the idea that she'd singled
him out to address. His friend was a lot more important
than he was, except perhaps to die-hard Rushers fans. As a
lowly assistant coach, he didn't get nearly as much attention as the players did. "Make it a Scotch and water," he
said. "Johnny? What'll you have?"

"A double martini," Hoag answered. He was a bit on the
sullen side, perhaps because being in Diamond's reminded
him of his missing ten grand. "Tell the bartender to mix it
with Beefeater's. And Liz—is there anything around this
place to eat?"

Liz told him she would bring over some mixed nuts and
an appetizer menu. After giving the bartender their order
she made a quick detour into the kitchen and picked up a
couple of shrimp cocktails as well. Hoag actually smiled at
her when she delivered them to his table. They began to talk
about *Main Attraction*, Liz responding to a question about
Hawaii with the remark that she'd probably eat so much
she'd never get into her costume again. The comment called
attention to her body, not that the men hadn't noticed it
before. They obviously had.

It took another round of drinks, but she finally got what
she'd been angling for for weeks—an invitation to a private
party, being held that night in Hoag's suite. It was an exciting breakthrough, but the first thought in Liz's mind concerned O'Dwyer. If she could get him some hard information, maybe he'd go along with her about Delaney. There
was no reason for him not to.

A couple of words from Hoag, and Corelli agreed to let her off early. Still, it was past midnight before she got to the party. She could hear the throb of rock music as she walked down the hall, even through the closed door. A redhead who worked for Whittaker answered her knock, but wouldn't let her inside until she gave her name and explained that Hoag and Johnson had invited her. At that point the redhead smiled and told her to make herself at home.

The suite's large main parlor was crowded, but not so packed you had to elbow your way through the bodies. Within ten seconds a man Liz had never seen before handed her a glass of wine. She giggled, saying she'd had more than her limit already, but eventually accepted it.

She spent the next half an hour nursing the wine and dancing. It was a mixed crowd—celebrities, well-heeled businessmen, lots of attractive women. Eventually she went off to use the bathroom, using the trip as an excuse to poke around the suite. She was on her way back to the parlor when Johnson came out of one of the bedrooms. He looked as if he could have taken off and flown without too much trouble. His gait was somewhere between a shuffle and a swagger and there was a cocky self-confidence that hadn't been there at dinnertime.

"Hey, Lizzie!" He put his arm around her and turned her to face the inside of the bedroom. "Look, who's here, Johnny. It's Zack's girlfriend."

Johnny Hoag was sitting on a couch, bent over a marble-topped coffee table. He was holding a razor blade, concentrating on the white substance heaped on the marble in front of him. He glanced at Liz, nodded and then went back to carefully chopping the crystals into a fine powder.

"Listen, baby, I've got to hit the john," Johnson said. "Go on in if you want to. Dessert's on the house." He weaved away, leaving Liz standing there.

She had a cigarette-pack sized tape recorder in her purse, sewn into the lining. She felt for the button to turn it on and then walked into the room.

There were eight people inside, three women and five men. The only one she recognized besides Hoag was Sy Whittaker, who was standing by the window, looking down at the traffic. Two of the other men were so big Liz wondered if they might be football players, but the introductions didn't go beyond first names.

Whittaker joined Hoag on the couch, then motioned for Liz to join them. She watched Hoag snort the drug up what looked like a solid gold straw and then offer it to the others. When the last line was gone, Whittaker pulled a foil packet out of his jacket pocket and tossed it on the table. Hoag invited Liz to take a turn as soon as the drug was ready, but she shook her head, looking tempted but determined to refuse.

"I'd love some, but coke and me—we go way back," she said. "For a while there, it was all I ever thought about. It took me a whole year to give it up. I stick to old-fashioned booze these days."

The explanation was accepted without question. Everyone except Whittaker was probably too high to care. She stayed for another thirty minutes, taping a conversation that got more and more incoherent as time went on. When she was ready to leave she asked Whittaker if she could take some coke for her boyfriend, mentioning all the usual facts—he was a pilot, he worked only part-time, he spent more than he could afford at the craps tables. After all the money he'd lost at Diamond's, she joked, the casino probably owed him a little entertainment.

The Sacramento office of the Drug Enforcement Administration was located in a suburban area of the city, in a complex containing small retail shops and commercial office space. If Liz hadn't been there before she would have had a hard time knowing where to go, because the agency wasn't listed in the building's directory and there were no signs on its doors. When your agents got tortured and murdered, you learned to keep a low profile.

She held up her tape as she walked into the meeting, saying she would play it first and explain it later. There were three people in the room—her boss, Jack O'Dwyer, who supervised the San Francisco district office, and the heads of the two smaller offices from Reno and Sacramento that shared jurisdiction over South Lake Tahoe. While the local investigation was focused solely on the Diamond's Hotel at Tahoe, other teams were looking into the company's casino/ hotels in Las Vegas and Atlantic City. O'Dwyer had gone to Washington for meetings to coordinate the various investigations.

Liz clicked on the tape, then sat back and let it run. O'Dwyer was smiling by the time it finished playing. "You're something else," he said. "I can't believe you strolled out of there with a free packet of cocaine."

Liz took the foil envelope out of her purse and slid it across the table to him. "It's only about a quarter full, but I got the feeling Whittaker can get as much as he wants. Still, there's no actual evidence that he's doing anything but giving it away to VIP's. He didn't seem especially interested when I went into my song and dance about Bill."

Bill Genaro represented what they hoped would be the next step in the investigation. People who trafficked in narcotics needed pilots to smuggle drugs into the country or move them around from city to city. As someone who not only used drugs but needed money to pay for a gambling habit, Genaro would be a natural for the role. It was Liz's job to find out who in the hotel might be interested in his services and make the introductions.

She'd mentioned Whittaker in passing before, so O'Dwyer knew who he was, but she'd never suggested he might be involved in anything illegal. She gave O'Dwyer her most recent impressions of the man, then added, "My gut instinct tells me he *is* involved in distributing and selling. I think I should continue along the same lines as before, keeping my eyes open for other possibilities, but also try to get as close to Whittaker as I can."

O'Dwyer said that sounded fine and then complimented her on her progress. With the immediate needs of the investigation out of the way, Liz decided to bring up the topic that had brought her to the meeting in the first place—Zack Delaney. O'Dwyer, of course, had no idea Liz was supposed to go to Hawaii with him. His name had never even come up on the tape.

She explained about the last-minute substitution that had led Gloria to switch her to Delaney's segment, then apologized for the blunders that had turned her into a winner. "It wasn't a total disaster, though," she added, "because one of the Rushers' coaches —Cal Johnson—came into the restaurant with a Las Vegas businessman named Johnny Hoag, and my connection to Delaney was what got me invited to the party. But now I'm stuck with this Hawaii thing. Believe me, I tried every way I could to get out of it. I even told Delaney I was an undercover agent for the hotel...."

O'Dwyer's head jerked up. "You *what?*" he barked.

"I told him I was an undercover agent for the hotel," Liz repeated defensively. "I said I was there to keep the employees honest. But don't worry, I told him I worked for corporate headquarters, and that nobody in the hotel knows my real job. He thinks I could get in real trouble for telling him about it. He won't check it out with management."

O'Dwyer muttered that he damn well hoped not and told her to go on. Liz sank down in her chair, very relieved. She wasn't used to having him yell at her. But then she realized that he wasn't only worried about corporate headquarters learning she'd claimed to be one of their people, but also about Delaney finding out her real job. A sinking sensation hit her deep in the pit of her stomach. Her original intention to ask O'Dwyer to level with the man was temporarily abandoned.

"I thought maybe you could call Delaney and the show's producer and tell them you're the head of security for Diamond's Hotel," she said. "You could say you'll need me where I am for another six or seven weeks. Delaney will be in training camp by then . . ."

"Having returned from eight fun-filled days in Hawaii with you." O'Dwyer tipped back his chair, folded his arms across his chest and grinned. "Aloha, Liz."

"Very funny, Jack." Liz gave him a pleading look, thinking that she had nothing to lose by returning to Plan A. "Come on, you're got to get me off the hook. I don't have time to run off to Hawaii and I don't want my face all over national television again. Would it be that much of a problem just to tell everyone who I am? That way, I wouldn't have to go at all."

It didn't take her long to suspect she was fighting a losing battle. The first nail in her coffin came when O'Dwyer pointed out that if she were recognized during a future assignment she could say she'd tired of working as a waitress and moved on to something else. It was right in line with the free-spirited character she'd portrayed. The Reno supervisor added that a week or so away from Tahoe wouldn't make any difference in a case that was expected to go on for months. He also pointed out that people around the hotel would expect her to go. She was in the middle of insisting that she would somehow come up with a story to explain that when the last man at the table, the one from the local office, pounded in what proved to be the final nail—he asked her to replay the tape.

"I think we need to identify the other people in the room," he said afterward. "First of all, where was Cal Johnson? Did you see him at the party?"

"He was on his way to the bathroom when I passed the bedroom," Liz explained. "He seemed to be high, but it could have been from liquor rather than drugs. He never came back to the room."

O'Dwyer was nodding his head, saying he saw his colleague's point. Liz didn't know what "point" they were talking about and had the feeling she wouldn't enjoy finding out. "I thought I heard the name 'Slammer' on the tape," O'Dwyer continued. "Can you tell us who that referred to?"

"I didn't recognize anyone but Whittaker and Hoag, but there were two men I thought might have been football players." Liz gave physical descriptions, adding that both had taken drugs in her presence.

At that point, all three men in the room were able to identify "the Slammer." He was a huge defensive end named Pete Slama whom the Rushers had traded to the Los Angeles Titans during the off-season. The man sitting next to him, whose name had been Willie, might have been Rushers' linebacker Willie Lee White, but there were other "Willies" in the league who fit the same general description. O'Dwyer wanted Liz to look at pictures, and sent a secretary to a nearby library to check through old sports magazines and reference books to see what she could come up with.

"The bottom line," he said once they'd thoroughly discussed the tape, "is that we have two and possibly three men associated with the Rushers who have been implicated in the use of illegal drugs. It's a lead I want followed up."

"Followed up how?" Liz asked, all but dreading the answer.

"By going to Hawaii with Delaney. By getting him to talk about his teammates, whether they use drugs, and where they get them." O'Dwyer paused, taking in the recalcitrant expression on Liz's face. His own expression got a lot harder. "I don't care whether you like it or not, Liz. What I'm about to say stays in this room. It comes out of my meetings in Washington, one of which involved the FBI. They've got a wiretap that alludes to attempts to bribe or blackmail professional athletes into deliberately blowing games. That's hardly a new concern, but now we've got a pair of football players in Diamond's getting free coke and I want to know more about it. The public has a right to expect clean sports, and it's part of our job to see it gets them. And before you get on your high horse and start lecturing me about how Delaney is an innocent bystander, you might remember what happened to your brother Tommy and why you joined this agency in the first place."

Liz felt her temper flare, making her whole body stiffen with reproach. "Just leave my brother out of this," she snapped. "Dammit, Jack, I liked Zack Delaney. He's a decent person—"

"Who probably has more brains than to use narcotics. A quarterback has to see too much and remember too much during a game to cloud up his mind with junk."

"That's not the point. You're asking me to get him to inform on his teammates."

"I'm not asking you, I'm telling you. I expect you to do your job."

Fuming now, Liz glared at him and muttered, "Yes, *sir!*"

O'Dwyer immediately softened. "Listen to me, Liz. We're not out to crucify any of the players. You know that. But maybe they can lead us to the men who really run things. Just follow this up and see where it leads. We don't have athletes like Delaney dropping into our laps every day."

"So let me tell him who I am."

"Not a chance. In the first place, I doubt he'd cooperate if he knew. And in the second place, we can't be absolutely sure he's not involved. I repeat, I expect you to do your job."

Although Liz knew it was pointless to argue, she couldn't bring herself to agree verbally. O'Dwyer took her silence for what it was—obedience. The queasiness in the pit of her stomach turned into a full-blown bellyache when the secretary returned with an old copy of *Sports Illustrated*. The "Willie" she'd met *was* Willie Lee White of the Rushers. One coach and two players didn't make a conspiracy, but the whole thing was beginning to stink. It was no longer a question of whether or not Liz would do her job, but of how much enthusiasm and determination she could bring herself to put into it.

Chapter Four

Zack Delaney knew how it felt to be stood up by a woman, but it hadn't happened for a very long time, not since the days when he'd been an ordinary mortal. As he waited for Liz Reynolds's flight to arrive in San Francisco from South Lake Tahoe, he tried to remember exactly how long it had been. Thinking back to his sophomore year in college, he recalled an intellectual redhead named Mary Jane Something-or-other and a fruitless two-hour wait at the local pizza place. He hadn't been so much disappointed as embarrassed on that occasion, but if Liz didn't show up... He looked out the window, watching a small commuter plane taxi toward the gate. He only hoped she was on it, because if she wasn't the media would be even more of a pain in the neck than usual.

The only communication between the two of them had been a letter he'd sent her about two weeks after the taping. It had taken him all that time to realize that the vacation plans he'd agreed to were totally unworkable, which just went to show that all the running around he'd done between January and June had left his brains a little scrambled.

There was no way he could go to three different islands in eight days, and he'd explained as much to the show's producer. He would need to stay on Oahu, and furthermore, he wanted his schedule left open through lunchtime every day. He'd stepped up his off-season conditioning program around the middle of June, but if he went off to Hawaii for eight straight days and didn't continue to get in shape he'd stroll into training camp as soft, fat and happy as a suckling pig before roasting time. As a professional athlete in an intensely physical sport, he couldn't afford that. Being out of shape meant poorer play, a higher risk of injuries and, maybe worst of all, Halliday benching him in favor of a tough young quarterback just itching for his job. Although Zack wasn't worried about unemployment, sitting on the bench was probably his least favorite activity.

He'd written to Liz in care of the show to explain all that and then apologized if the change in schedule inconvenienced her. When she didn't write back he toyed with the idea of following up the letter with a phone call, but in the end he decided to leave well enough alone. The last thing he needed was more arguing from her about going away with him.

He'd been busier than ever during the past five weeks or so, primarily with business matters. Although his older brother Brian, who lived in Los Angeles, managed his investments, he'd taken a lot more interest in them over the past year or two. Still, as June gave way to July and the fall approached, his thoughts had turned more and more to football and the season that lay ahead. Training camp, with its two-a-day practices and summer heat, could be physically exhausting, but he was looking forward to it with an eagerness that surprised him. Certainly there was nothing to make him want to stay in San Francisco, the way Allison had the first summer he'd known her. The week in Hawaii with Liz had come to represent more of a duty than a pleasure by then, and all he wanted was to get through it in as civil a fashion as possible.

As he waited for the first passengers to emerge from the plane he found himself hoping that, for once, people would be too wrapped up in their private comings and goings to approach him. There had been quite a few double takes as he'd walked down the corridor to the gate, but nobody had tried to stop him. He was grateful for that, because the situation was making him feel awkward and nervous. Women were so damn moody, and Liz had been reluctant from the start. The last thing he needed was five hours on a plane with a sullen, even hostile companion.

Even so, he was undeniably relieved when he saw her walking through the jetway. *Main Attraction*'s publicist hadn't made any secret of which flight they'd be taking to Hawaii, and there were bound to be reporters at the Transpacific Airlines gate. At least he wouldn't have to show up there alone, and then attempt to explain what had happened to his date.

She kept her eyes set straight ahead. He hadn't told her he'd be meeting her plane, so there was no reason for her to look for him. He had come for two reasons. He didn't want to see her for the first time in more than a month in front of a bunch of reporters, and even more important, he'd been raised to have better manners than to leave a woman on her own in a situation like this.

She was wearing a white linen suit, red blouse and navy shoes, with a gray tote bag over one shoulder and a navy purse over the other. Looking at her, Zack wondered how he could have remembered her as merely "pretty." With her silky hair pinned into a ballerina's knot at the nape of her neck and her makeup a lot less heavy than it had been for the taping, she looked sophisticated but fresh, a total knockout. Eight days of mere civility began to have as much appeal as a three-game losing streak.

He trotted up behind her, calling out her name as he raised his hand to take the tote bag off her shoulder. "I'll carry that for you," he said as she jerked around. He could tell that he'd startled her. "How was your flight?"

Liz had been lost in a world of her own, wrapped up in emotions that ranged from worry to guilt to nervousness. To begin with, she'd hated walking out in the middle of such a promising investigation. Bill Genaro, her fellow agent, had gotten the job offer they'd been waiting for. It hadn't come from Whittaker, but from Coach Johnson's friend, Johnny Hoag. On the surface, at least, Hoag was a legitimate businessman. His company provided first-class hotels with all the little extras they were always giving away to guests— soaps, toiletries, shampoo, shower caps, and so on. Bill was making several runs a week now, flying supplies between Hoag's Las Vegas warehouse and other Western cities. The cargo had been strictly legitimate so far, but they doubted it would stay that way.

Liz, meanwhile, had carried on her previous routine. She'd attended quite a few private parties over the weeks, seen a lot of drugs exchange hands and gotten more and more friendly with Sy Whittaker. She had the feeling he was sizing her up before trusting her with anything more important than helping entertain VIP's, but that might have been wishful thinking on her part.

Only the week before, O'Dwyer had received additional evidence linking drugs to attempts to rig sporting events. The DEA and FBI were more interested in the subject than ever. So here she was, expected to wring information out of a perfectly pleasant man who'd never done her the slightest harm, and feeling miserably guilty about it.

O'Dwyer had told her she was overreacting, but he wasn't the one who'd received Zack's letter. The man had such flawless manners that he even apologized for the simple need to do his job. She could remember the last few sentences verbatim. "I promise, though, I'll try not to let the workouts get in the way of what we're going to Hawaii for. After two Pro Bowls, I know my way around Honolulu's night spots better than I should probably admit, and I guarantee you a good time—assuming we can lose the watchdogs. So grit your teeth and resign yourself to having some fun, and I'll see you on July 11th."

That fun of his made Liz extremely nervous. Nobody had ever suggested that Zack Delaney was in the same class as Joe Namath, who had written the book when it came to high-living bachelor quarterbacks, and he didn't strike Liz as shy and retiring, either. All that talk about showing her a good time and teaching her how to have fun made her wonder about his plans for their relationship. She had no intention of getting involved in a one-week affair, especially not with a man who'd become part of her job.

Her strategy for keeping him at a distance was based on the hope that a cool, unresponsive woman with ice water in her veins would have very little appeal for him. Lord knows it was a role she'd played often enough in the past, usually with good results. The only trouble was that she'd never played it opposite anyone as attractive as Zack.

If his touch had startled her, a single look at his face made her want to bolt right back to the plane. No man had a right to be so handsome, much less smile in a way calculated to leave any normal female weak in the knees. Temporarily off balance, she allowed him to take her tote bag and then answered his question about her flight. "It was fine, but I'm afraid I'm a nervous flyer, especially in small planes. I'm glad we're taking a DC-10." She immediately felt like kicking herself, because cool, bored ladies didn't go around chattering about their hang-ups.

They started down the corridor, with Zack attracting more than his share of whispers and stares. Outwardly oblivious to them, he told Liz he knew exactly how she felt, only with him it was closed-in places. "Once I got stuck in an elevator and I was covered with sweat by the time they got me out half an hour later." He shook his head, looking embarrassed even to remember it. "The only other person in there with me was a pregnant woman. She was due any day, but she wound up reassuring *me* that everything would be all right. It doesn't exactly fit the image I try so hard to cultivate."

Liz fought a losing battle with her curiosity. "And what image would that be?"

"The fearless quarterback, disdainful of physical danger. I'm not crazy about getting sacked, but what I really hate is winding up on the bottom of a pileup, trapped under half a ton of bodies. Fortunately it almost never happens. I take my offensive linemen out to dinner a lot. I want them to love me like a brother."

Liz didn't know if they loved him like a brother, but they certainly took pride in protecting him. She'd spent a lot of the past week skimming every football book and magazine article she could get her hands on, looking for information on Zack, the Rushers and football in general. She hadn't understood even half the technical details in all that reading, but one thing had come through loud and clear. Zack Delaney was a leader. His teammates paid careful attention to his opinions and had a unanimous confidence in his ability to win. One player had remarked to a journalist that Zack never yelled when somebody's sloppy play or lack of concentration allowed the opposition to get to him, but just looked at him as if he were knee-high to a snake's belly. That look, the player insisted, was as bad as anybody else's screaming tirade and Zack's teammates cringed when they saw it coming.

Liz was intensely curious about what sort of man could inspire such loyalty and exert such influence, but the last thing she wanted was to show too much obvious interest. The closer she let herself get to Zack Delaney, the more difficult the next eight days were going to be. She had enough problems already without taking on any more of them.

Deliberately discouraging him, she didn't make the slightest response to what he'd told her but kept her eyes straight ahead and her feet on the move. After a few silent seconds he asked her how she'd been. She answered "Fine." He asked her how her work was going and she told him "Okay." When her answers to his next couple of questions were equally abrupt, his face tightened in annoyance and he gave up trying to make conversation.

Picking up the pace of his steps, he walked briskly through the concourse and out of the building, his head down and eyes straight ahead, rather like a charging bull. He didn't seem to notice that Liz had to scramble to keep up with him. She was grateful for the long line at the Transpacific security check, because standing in it would give her a chance to catch her breath.

She went through the metal detector first. There was a loud beep a few seconds later as she collected her purse from the conveyor belt. Turning around to look, she saw Zack back up a few steps and take off his navy blazer. The line was even longer by then and a couple of people began to grumble under their breath about the delay.

He handed the jacket to an apologetic-looking security guard, murmuring something about the buttons. It was a common enough event—everyone had seen buttons, keys and change set off the machines—but suddenly, as Liz was picking up her tote bag, an everyday occurrence turned into an incipient mob scene.

It started when two teenage boys shouted out Zack's name and ran down the corridor. He barely had time to get through the metal detector and take back his jacket before the eager boys were shoving a paper bag under his nose and asking him for an autograph. His agreement attracted a flurry of attention, the crowd around him growing until it threatened to block the corridor. People didn't seem to care what he signed—airline ticket envelopes, spare scraps of paper, even magazines they'd bought to read on the plane. He patiently scrawled his name, a stoic smile on his face, while Liz stood on the fringe of the crowd and waited.

She was beginning to think he would never get away when a pair of airport security men showed up to disperse the crowd. In the meantime, the flock of photographers and reporters who'd been waiting by the gate realized what the commotion was all about and hustled down to get the story. The photographers wanted Zack to recreate being stopped by the metal detector for their cameras, but he refused. Outwardly at least, he seemed half amused, half regretful as he flashed a smile and apologized, "I'm afraid not, fellas. I think I've caused enough trouble already," but Liz was beginning to see beneath the surface charm by now. His smile was a little strained and he wasn't nearly as relaxed as he pretended to be. Liz could spot the difference because she remembered how he'd been in her dressing room. There was a lazy, almost careless grace about Zack when he was genuinely enjoying himself, but at the moment there wasn't even a hint of that. Unless she missed her guess, he was deeply uncomfortable, so much so that she wanted to take him by the arm, order his fans to leave him alone and march him off to safety. Instead, she stood there in frustrated silence while he placated the journalists by promising to meet them by the gate for an interview and pictures.

Nobody paid her any attention until he called out her name and told her to join him, but then somebody yelled,

"Hey, look! There's the girl from the show," and people started craning their necks to locate her. She was aware of their curious stares as the security men muscled their way into the crowd to clear a path for her, but she did her best to ignore them. The only thing on her mind was to make this whole sideshow as easy as possible for Zack to endure. She took his outstretched hand and the two of them followed after the security men.

When they reached the gate, Zack got her settled in an empty seat and then walked over to where the television cameramen had set up their lights. The questions came rapid-fire, and there was nothing the reporters didn't want to know. Had he and Liz seen each other since taping the show? What would they be doing in Hawaii? Where would they be staying and what would the sleeping arrangements be? Was he predicting another trip to the Super Bowl? Did he think the Rushers had a harder schedule this year? And what was his opinion of their number-one draft pick, a glamour boy running back with a reputation for being as erratic as he was talented?

He'd obviously had a lot of practice with the press. He answered their questions with such smooth self-assurance that Liz decided he must have heard it all before. The only exception was the question about the sleeping arrangements. Personally she thought the man had a hell of a nerve asking something like that, but she wasn't the one on the firing line so she kept her mouth shut. As for Zack, he stared at the reporter in apparent amazement for several seconds but then grinned. "Get your mind out of the gutter, McCleary. Any more questions like that and the lady will probably decide to stay in a different hotel. Maybe even on a different island. Why don't we talk about football?"

He cut things off about fifteen minutes later, once the questions began to get tediously repetitive. The reporters promptly descended on Liz, reminding her of a flock of swarming locusts. She began to answer the first question she heard, which was something about what her family thought of her winning the trip to Hawaii, but found it hard to concentrate with so many flashes going off in her face. All she could think about was having her picture splashed across the front pages of the next day's papers.

At that point she saw a side of Zack Delaney that she'd previously only read about. With a crisp "Excuse me," he waded into the crowd of reporters, cutting through it like a Midwestern twister. The next thing she knew, he was standing by her side with his arm around her shoulders. One look at his face and she understood all those articles a lot better. His expression was cold enough to make a polar bear shiver. The reporters abruptly quieted down, and some of them even backed up a step or two.

When he finally spoke, however, his tone was surprisingly mild. "Come on, fellas. She's a civilian. No more questions, but you can take a couple of pictures. Then we've got a plane to catch."

Liz tensed as the cameras started flashing again, but it was all over within ten seconds. "Okay, that's it," Zack said. "I'll see you later this month, at Marshal College." She felt the muscles in his arm press against her back, directing her toward the jetway, and automatically went where he wanted. Through all of this it had never occurred to her *not* to go and do what he wanted.

She didn't know whether it was the look in his eyes or the way he carried himself, but the message was as clear to her as it had been to the reporters. He'd made certain decisions and they weren't open to discussion. On the surface he was the most easygoing, low-key guy in the world, but you didn't have to dig down very far to find the will of pure steel underneath.

There was nobody by the tunnel to check their tickets, but that didn't stop him for a moment. He didn't even seem to care that the gate attendants weren't boarding the plane yet, or that airline personnel were sticklers for following established procedures. When one of them came running through the jetway, calling out Zack's name, Liz half expected to be led back out to the waiting area. Zack stopped, but only to ask Liz for her ticket and take out his own.

He held the two envelopes out to the gate attendant, who smiled and tore off their boarding passes and San Francisco-Honolulu tickets. A few seconds later a flight attendant hurried out of the plane and led them on board. *Main Attraction* was sending them first-class, a new experience for Liz but evidently old hat to Zack. He seemed to take special treatment for granted.

When she asked to sit by the aisle, he smiled sympathetically and asked her if she wanted him to pull down the window shade. Her answer was yes. She admitted she hated being by the window and hated looking out at the ground even more, but that was as far as the conversation got. People had started filing onto the plane, and not a single one of them, in either of the twin aisles, seemed capable of passing their seats without slowing and gawking.

Zack immediately took out the airline's in-flight magazine, buried his nose in it and slumped down in his seat. Liz felt like handing him dark glasses and a stick-on mustache. The whispers and stares continued unabated, but at least people weren't bumping their carry-on bags against *his* shoulder, or stopping right by *his* seat for a better look.

As much as Liz disliked the secondhand attention, she eventually realized that the situation was actually kind of funny. Zack Delaney was as intimidating a man as she'd ever met, at least when he wanted to be, and here he was, trying to hide from the public behind a Transpacific Airlines magazine. Maybe it was just his way of telling people he wasn't available for autographs or conversation just then, but Liz doubted it. She suspected he was a lot shyer than she'd realized, uneasy with all the hoopla, and sorry about subjecting her to the consequences of his fame. She'd never doubted he was human, but to be *so* human made him doubly attractive. She couldn't help wanting to make it less awful for him, or at least to assure him that she would survive the ordeal.

She leaned in toward his seat, turning her back to the passing crowd. "Now I know why you smiled when I asked to sit by the aisle," she hissed. "I thought you were sympathetic because of your claustrophobia, but you were actually trying not to laugh. I'll bet you wanted the window seat all along."

His gaze shifted to the aisle. People were still shuffling past, but the line was finally thinning. "Did I?" he asked.

Liz nodded. "Yup. You wanted to put *me* into the line of fire instead of you. Quarterbacks are the biggest chickens in the world. I know that because I've been reading all about football. Guys become quarterbacks because they hate hitting and getting hit, and other than a kicker it's the position with the least physical contact." She forced back a smile. "Although come to think of it, there's something a little weird about the way you guys put your hands under the center to get the snap."

Zack put down his magazine. He hadn't been paying much attention to it anyway, since it was hard to concentrate on reading when people were using your face for visual target practice. The kindest thing he could say about constantly being recognized was that it was a result of his success, and therefore to be tolerated as graciously as possible. The one thing he *couldn't* tolerate was the public's insatiable curiosity about anyone who happened to be with him. He hadn't missed the look of panic in Liz's eyes when all those flashes had gone off in her face and he was still a little angry about it.

He'd planned on offering her an apology as soon as the plane was in the air and they had a little time to themselves, but she'd obviously made a complete recovery. Not only that, but she was even teasing him about diving for cover behind a magazine. He liked it when she teased him. He especially liked the mischievous look in her eyes and her deadpan delivery. Very few women he knew had such a good sense of humor about having their privacy invaded.

At that moment there was nowhere he would rather have been than on that particular airplane with that particular woman by his side, unless it was in a large, comfortable bed with her moaning in his arms. The image made his stomach muscles tighten in anticipation. Back in the airport, when she'd answered all his questions with curt, one-word replies, he'd told himself that thoughts like that were strictly in the realm of fantasy, but now he wasn't so sure. She'd warmed about fifty degrees in the past forty-five minutes.

Now she had broached the subject of physical contact. He didn't touch her, but he didn't hide his interest in sleeping with her, either. "I'd like to be clear about what you're suggesting," he said. "Which are you questioning? My physical courage, my psychological toughness or my heterosexuality?"

She edged away from him and straightened up. Something, either the look in his eyes or the suggestiveness in his tone, had evidently made her nervous. "None of the above. It was just an idle observation. Obviously I was wrong."

The last few passengers straggled onto the plane, moving even slower than the others. Zack was put off by the idea of being a sideshow for a bunch of rubberneckers, but at the same time, he wasn't about to give up the advantage he'd gained. Liz held his gaze for another moment or two, then looked into her lap.

"Obviously you were," he said, and ran his fingertips up and down her cheek. She had a beautiful complexion, the peaches-and-cream skin a delight to caress. He even had the satisfaction of seeing her redden a little. Leaning close to her ear, he murmured, "But I wouldn't expect you to take my word for it. I'm used to proving myself. I do it every time I step on a football field."

For a few long seconds, Liz had no idea what to do. She could handle out-and-out propositions with very little trouble, but had never had a man look at her, speak to her and touch her the way Zack did. The intensity of his gaze, the husky self-assurance of his words, the teasing delicacy of his fingers—all sent her pulse rate soaring, and the worst part was the hot excitement that licked at her skin whenever he got too close. She cursed the chemistry that made him so appealing and forced herself to stop acting the way Michelle probably would have.

She shook her head, then rolled her eyes in disbelief, as though nobody in the world could have expected her to take such drivel seriously. "That's some line you have, Delaney. But don't you think you should save it for someplace less public?"

He grinned at her. "Hey, listen, Liz. The last time I tossed a pass, it was in front of ninety thousand people. Millions if you count TV. This is intimate by comparison."

Liz wouldn't have called it intimate, but at least everyone was finally seated by then and the flight attendants were closing the door. "Mmm." She gave a thoughtful nod. "I suppose you're talking about that pass you threw against the Dolphins, to Travers in the end zone for a touchdown. I hate to be the one to tell you this, but your performance in front of the crowd was a whole lot better."

"But you've never seen me operate in private," he pointed out. "I'm very persuasive."

Liz raised her eyebrows. "What a terrifying prospect! Remind me not to let you get me alone. I wouldn't want to run the risk of getting talked into anything."

"Good game plan. One-on-one, I'm unbeatable." He curled his fingers around the back of her neck and stroked the sensitive skin there. "There's one problem, though. It won't work. I have every intention of getting you alone, and when I do, there's no limit to what I plan to talk you into."

He made a claim that would have been laughable from any other man Liz knew into a rather alarming promise. She was sorry by now that she'd ever started in with him. It was too damn dangerous to let it continue, even if the only alternative was to shut him up in a way that was going to make her feel like an absolute bitch.

She stiffened, giving him the kind of look she usually reserved for the scum she sent to jail. "Mr. Delaney, please get your hand off my neck. I've tried to be nice about this, but you don't seem to be getting the message. I'm not a football and I'm not out for a good time, so you have no further reason to touch me. The sooner you get that through your thick, conceited head, the less unpleasant this so-called vacation will be for me."

Zack took away his hand, shaken by the sheer strength of her distaste. In twenty-eight years no woman had ever spoken to him like that, and his first instinct was to forget her. She was driving him straight up the wall, turning him on with smiles and teasing one moment and slapping him down with six different kinds of rejection the next, and he of all people didn't have to put up with it. But then he remembered her skittishness whenever he got too close and the way she flushed whenever he touched her, and told himself he was probably just as dense and conceited as she'd said. After so many years of women dropping into his lap like so many ripe apples, he was spoiled rotten. Maybe she was scared. Maybe she just wanted to be friends. Obviously he'd gone too fast.

He picked up his magazine, saying he was sorry, but her only response was a clipped, "Good." With a sigh, he started thumbing through the pages again. As soon as the plane was in the air he ordered a Bloody Mary. He sat there sipping it, waiting for her to unbend a little, but she didn't. She'd taken a paperback out of her tote bag and was no longer even acknowledging his existence. Having no choice, he let the matter drop.

He tried again over lunch, an excellent slice of prime rib that Liz only picked at. He told her he was sorry if he'd upset her. He assured her he'd only meant to tease her, not to suggest he actually expected anything. He was used to women who lived in the fast lane, but he understood she didn't and would remember it in the future. She did a lot of nodding but very little talking.

By the time lunch was over Liz felt like a criminal. Zack Delaney was too damn sweet for words, and she hated being so nasty to him. She picked up her book again, but couldn't begin to read it. Hadn't he said he wouldn't expect anything? That he knew she was out of his league and wouldn't press her? So what was her problem? They understood each other perfectly now, didn't they?

When the lights dimmed for the in-flight movie, she touched his arm and gave him a forgiving smile. "I've heard this is good. Michelle just loved it."

He picked up his headphone. "Can you trust her opinion?"

"Well—she thinks *you* walk on water."

"Smart girl," he murmured.

The movie *was* good, maybe too good. It was one of those plots where the hero and heroine are thrown into a dangerous situation and desperately start to want what they can't have, namely each other. The two actors radiated a tension and frustration that burned up the screen. Assuming you were a healthy adult with all the normal instincts, it was impossible not to feel the heat. By the time they got to the first illicit kiss, it was like watching a long-delayed explosion of fireworks. Liz didn't even want to think about how she would react if the hero and heroine ever made it into bed together. She was already much too conscious of Zack sitting by her side, very real, very warm and probably very willing.

Zack was willing, all right, and so worked up by then he found himself hoping the projection system would break down. He didn't have the self-discipline to stop watching the blasted movie, but the more he watched the more turned on he got. He decided there was only one possible explanation for the fact that they were showing this particular film—somebody was deliberately torturing him.

He watched the plot unfold with agonizing predictability. Shared danger, a narrow escape, a desperate effort by the hero and heroine to forget their fears by losing themselves in physical pleasure . . . It was all totally inevitable. It was also inevitable that the sight of the two of them all but devouring each other in bed would make him ache with frustration. After all, there was a beautiful woman by his side who was finally smiling at him again. He longed to kiss her, or even just to touch her. Up on the screen, the two actors were twined around each other's bodies under a quilt, moving suggestively. Zack closed his eyes and cursed silently, wishing he couldn't smell Liz's delicate perfume. How in the hell was he going to keep his hands off her? He wasn't.

On the face of it, the idea of touching her was close to suicidal, but Zack Delaney wouldn't have been an All-Pro quarterback if he hadn't been willing to take risks every now and then. Sometimes the only way to win a game was by forgetting the usual percentages and trying the daring or unexpected. Successful football, after all, was largely a matter of outsmarting the opposition.

He considered his options, which ranged all the way from silent suffering to the romantic equivalent of a Hail Mary pass—one of those long bombs you throw down the field in the final seconds of a game, when only a touchdown can give you the victory. The more he thought about it, the better he liked the odds. In a football game your opponents knew what you would try and made sure to cover your receivers, but Liz was out there all alone, totally off her guard. Assuming she was even half-human, the movie had to have had some effect on her. It all came down to a simple question: was she attracted to him or wasn't she? In the end he couldn't stop himself from trying to find out.

Liz didn't even notice Zack take off his headset, so it came as a complete surprise to her when he put his arm around her shoulders. Half of her—the logical half—instantly froze, but the half that responded to his every look and touch felt as if the first-class section of the plane had turned into a sauna. The picture that flashed into her mind had a lot in common with what was happening on the screen, but the lead characters were different. She wondered how Zack kissed. She wondered how his hands would feel on her body. Knowing it was insane even to speculate, she reached for the fingers that had begun to burrow their way under the collar of her suit jacket, intending to firmly remove them. The time to call a halt was right now.

Unfortunately, he was much too quick for her. While she was busy fumbling for his elusive fingers, he leaned closer, pulled her around to face him and pulled off her headset. Trapped in his arms now, she had nothing to show for her troubles but a scratched palm, the victim of an encounter with his diamond-studded Super Bowl ring.

Given the things she'd said to him only hours before, he was either incredibly forgetful or just plain arrogant. Annoyance rippled through her body when he tightened his hold in response to her attempt to pull away, but his high-handed insistence on keeping her exactly where he pleased was also intensely exciting. No man in Liz's experience had ever moved in and taken over this way, and it was just her lousy luck that the first one to try it would be somebody she was so attracted to. Even worse, it was all happening so fast that she never had time to stop, catch her breath and talk a little common sense into herself.

The next thing she knew, his lips were against her throat. They were soft and gentle, but there was an urgency about the way they moved hotly up her neck that alarmed her as much as it aroused her. There was nothing playful or teasing about any of this. It was raw, unapologetic desire, and all the time she was fighting it, she also found herself responding to it. She shuddered, feeling the situation spiral further and further out of control.

"Zack, please..." She took a quick, unsteady breath. "I want you to stop that. I've already told you..."

"You'll have to speak up," he murmured as he kissed his way along her jawbone. "I can't hear you."

He knew darn well she wasn't going to shout, not when there were other people around. The plane might have been dim and the seats in the rest of the row unoccupied, but it wasn't as dark as a regular theater would have been and Zack's presence wasn't exactly a closely held secret. He nipped her earlobe, sending shock waves of pleasure down her body. By the time his tongue began to explore the sensitive folds and hollows above, she was almost too dazed to think straight. None of this could really be happening. Sensible, adult women didn't go around necking in airplanes. They didn't go crazy just because some guy made a pass at them. She was a hard-nosed federal agent and she was supposed to be able to handle anything—or anyone.

She groped for her seat belt, telling herself she had to get up, but before she could undo the buckle Zack caught hold of her hand and pulled her arm up around his neck. A moment later his hands were on her face, holding it captive for his mouth. She hadn't realized how long and sensuous his fingers were until she felt the roughly callused skin caress her throat and cheek. With his lips poised above her mouth and his breath fanning her face, all she could think about was how badly she wanted him to kiss her.

One soft brush of his lips and she was lost. She waited tensely, her heart beating wildly in anticipation of the next erotic touch, and finally felt his tongue slide along the space between her lips. She parted them a little, inviting him to taste the softness inside. But he didn't just taste; he fed like a man who'd been starving, probing her mouth with a deep, explosive passion that swept her up and carried her along for the ride. Overwhelmed, Liz gave him everything he wanted and more. She wrapped her arms tightly around his neck as he crushed her against his chest, and her mouth fed every bit as greedily as his did. By the time he pulled away his lips and buried them against her neck, she was wishing they were someplace else, someplace totally private. She twisted her head, blindly seeking his mouth again, but he caught her by the shoulders and gently eased her backward. She sought his eyes, saw that he was smiling, and didn't know what that meant. Triumph, maybe. Pleasure at calling her bluff so completely. Without breaking eye contact, he picked up her headset and slid it back in place. Liz didn't know which was worse—her confusion, her frustration or her embarrassment. She looked away first.

She sat there wishing the movie would never end, but it did, and the lights came back on, and a flight attendant came around with an offer of still more food. Zack asked for a beer along with the snack, then said casually, "So what did you think of the movie?"

Try as she might, Liz couldn't hear any needling double entendre in the question. To look at him, you would never have known that only minutes before they'd been locked in each other's arms. "It was fine," she answered.

He took the beer, set it on his tray and stretched out his arms. Once the stewardess had moved down to the next pair of seats, he remarked, "You know what I want to do when we get to Honolulu? Exercise the stiffness out of my muscles and then soak in a Jacuzzi for about an hour. After that, dinner at the hotel and a quiet walk along the beach in the moonlight. How does that sound?"

It sounded just fine, but not to do together. Liz stared at her food, more unsure of herself than she'd been in years. "Zack, about what happened before . . ."

"You mean the way you jumped me when I was least expecting it?" He brushed his knuckles across her cheek and she gave him a quick, uncertain look. She wasn't surprised to see a smile on his face, an unmistakably teasing smile. "Don't worry about it. I understand about the movie."

"If you would be serious for a moment . . ."

"I *am* being serious. Totally serious. You don't have to apologize. It's a myth that women aren't affected by visual erotica. A study by two Stanford psychologists—"

"Zack, if you don't cut it out I just might pick up your beer and pour it over your head." She gave the can a meaningful stare. "I want to get this settled right now."

"Okay." Laughing, he pushed the beer as far away from her hand as it could go. "Tell me what we need to settle. I mean, I assume we're not talking about ending the arms race here, or deciding the future of Central America."

Liz reddened, but she wasn't about to let him embarrass or tease her into dropping the subject. "You know perfectly well what we're talking about. You and me. This whole situation."

He nodded, outwardly sober now. "Right. We're going to relax, have some fun and do our best to slip away from things like cameras and chaperons. Do you have a problem with that?"

"Of course I don't. But you're not exactly being honest about it. You haven't said what happens during that moonlit walk you mentioned, or afterward, for that matter."

She expected another evasion, but what she got was dead silence. He didn't have to say a word, though, because the look in his eyes said it all for him. He wanted to pick up where they'd left off. After a few long moments he picked up his beer and sipped it. "I suppose it depends on you. What do you *want* to happen?"

"Not that," Liz said in a low voice.

"Then it won't." He reclined his chair, looking relaxed and a little amused. "Your reading seems to have left you with certain misconceptions about quarterbacks, Miss Reynolds. We aren't chickens. We aren't any kind of animal at all. On the contrary, we're perfect gentlemen who confine our aggressiveness to the playing field."

"You mean like during the movie?"

He gave an ingenuous shrug. "I plead temporary insanity. I doubt it will happen again."

And Liz doubted it wouldn't, but she didn't say so. The first period of play was over, and it was a little late to register a protest.

Chapter Five

Gladys Tibbs was a middle-aged woman with steel-gray hair and a stocky build. Despite the welcoming smile on her face and the flower leis in her hand, she reminded Liz of a roughneck character from one of those 1940s prison movies about bad girls and what becomes of them. Zack obviously had the same impression, because he leaned over as they were walking down the steps toward the exit and murmured in her ear, "I think I saw her in *Female Hellions of Alcatraz*. She played the role of the vicious matron. Giving her the slip may be harder than I thought."

"Even for the man who can scramble away from a pass rush better than anyone in the NFL?" Liz teased.

"I never said I could do it on my own." He looked at Gladys in pretended terror. "It's a good thing you're around to block for me."

"Not me!" Liz said.

"Yeah, you." He winked at her. "Both of us know you're a lot tougher than you look."

Liz chose to interpret that as an admission that she'd fought him to a standoff. After all, he'd spent the past hour acting like the perfect gentleman he'd claimed to be, telling her about his favorite spots in Hawaii and some of his more repeatable adventures. The conversation had been so completely impersonal that Liz had slowly relaxed and dropped her guard.

Gladys met them at the foot of the steps, welcoming them to Hawaii on behalf of *Main Attraction*'s producer. She introduced them to her cameraman, a local free-lancer named Danny Fong, and then swung into action. Their fellow passengers were extremely cooperative about helping to stage what happened next. Gladys repeated her greeting and put leis around their necks while everyone around them stopped and gawked. She was surprisingly soft-spoken for someone as imperious as Cecil B. DeMille, but equally intimidating. They had to repeat the welcome twice more before she was finally satisfied.

Afterward she ushered Zack and Liz out to a white limousine while the cameraman climbed into a van parked directly behind it. As they drove to the baggage claim area, she told them she was a full-time employee of *Main Attraction*, with a whole season's experience in showing celebrities and their dates the country's vacation spots. If she'd ever allowed any of them to get the better of her, it certainly didn't show.

She filled them in on their schedule as soon as their baggage had come through and they were on their way to the hotel. All of Zack's mornings had been left open, but every tourist attraction on Oahu had evidently been squeezed into the remaining afternoons and evenings. Every now and then she would glance back at Zack to check his reaction, but he never did more than nod or smile politely. Liz thought he looked more resigned than enthusiastic.

Their hotel, the Maunaloa Bay, was located well beyond the bustle and crowds of Waikiki on beautifully landscaped grounds that included a private beach, an eighteen-hole golf course and as much seclusion as anyone could want. Danny filmed their arrival, then followed them to their oceanfront suite on the fifteenth floor. It had two bedrooms with a lounge between them, all with their own entrances from the main corridor. The bedrooms were also connected to the lounge by means of back-to-back doors that could be locked from both sides, insuring privacy. Between the spectacular view and luxurious furnishings, the place had to cost a fortune.

There were two enormous baskets of fruit in the lounge, one from *Main Attraction* and the other from the hotel. While Liz read the cards, Gladys opened the sliding glass door to the balcony and ordered everyone outside. Zack started to object—Liz had the feeling he thought she'd take one look at the ground and keel over—but she assured him it was only airplanes that bothered her, not heights per se. They spent a very long time gazing raptly at the ocean for the benefit of Danny's cameras.

"I'll leave you two to relax," Gladys said afterward. "You've got dinner and a show in the hotel nightclub starting at seven, so please be there at six forty-five. We'll be filming you, of course." She paused and smiled, a little ominously, Liz thought. "If there's anything I can do for you, ring up my room and ask. That's 215. All of us at *Main Attraction* want you to enjoy your stay here."

"I'm sure we will," Zack said, and escorted her and Danny to the door. The moment they were out of the room he began to laugh. "I wonder what happens if we *don't* enjoy our stay? Solitary confinement? Detail to chain gang? Six extra months at hard labor?"

"Maybe you could bribe her into going easy on us," Liz said. "Don't players get tickets to home football games to give out? She looks like the type who enjoys football."

"She looks like the type who *plays* football," Zack corrected, "but we'll leave that aside. The fact is, next year's tickets have been promised to people since the middle of last October. Any other bright ideas about how to get away from her?"

"None at all, other than running as fast as you can. Why don't you think of her as part of your conditioning program?" Liz grinned at him and started toward her bedroom. "You'd better get to work, Zack. Miss a single day of training and Tibbsie will walk all over you. I'll see you later."

Zack trailed along after her. "You mean you're not coming down to the health club with me?"

"No way. After all, *I* don't have to get in shape for the football season." Still smiling to herself, she pulled the inner door closed and turned the lock.

Zack stood in front of the closed door for several moments, then sighed and went to his room. He was beginning to realize that Liz had the capacity to drive him absolutely crazy. Her face, her body, her sense of humor—the woman was a threat to his sanity. She didn't play fair.

Between the media and his fans, he wasn't an easy man to be with. He knew that. Women seemed either to resent the outside attention, fear it or try to control it. Liz did none of those things. She deferred to him when he wanted her to, as with the press, but she also picked up on his discomfort with crowds and tried to help him relax. Most damning of all, she kissed him with a reluctant but heated passion that said she didn't want to respond but couldn't help it. He couldn't even remember the last time he'd held a woman in his arms and known beyond all doubt that he could have been Joe Jones from Brooklyn and gotten exactly the same response from her. After Allison, his ego had loved every minute of it.

He changed into shorts and a T-shirt, thinking he would just have to be patient with her. The two of them had finally clicked, hadn't they? He'd settled the question of whether the attraction was mutual, hadn't he? True, something kept stopping her from letting things happen naturally, but she couldn't stall him forever.

He went downstairs to the health club, loosened up with some stretching exercises and then worked out on the Nautilus machine for a while. A quarterback didn't need the same great power in his upper body as most other players did, but he'd found that a moderate amount of weight training improved the speed and accuracy of his throws, particularly on longer passes. It was beside the point that working out with weights was his second least favorite activity in the world, next to sitting on the bench. He wanted to be the best, and that took determination and discipline.

A couple of people in the club recognized him, but they were too serious about their own exercising to interrupt a professional athlete at work. It was a welcome respite from being pawed and gawked at, as was the run he took afterward along a golf course marked with signs reading "Golfers Only. No Observers, Please." Zack wasn't averse to obeying rules and regulations—God knew the average football coach had enough of them to drive a marine half-nuts—but he'd also been known to ignore them. With the money he made, he could afford to shrug off the resulting fines.

He was dripping with sweat by the time he got back to the hotel. He looked totally disheveled but felt really good, the way he always did when he'd used his body enough to loosen it up and tire it out. An elegantly dressed woman stepped into the elevator ahead of him, regarding him with horror the moment she turned around. When she shrank back into the corner and clutched her purse to her chest, Zack experienced a strong urge to growl at her. He introduced himself instead, but she didn't look especially impressed.

He was still smiling about the incident as he unlocked the door to the lounge, but the sight of Liz curled up on the couch was enough to sober him up instantly. She was reading a magazine, dressed in a silky, jade-green robe that covered her from wrist to ankle but could have been removed with a single swift tug on the sash around her waist. Without really thinking, he walked over and picked up the iced drink sitting on the table beside her. He was very thirsty.

She watched him drain the glass, then asked, "Was it good?"

"I don't know. All that matters is that it was wet." It took him a moment to realize that he'd just stolen her soft drink. "Let me get you a replacement. Which way is the soda machine?"

"You see that bar?" She pointed to an alcove to the right of the door. "It's fully stocked, complete with macadamia nuts, pretzels and a refrigerator full of soda and beer. The soda you just swiped was a Berry's Natural Cola, by the way, so you should try to show a little enthusiasm." Her eyes slid down his body, her scrutiny making him wonder what she was wearing under her robe. "If I didn't know you were harmless, I might worry about being in the same room with you. Given how disreputable you look, I'm certainly not going to complain just because you helped yourself to my soda."

Zack felt like proving he was anything *but* harmless, but figured it would be better to try it some other time when he wasn't soaking wet and didn't smell like a locker room after a tough game. "A woman in the elevator shared your low opinion," he said. "She couldn't decide if I was going to rape her or just snatch her purse. I told her who I was, but she'd obviously never heard of me."

"Was it a blow to your ego?" Liz asked.

"I think maybe it was." Laughing at himself, he went over to check out the refrigerator. The beer was a brand he liked, so he grabbed a can to take into the bathroom with him. It was past six, too late to do anything more than clean up and dress for dinner.

Liz watched Zack walk into his bedroom, getting a perfect view as he pulled his shirt over his head and tossed it onto the dresser. One look at the glistening, rippling muscles in his back and she was on her way to her room. Apparently nobody had ever told the man that the whole point of doors was to close them. Modesty didn't seem to be his strong point, but with a body that good, there was no reason it should have been.

She'd never seen him look so much in his element as in the past five minutes and couldn't help thinking that a man who made a living with his body had to know every inch of it, had to feel comfortable with it, had to be in control of it. It was like a finely tuned instrument, and if he used it with the same confidence and finesse in bed as he did on a football field . . .

She shook her head and picked up her curling iron. Thoughts like that had gotten her into more than enough trouble already.

The Kahala nightclub was on the sixteenth and topmost floor of the hotel. By six forty-five Liz was both tired and hungry. All she wanted to do was have a quiet evening and get to bed early, but Gladys and her cameraman had other plans. They were lying in wait as Liz and Zack entered the foyer and photographed them as they made their way to their stage-side table. Danny was using a high-speed film designed to produce a good picture with normal indoor lighting, but the club was on the dark side so Gladys was carrying portable spots for him. Their light was so bright that Liz could still see the glare even after Gladys and Danny retreated to the foyer.

She buried her face in the oversize menu. The presence of a camera and lights had attracted even more attention to Zack than he normally received, including the stares of foreigners who wouldn't have known a football from a hockey puck. He shifted his chair closer to Liz's so that his back was to all those curious eyes, and picked up his own menu. After two or three minutes the wine steward approached them, but not to take their orders. He was carrying a silver ice bucket containing an expensive bottle of champagne.

"With the compliments of an admirer, Mr. Delaney." He set the ice bucket on their table. "He would like you and Miss Reynolds to join him and his wife for dinner."

Both Zack and Liz looked around, but the wine steward told them the man's table was all the way in the back, too far away to see through the crowded room. "Thank him for the champagne but tell him we have to stay where we are," Zack said. "They'll be filming us during the show."

"Of course, Mr. Delaney." The wine steward gave a formal little bow of his head. "Would you like me to open that for you? It was quite well-chilled before I brought it over."

Zack told him to go ahead, nodding his approval after taking the ritualistic first taste. It was only afterward that he admitted to Liz that he would have preferred beer. "Maybe I should tell that to our friend in the back of the room," he added. "He'd probably send over a whole case."

"Does this kind of thing happen often?" Liz asked. "I mean, people sending over drinks and inviting you to eat with them?"

"Often enough. Usually they want to talk football. Once in a while you get someone knowledgeable enough to be interesting, but mostly it's a real pain. They give you their opinions of your teammates, they tell you which college players your team should draft, and they explain why you make all the mistakes you do and how you can manage to avoid them.''

Liz could tell how restless he was by the way he kept fiddling with his Super Bowl ring. It was a gaudily expensive little number all done up in the Rushers' colors. The setting itself was gold, there was a football outlined in blue sapphires and a date inscribed inside the football was fashioned out of tiny diamonds. ''But do you want to know the worst thing they do?'' he went on. ''They suggest plays. Even Dirk Denning had a play. I thought I'd escaped finding out about it when time ran out and he had to start the show, but he mailed it to me in San Francisco. It was this screwball pass-option that probably would get me crippled against any competent NFL defense and killed against any good one.''

What Liz knew about pass-option plays could have been engraved on her smallest fingernail. It took her a moment to come up with a halfway intelligent comment. ''Why don't you tell them to send their plays to your head coach? Doesn't he call them during a game?''

''Most of the time, yes. Ben gets reports from an assistant coach sitting up in a spotting booth near the press box, and from other people at field level, and from me, of course. So he has a more complete sense of what's going on during a game than I do. After calling my own plays in college it was a big change to switch to his system, but you can't argue with success.'' He flashed the symbol of that success—his ring—and then smiled crookedly. ''The more I think about it, the better I like your idea. People keep suggesting my IQ must be mildly subnormal because Ben calls our plays, so I might as well take advantage of it. Let 'em think I'm too dumb to understand what the hell they're talking about.''

Liz knew he was anything but dumb. He'd majored in economics at Colgate, which was a first-rate school, but

even more than that, professional football was too complicated a game for a stupid athlete to succeed at. A quarterback needed to memorize and execute a hundred or more
different plays, and the good ones, like Zack Delaney, knew
everyone's job in addition to their own. If a teammate
needed his memory refreshed in the huddle they could do it.
They also made it their business to learn the strengths and
weaknesses of every opposing player in the league. They
would check out the other team at the line of scrimmage,
trying to sense if the defense had anticipated their plans. If
necessary, they would adjust those plans or even call a
completely different play—an "audible"—before taking the
snap. Although Liz couldn't imagine devoting her own life
to something like professional football, she didn't underes-
timate the skill it took to play the game well.

She smiled and told Zack she was glad she'd been of help
and then went back to studying her menu. She was still de-
bating her choices when the wine steward approached their
table for the second time. Unlike before, he wasn't bearing
any gifts.

"I'm sorry to disturb you again," he said to Zack, "but
the gentleman who sent the champagne insisted that I come
back. He said—let me quote him correctly, now—he said he
was a major supporter of your team who saw every game
last year, including the Super Bowl. He's a close personal
friend of your head coach. And he's on a first-name basis
with all the sports reporters in the San Francisco area and
frequently discusses the team's performance with them."

Zack lazed back in his chair, outwardly at ease, but Liz
wasn't fooled for a moment. He was simmering underneath. The big shot with the champagne seemed to be
threatening to tell the press how uncooperative Zack was if
he didn't toe the mark, and Liz didn't like that any more
than he did. He instructed the wine steward to thank the
gentleman for his support but repeat that they couldn't have

dinner with him. "You can tell him he's welcome to take back the rest of his champagne if he wants to," he added coolly.

The wine steward looked horrified. "No, no, of course he wouldn't want it back. But perhaps you would consider having a drink with him? It might—mollify him."

Zack didn't see why he should do anything of the sort, especially not for a pushy pain in the ass who thought that dropping a name or a threat would get him what he wanted. Mostly, though, he didn't want to subject Liz to that sort of self-important jerk. He looked across at her, saw that she wasn't going to say a word and felt a quick rush of gratitude. Allison had never failed to tell him what to do in unpleasant situations like this, and her interference had never failed to annoy him.

Since he didn't want to cause any scenes, he softened his refusal by suggesting an alternative. "Remind the gentleman that Miss Reynolds and I just flew in from California today. There's a two-hour time difference and both of us are tired. We wouldn't be especially good company right now, but I'd be glad to have a drink with him tomorrow evening, before dinner. If you get me his name and room number, I'll leave a message telling him what time I'll be available."

The wine steward thanked him and left the table. Zack fully expected that to be the end of it. In his experience, the football fans of the world just weren't that persistent. The man would be happy as long as he got his half an hour tomorrow night.

He found out how wrong he was a few minutes later, after he and Liz had ordered dinner. This time, the intermediary wasn't the wine steward, but a tall, patrician-looking man named Daniel Reid. Reid ran the company that owned the hotel, and Zack and some of his Pro Bowl teammates had been guests at his Kahala district mansion only the previous January.

He stood up to shake Reid's hand, introduced him to Liz and then pulled over a chair so Reid could join them. He was hoping that the visit was purely social, because having eaten Reid's food and enjoyed his tennis courts, there was no way Zack could say no if he asked for a personal favor.

He knew his hope was a vain one by the intimate way Reid leaned across the table. "We seem to have a problem here," he said softly. "Mr. Smith won't take no—"

"Smith?" Zack interrupted incredulously. "Come on, Daniel, the guy's name can't really be Smith."

Reid shrugged. "That's what he chooses to call himself. Do me a favor, Zack. Go over, say hello to him and tell him how much you appreciate his champagne. Frankly, I'd rather not have his kind in my hotel, but it's a free country. I'll see it doesn't take more than a few minutes of your time, even if it means calling in my security people. I don't approve of his type of pressure any more than you do."

The conversation was conducted in such hushed tones that Liz had to strain to hear it. If she understood Reid correctly, "Smith's" business interests were something less than legitimate. When it came right down to it, she couldn't separate herself from her job. She wanted a look at this "Smith." She wanted to know why he was so interested in Zack Delaney, especially given the reports that linked organized crime to professional sports. Most of all, she didn't want Zack going over there without her. If the man sent his wife away, the two of them would be alone together. There would be no constraints on the conversation, and even worse, Zack would be in the position of publicly rubbing elbows with a known thug. Maybe he and Reid didn't appreciate the delicacy of his situation, but Liz did. Zack had his reputation to think about.

A part of her knew he could take care of himself perfectly well—she recognized the flinty look in his eyes because she'd seen it once before, at the airport—but she still felt compelled to intervene. This was *her* territory, not his. She even wished she'd had her gun with her. Ever since the stabbing, its hard presence had made her feel more secure. Unfortunately, it was back in her house in California, locked up in the safe.

Zack agreed to Reid's request and pushed back his chair. Liz knew he was too much of a gentleman to allow her to get mixed up in this, and that meant she'd have to be clever about it.

She reached across the table and placed her palm over his hand. "I see a lot of his type in the casino. They may be tough, but they also humor their women, at least in social situations. If he thinks your girlfriend is cranky or resentful of the whole thing, he won't try to keep you."

She could see Zack was about to refuse, but Reid jumped in before he had the chance. "That's a good idea. I'll show you where he's sitting."

Zack removed her hand and stood up. "It's a lousy idea and she'll stay where she is."

Liz was standing by his side in two seconds flat. Linking her arm through his, she said flirtatiously, "Of course I won't. I refuse to be abandoned, Zack. I'm not letting you out of my sight for a moment." She gazed up at him, a seductive look on her face.

If Liz refused to be abandoned, Zack refused to be manipulated. The look in Liz's eyes went straight to his groin, but he wasn't about to let a woman half his size run interference for him.

Fortunately, he knew exactly how to handle her. "Oh yeah?" he demanded. "Does that include tonight, up in the suite?"

Liz stayed right where she was, even though Zack's clipped question put her on the defensive. "Of course it does. You can sleep in my room—in the other bed."

"Let me that close and there's no way in hell you're going to stop me from getting closer," he retorted. He suddenly remembered about the existence of Daniel Reid, and reddened. Maybe it was the grin on Reid's face, but the situation started to seem ridiculous. What was he so worked up about? For some inexplicable reason Liz had dug in her heels, and he really didn't want to fight with her about it. "Smith" wasn't going to try to compromise his integrity, not in a public restaurant. So they'd chat for a while, Liz would stand there looking bored and they'd make a graceful escape. End of crisis.

He believed that for all of five seconds, which was as long as it took for Gladys and Danny to hurry over with the lights and camera. With half the nightclub watching there was nothing he could do to stop them, but he had no intention of letting them use the film—not even if he had to rip it out of the camera.

Irritated or not, he still couldn't resist putting his arm around Liz's waist as they walked across the room. Her body tautened under his touch, but he wasn't sure why. It could have been the physical contact, but it could also have been the prospect of confronting Mr. Big.

For a man who used muscle to get his way, "Smith" proved surprisingly camera shy. When they were halfway across the room, Reid cut to his right and pointed straight ahead, but all Zack could see was a pair of menus and the very top of one male head. There was a thatch of brown hair there, which was equally surprising. Zack had always pictured Mafia dons as either graying or bald.

The closer they came, the more he could make out. The man's elbows were resting on the table, clothed in fine, beige wool, and his hands were curled around the edges of the menu. Zack noticed a plain gold band on one ring finger and a diamond and sapphire ring on the other. It looked very familiar, as well it should have. Zack had one exactly like it.

It was hard not to burst out laughing. He would have loved to let loose with the kind of scatological greeting so typical of the average locker room, but they were in a public restaurant, women were present and a camera was running. "Well, well, well," he drawled. "You just never know what kind of scum is going to turn up in Honolulu. How's the crime business these days, Don Corleone? Racking up record profits?"

Standing by his side, Liz tensed and sucked in her breath. She was sure Zack had gone crazy. You just didn't talk to these people that way, no matter who you were.

She was a good fighter and an even better talker, but she didn't want to have to do either. She prayed the man at the table would have a generous sense of humor. When he lowered his menu with slow menace, every sense came fully alert. She took a quick step forward, prepared to get between him and Zack if necessary. Swinging fists had a way of leading to broken hands. But the face behind the menu wore a grin a mile wide, and it was also hauntingly familiar. She'd never felt so foolish in her life as when she noticed the ring he was wearing.

The two men laughed and embraced each other. The woman at the table had laid down her own menu by then, and Zack went over to pull her into his arms. She pretended to swoon from sheer rapture when he kissed her on the mouth, but then, when he was least expecting it, she playfully tousled his hair.

Liz had figured out who they were by that point, and Zack's introduction confirmed it. "Paul, Jenny...this is Liz Reynolds. Liz, Paul and Jenny Travers. As you know, Paul is one of my teammates. He's a little over the hill by now, so every now and then I throw him one of my perfect passes so he can look good and keep his job. He's even been known to catch a few."

"More than a few, I think. He might claim he makes *you* look good." Liz gave Zack a mischievous grin and then shook hands with Paul and Jenny. Both of them were tall and slender with dark hair and eyes, California suntans and the kind of healthy good looks that advertisers love. With two exceptions, they reminded Liz of a matched pair. First, he was lanky where she was fine-boned, and second, she was either pregnant or loved loose-fitting clothes.

"A woman of rare perception," Paul said to Liz. He turned to Reid. "Thanks for your help. Didn't I tell you nobody but you could get Delaney over here?"

"I'm flattered—I think," Reid answered. "Lani and I will expect you all to come to dinner later in the week. She'll call to set a night. In the meantime, enjoy the hotel."

"We will," Zack told him. "As a matter of fact, I went running on your golf course today, Daniel. It was very relaxing."

"And also very much against the rules," Reid said, "but okay, we'll make an exception for you and Paul—as long as you don't bounce any footballs off the golfers."

Zack swore that they wouldn't but Reid was laughing and shaking his head as he walked away. "About dinner," Zack said to Paul afterward. "Our seats are by the stage, and it would mean giving them up."

"Why do you think I took a table at the back? Both of us know how you hate getting stared at." Paul looked at Liz. "Do you mind switching seats?"

Liz didn't. Like Zack, she was just as glad not to be where people could watch her, and besides, he was obviously very pleased to see his best friend. Paul signaled a waiter, who brought over two more place settings and a pair of chairs. Through it all, the cameraman kept right on filming, at least until Zack placed his hand over the lens and told Gladys he wasn't posing for any more pictures that night. She, in turn, started to lecture him about his responsibilities to his fans,

to the audience and to the Berry's Natural Soda Company.
In the end they compromised. The dinner would be private
if Zack and Paul agreed to take part in the nightclub act.
Gladys went off to try to arrange it, leaving no doubt in
anyone's mind she would succeed.

As soon as everyone was seated, Zack told Paul he'd had
visions of seeing himself plastered all over national TV with
a Cosa Nostra godfather whispering in his ear. "One bad
game and they'd say I'd taken a bribe to fix the point
spread. You were right in thinking I couldn't say no to Reid,
but I was also planning to yank the film out of the camera
as soon as we were through talking."

"Mmm." Paul was slowly nodding his head. "You know,
there's not many guys conceited enough to turn down a fan
who sends over Dom Perignon. What did you want? A
dozen roses and a singing telegram?"

Zack replied that Paul might have come over himself, but
Jenny only laughed. It was obvious to Liz that the two men
enjoyed playing practical jokes on each other, the more
elaborate, the better.

"So what are you doing here?" Zack asked. "I thought
you were staying in San Francisco till training camp begins."

"I couldn't let you work out with a bunch of college kids.
I have to protect the team's investment." Paul paused, then
explained to Liz, "The man has great talent but no self-
discipline. Without me to keep an eye on him, he'd still be
playing backup."

Zack insisted it was the other way around, prompting
Jenny to throw up her hands in mock dismay. "They both
have monumental egos, not to mention one-track minds.
Put them in the same room and all they talk about is football. They're capable of spending an entire evening on a
single play. They'll go through every team in the league, one
by one, and talk about every defensive formation the team

might use against that play. And then they'll talk about how to adapt the play to beat that specific defense.'' She gave Zack a warmly teasing look. ''Zack lived with us for a few months last fall, Liz. It was the most scintillating period of my life.''

Liz didn't really believe the two men had gone on night after night that way, but Zack was just sheepish enough to tell her there was a germ of truth to Jenny's claim. In the end they didn't talk so much about football as about what friends usually talk about when they haven't seen each other for a while—what they'd been doing, how their work was going and which mutual acquaintances they'd seen. Liz couldn't contribute much to the conversation, but she didn't mind sitting and listening. There was a lot of warmth and love at the table, and it was natural to respond to it.

She even let herself believe that the evening was purely social, at least until the conversation turned to Zack's teammates, and to who would probably would make the team that year. One of the first names to come up was that of Pete Slama, the defensive end Liz had met at Johnny Hoag's private party. It was no secret he'd been traded to the Titans, but Paul told Zack he'd heard rumors that the reason behind the trade was drug use. Coach Halliday evidently didn't have any proof of that, but he did know his player had been irritable, paranoiac and even dangerously aggressive at times. Liz had seen Slama with cocaine, but the list of problems Paul reeled off made her think he was doing speed as well. The symptoms could be similar, but amphetamines had a longer-lasting effect.

Paul had handed her the type of lead she felt compelled to follow up on. As much as she'd disliked listening to O'Dwyer's lecture, she knew he was right. If drugs were being used in an attempt to bribe or blackmail football players, they needed to put a stop to it.

''Do other guys on the team take drugs?'' she asked Zack. ''I mean, every now and then you read about an athlete getting in too deep, and I wondered if it's really a problem, or if the media just sensationalize it.''

"It's been a problem on other teams, but not on the Rushers," he answered. "At least, not in the six years I've been there. If there's dealing in the locker room or pills being swallowed in the john, I've never seen any of it."

Liz pressed him a little harder. "But you wouldn't have to actually see it. You could tell by the way people behave. Like Slama."

Paul laughed at that. "Maybe or maybe not. Some of those guys are so naturally crazy they'd slam into a brick wall just to show how tough they are. When I was in college one of my teammates decided to hit the goalpost one morning to prove he could tackle anything. He wasn't high, just weird. Jarred it loose, too."

Liz would have liked to throw out a pair of names—Cal Johnson and Willie Lee White—but didn't dare. She wasn't supposed to know about ordinary players and coaches, just about the stars. Instead she remarked, "I guess I can understand how even a sensible player might get hooked. You're under so much pressure to win every week. You play with pain so often. Then you go to bars or parties where even average players are fussed over and offered drugs, and it must be tough to say no. I know all about cocaine. It makes you feel too damn good. You think you can do anything."

There was a sudden, uncomfortable silence at the table. At first Liz thought they'd interpreted her remark as meaning *she* used drugs, and felt awkward about openly disapproving. But then she picked up on the look Jenny and Paul exchanged, and noticed the grim way Zack was staring at his plate. She felt herself go pale. She didn't want to hear what was coming next, not about Zack Delaney. And dammit, she wasn't going to tell O'Dwyer about it even if it was awful. Enough was enough.

Finally, looking more serious than she'd ever seen him, Zack nodded slowly. "I know what you mean about drugs. A couple of years ago I was having a problem with my arm. It hurt to throw, so I didn't throw well. Every game was a struggle. When exercise didn't help, the doctor prescribed some painkillers. They had a pretty good kick to them, and without quite realizing it, I got to like them so much I started telling myself I couldn't play without them, even after my arm was more or less better. I don't know what would have happened if it hadn't been for Paul and Jenny. It taught me to be a little more tolerant of other people's weaknesses."

Jenny put a comforting hand on his arm. "You would have been okay. It might have taken you a little longer to stop, but we weren't telling you anything you didn't know. Come on, dance with me. I'll make you feel like Fred Astaire."

Liz watched them walk to the dance floor, pensive now. Zack had a very special relationship with these people, and she rather envied him that. "He's lucky to have two such good friends," she said aloud. "He's uneasy with all the attention, isn't he, Paul?"

"Yes, but there are some good reasons for that. Take that business about hurting his arm. He'd come off a great year the season before. We'd almost won the Super Bowl, and the fans' expectations were enormous. When he didn't meet them—*couldn't* meet them—he got hit with some of the worst booing I've ever heard, game after game after game. It would start the moment he walked on the field. An experience like that puts the cheers in perspective."

He pushed back his chair, stood up and held out his hand. "I can't promise to make you feel like Ginger Rogers but I won't step on your feet, either."

Liz smiled and let him lead her to the dance floor. She was being pulled in opposite directions, her common sense warring with her emotions, and it frightened her to realize that the first might be losing.

The song was a slow one, the music soft and dreamy. They continued talking, Liz eventually asking the question that had been on her mind ever since she'd first set eyes on Paul and Jenny Travers. What were they *really* doing in Hawaii? Surely they hadn't come all this way just so the two men could spend a few hours a day practicing together.

Paul's answer was blunt, but it also poked some good-natured fun at his own overprotectiveness. "Rescuing Zack from a horrible week. Of course, now that I'm here, I can see just how necessary my presence will be."

"You thought I'd be—difficult," Liz said.

"Not difficult, impossible. You didn't want to win the trip, you didn't want to go away with Zack and you never even answered his letter. Jenny was starting to feel better after a few months of morning sickness, and Hawaii is one of our favorite places. It wasn't exactly a hardship to fly out here for a week, especially not for a man who's been there every time things got tough in my marriage and my career." He loosened his hold so he could look Liz in the face. He wasn't smiling, but there was a definite twinkle in his eyes. "You have my permission to tell us to get lost wherever and whenever you want to. That is, if Zack doesn't tell us first."

"It wouldn't do any good unless you took out Tibbsie and her cameraman, too," Liz joked. "Personally, I'm resigned to continuous surveillance."

"And that suits you just fine, doesn't it?" Paul took her back in his arms, then added softly, "I can see you holding back with him. You're afraid of letting him get too close. Why?"

Liz grabbed the first excuse that came to mind, thinking he was much too perceptive. "He's a celebrity. I'm a nobody."

"And you think you'll be hurt. You think he'll have a little fun and then go on to somebody new."

"We live in two different worlds," Liz said.

"That's true, but I can guarantee you Zack doesn't give a damn about that. I've been watching him with you, Liz. He likes you a lot. He feels comfortable with you. Most women want something from him, but you don't. Don't mix up the real person with the media hype because they're two different things, and Zack knows the difference better than anyone."

The song ended and they walked back to the table. Liz felt guiltier than ever, and also more confused. The only way she could deal with the conflict raging inside of her was to remind herself firmly that her work was important, not just to her but to the country. It had to come first.

The silent lecture helped, but only until Zack asked her to dance. The room was much too dim, the dance floor much too crowded. He didn't hold her especially close, but she could still feel the intimacy of the situation along every nerve-ending in her body. Under the circumstances it was tempting fate to repeat the experience, but when he asked again she agreed again. He pulled her closer this time, nuzzling her hair as the orchestra swung into the final chorus of the song. The third time he suggested dancing, she told him she was too tired.

The tension between the two of them grew, easing off only when the show began. The warm-up act was a magician who mixed a lot of comedy into his routine. He called on Zack and Paul to help with a couple of his illusions, and the audience loved it. Gladys got her film, so everyone was happy. By the time the show was over, Liz was yawning. It was past midnight in California and she felt every hour of a very long day.

The two men arranged to meet on the golf course at seven to go running together, and Jenny said she would order breakfast sent to their room at eight. The Traverses were staying in the low-rise wing of the hotel, in a luxury suite overlooking the golf course. They continued down to the lobby after Zack and Liz got off the elevator. The moment the two of them were alone together, all the tension Liz had felt earlier in the evening came back even more strongly. It was unnerving to have no idea whether he planned to make another pass at her.

Zack unlocked the door to the lounge and followed Liz inside. He wouldn't have tried to deny that making love to her was very much on his mind, but he'd already decided it wouldn't be tonight. He'd felt her response to him, both physical and emotional, but he'd also felt how reluctant she'd been to give it. Push her and maybe she'd give in, but she'd also hate herself in the morning. He knew he'd eventually have his way. He intended to make sure she knew it too, but he could also afford to give her some time to get used to the idea.

He clicked on the light and casually stretched out his arms. "God, I'm tired. I had a good time, though. I hope you don't mind about Paul and Jenny."

Liz gave him a wary look. He seemed about as dangerous as a well-fed tomcat, but tomcats had been known to turn into tigers when the right prey crossed their paths. "I don't mind at all. I enjoyed meeting them. Do you think Tibbsie would have a fit if they joined our vacation?"

"Why should she? She gets two football players for the price of one." He raised his hand, but only to brush a strand of hair off Liz's cheek and tuck it behind her ear. His fingers grazed her neck and settled on her shoulder, lightly caressing the bare skin. Her mouth went dry as they stared into each other's eyes. She'd never had a man look at her with such open desire.

"I forgot to tell you how beautiful you look tonight," he said. "If you change your mind about what you want..."

"I'm not going to change my mind," Liz said hoarsely.

"We'll see." He moved away, the tiger disappearing as quickly as he'd come. "Unfortunately, by the time Travers gets done working me out every day, I'll probably be too tired to do much about it. Sleep tight, Liz. I'll see you at breakfast." He flashed a grin at her and strolled off to his room, just as though those moments of heart-stopping excitement had never taken place.

Liz switched off the light and walked into her room, locking the door behind her. She was relieved nothing had happened but also very unsettled. She had the feeling she'd become the target of a well-planned campaign, and at the moment her troops were decidedly demoralized. She couldn't switch her emotions on and off like a light bulb and she doubted Zack could, either. His touch had left her aroused and restless, which meant that a well-timed ambush had every chance of success.

Gladys Tibbs and her cameraman wouldn't protect her. Even the presence of Jenny and Paul Travers wouldn't help her. She stood there wondering what Zack would say if she invited the entire defensive line of the San Francisco Gold Rushers to come to Hawaii and bunk out in their lounge.

Chapter Six

Watching Zack and Paul from the sidelines of the University of Hawaii's practice field, Liz remarked to Jenny that she'd never realized how hard professional football players had to work in order to get and stay in shape. With the weather so warm and humid, the two men had already been drenched with sweat when they'd returned to the Traverses' suite for breakfast. After Paul and Zack had changed into practice clothes, the four of them had driven over to Cooke Field in the Traverses' rented car. The men had done some more running—short, quick sprints this time—and then loosened up with calisthenics. A workout on a make-shift obstacle course had followed.

Jenny told Liz that Ben Halliday, the Rushers' head coach, was a great believer in physical conditioning. The routine they used in training camp was even longer and more taxing. Even worse, it was only a prelude to a session that would last several hours. Then, when everyone was ready to drop from fatigue, they would go in for lunch, rest for a while and head back out and start all over again.

There were five awestruck college players working out with the two pros: a center, another quarterback and wide receiver and a pair of running backs. After the preliminary warm-ups, Zack loosened up his arm by playing an easy game of catch with Paul and two of the college students. The four of them stood in a rectangular formation. Zack threw the ball downfield to Paul, who tossed it to the college quarterback a few feet to his side. The college quarterback, in turn, threw the ball to the receiver next to Zack. A gentle toss to Zack and they started the routine again. According to Jenny, you never risked a quarterback's fingers by throwing him the ball too hard, just as you never risked the rest of him by having him take part in the blocking drills most of the other players had to do during practice sessions.

Once the two quarterbacks were loose, they ran through a series of drills—throwing on the run, throwing over the crossbar to simulate going over the heads of defensive players, looking for an open receiver while trying to elude a simulated pass rush, and so on. At one point the college center said something to Zack about how easy it was to snap the ball to him, and the other quarterback walked over to see exactly how he held his hands and feel exactly how much pressure he applied. Jenny remarked to Liz that Zack was superb on the fundamentals, in part because he was willing to practice them over and over again. For example, when he handed off the ball to one of his running backs, he didn't just hold it out and expect the runner to grab it on the fly. He tucked it directly into the protective pocket made by the runner's hands as the runner swept by.

"When you see a fumble on a handoff it's almost always the quarterback's fault," Jenny added. "It's a mistake you won't see on the Rushers—not when Zack is in the game, anyway.''

"Never?" Liz asked.

"Almost never," Jenny corrected. "Nobody's perfect, but even so, these kids are going to get spoiled playing with him.''

The two women paused to watch Paul cut across the field, put on a sudden burst of speed and stretch up high to haul down a pass from the college quarterback. Liz was beginning to understand that if Zack had thrown that ball, it would have reached the proper place at the proper time, coming in waist-high to Paul's arms rather than far over his head. And if somebody less talented than Paul had been trying to catch it, he would never have managed to reach it.

Jenny kept up such a knowledgeable running commentary throughout the session that Liz finally asked her if she'd made it her business to learn all about football after marrying a professional athlete. It turned out that her father had been Paul's coach at Notre Dame. She'd been raised on a diet of play diagrams, daily workouts and Saturday games, and for years had been something of a team mascot. By the time Paul had come on the scene she was attending a nearby women's college but still hanging around her father's stadium every chance she got. Paul had been too terrified of her father to ask her out at first, but they'd finally started dating in their sophomore year and married after graduation. They'd lived in San Francisco ever since. She'd established a successful career as a photographic model over the past seven years, but was taking some time off now in order to start a family. Liz liked her very much. She seemed to know exactly where she was going but also had time for other people.

The four of them had lunch back at the hotel, in a restaurant overlooking the golf course. Zack's expression grew more and more wistful as the meal progressed and one golfer after another arrived at the eighteenth green to putt. Liz had no doubt about what he would have liked to be doing that afternoon, and it wasn't going to Pearl Harbor with her. Far from minding, she sat there musing about how she could gain him his freedom.

When Gladys Tibbs came sailing into the dining room, Liz gave Jenny a gentle kick under the table and started waving enthusiastically. "Over here, Gladys!" she called out. "Come join us! Where's Danny?"

Gladys waved back and made her way to the table. She was smiling, but Liz had the feeling her mind was fixed firmly on keeping her two charges on schedule. "He'll be here soon. Did you have a pleasant morning?"

"*I* did, but I was only an observer." Liz gave Zack a sympathetic look. "Poor Zack. He developed a most awful problem with a muscle spasm in his leg. He's had a tough time of it. Jenny keeps telling him that she'll go on the Pearl Harbor cruise with me while he stays here and rests, but you know Zack. He's worried about his commitment to you."

Jenny, who was quick on the uptake, gave Zack a stern look. "It isn't even open to discussion, Zack. I've been through this with Paul. The damp salt air is the worst thing in the world for you. You're staying in the hotel." She turned her attention to Gladys. "We'll meet you outside as soon as we finish our coffee. All right?"

Gladys didn't look too happy about the change in plans, but she didn't argue about it, either. "I suppose there's no choice." She glanced at her watch. "Please don't be more than ten minutes. And Zack—rest that leg. We wouldn't want you to miss dinner tonight." She gave him a bracing pat on the shoulder and strode away from the table.

Liz had to bite her lip to keep from breaking up, but burst out laughing the moment Gladys was out the door. It didn't take long for the others to join in. "You know what's a sure cure for muscle spasm?" she asked Zack once she'd managed to contain herself. "Eighteen holes of golf."

"You're an angel of mercy," he said. "Also a genius. Do you think I can milk the injury for another few days of freedom?"

"Not if you go to practice tomorrow morning." Liz grinned at him and pushed away her coffee cup. "I'm going upstairs to get my windbreaker, Jenny. I'll meet you out front. Enjoy your golf game, fellas."

Zack watched her walk away, thinking she had to be the most understanding woman in the world. "Now there goes a first-class lady," Paul remarked. "Give her half a chance and she'd spoil you rotten."

"I'd love her to," Zack admitted. "If you want the truth, I'm beginning to get seriously hung up on her. It's wreaking havoc on my nervous system to have her sleeping only thirty feet away. If I didn't like her so much I'd probably be breaking down her door, but I'm afraid to push her too hard."

"I doubt she'd say no if you did," Jenny insisted. "She couldn't take her eyes off you this morning."

As much as Zack liked hearing that, it didn't really change anything. "Having her say yes and regret it afterward would be even worse than having her say no. Maybe it's just too soon. The attraction is there, but not the trust." He gave Jenny a smile. "Do me a favor, Jen. Convince her I'm the most terrific guy you know when you're out on the boat this afternoon."

Jenny gave it her best shot. She told Liz what a good friend Zack had been and spoke about how much time he gave to Bay Area charities. She gushed about his talent, his professionalism and his leadership abilities and made it clear that the woman who shared his life would be very lucky indeed. Liz listened politely, but Jenny wasn't telling her anything she couldn't have guessed. Zack's generosity and

decency shone out of every pore. They were part of what
made him so special—and so dangerous.

The rest of what made him so dangerous was on full display later that day, when the four of them had dinner together. Zack had a wealth of funny stories from his years
with the Rushers and he told all of them well. He took a
boyish delight in thinking up improbable schemes to elude
Gladys Tibbs and soon had everyone laughing and joining
in the game. Every now and then somebody would interrupt them for an autograph, but Paul had a talent for satisfying such people and getting rid of them quickly. He was
comfortable with being a celebrity in a way Zack wasn't,
perhaps because he'd grown up with it. He'd been a star
player in high school, a Heisman Trophy contender in college, and a high first-round draft pick. The fact that he was
around to share the spotlight with Zack took some of the
pressure off and helped him relax. Unfortunately, a relaxed
Zack Delaney was altogether too charming for Liz's peace
of mind.

After dinner they went to one of the night spots Zack and
Paul had discovered during Pro Bowl week the previous
January. The place was too raucous and noisy for any real
conversation, but the throbbing music and charged-up atmosphere made Liz feel wonderfully and totally alive. She
did a lot of fast, exhilarating dancing, laughed at jokes even
when she didn't quite catch the punchlines and thoroughly
enjoyed herself. She was still going a hundred miles a minute as they drove home. The men were in front, the women
in back, so there was no real feeling of intimacy.

The atmosphere changed with shattering abruptness the
moment she and Zack stepped into the elevator together. It
was very late and nobody else was around. She could feel his
gaze scorching its way into her blood but didn't have the
nerve to look back. She kept her eyes on the door. Neither
of them spoke. By the time they reached the fifteenth floor

she was acutely aware of the fact that there was such a thing as having too good a time with a man. It gave him romantic expectations. It made her long to fulfill them.

Zack unlocked the door to the lounge, then stood aside to let her go in first. She wasn't taking any chances; she switched on the lights and walked briskly toward her room. It was a shock when Zack dashed past her and darted into her path, putting his body between her and the door. The crooked smile on his face made the situation even more impossible. She'd always had a problem resisting it.

She stopped a safe couple of feet in front of him. He didn't move, but folded his arms across his chest and kept on smiling. "Did you have a good time tonight?" he asked.

"You know I did," Liz answered.

"Umm." He nodded to himself. "You know, it's a lot of work being the perfect date. All those funny stories, all that dancing." He paused. "It really took a lot out of me, especially after that practice session this morning. I don't know if I'll be able to keep up the pace." His voice dropped to a husky murmur. "Of course, I respond very well to encouragement. Why don't you come over here and encourage me?"

Liz wasn't about to do anything of the sort. His seductive tone affected her like an electric charge—it made every last nerve ending tingle—but she still had a healthy instinct for self-preservation. "I've already told you, I'm not interested in that," she said.

"I know what you told me. I also know it's not the truth." He pointed to a spot directly in front of his feet. "Here. Now. I'm only going to kiss you, not wrestle you to the ground and rip off your clothes."

"You're not going to do either one," Liz insisted. "What you *are* going to do is move out of my way so I can go into my room—alone."

He shook his head. "No. I don't think so."

Liz decided to let him have the last word. She was afraid that if she stood there arguing, she'd give in and do exactly what she longed to—walk right into his arms. She silently repeated all the arguments against it. He was part of her job. She barely knew him. It was stupid to get involved with him. He didn't fit into the life she'd chosen for herself and never would.

The lecture worked. With only a dull pang of regret, she turned on her heel and marched out of the lounge.

Outside in the hall, she unlocked her bedroom door and pushed it open. Her hand was unsteady and her heart was beating heavily. Suppose he'd come in through the other door? How was she going to handle him?

She looked around. The room was dark and the door from the lounge was still firmly shut. Taking a deep, relieved breath, she turned on the light in the entryway, flipped the door closed and started across the room. She doubted Zack would give up so easily, but at least he wasn't going to be physically aggressive with her. It was hard enough to resist his voice and his smile, much less the warmth of his arms and the urgency of his lips.

She threw her purse on the bed and started to unbutton her blouse. The room was shadowed and the hotel so utterly silent she could hear the pounding of the surf fifteen stories below. She decided to open the door to the balcony later, and let the soothing, rhythmic roar lull her to sleep.

She'd just reached the third button on her blouse when something slithered across her belly and began to drag her backward. Her eyes snapped down and saw a hard, male arm against her waist. Her instincts took over so quickly that she came within only a second or two of not being able to check them. It wasn't that she didn't recognize the light blue sleeve of the shirt Zack had worn that night, but that she really didn't take it in and realize there was no danger until she was already moving to strike back.

For a moment she was sick with horror at the thought of what might have happened, and then she was just plain furious. She shoved away Zack's arm and spun around, her face flushed with emotion. "Of all the damn fool stunts to pull!" she yelled at him. "Do you have any idea what I could have done to you?"

He was smiling at her, but for once the smile had no effect. "It would have been worth it," he said. "Did you really think I'd stay away?"

"You idiot! I'm not talking about a knee in your groin! I'm talking about slamming you onto the floor. I'm talking about things like dislocated shoulders and broken arms and ruined seasons." Her hand was shaking as she ran it through her hair. "Don't you ever play that kind of game with me again."

The smile faded into a look of abject apology. "I'm sorry I scared you, Liz. I figured you'd expect me to come after you."

"You haven't heard a word I've said, have you!" Liz was so distraught she wanted to grab him by the shoulders and shake some common sense into him. What did the man have for brains? Sawdust? "Listen up, Mr. Delaney. I know how to defend myself, and I'm not talking about one of those nice little classes you take at the Y. I'm talking about years and years of training. You got that?"

His expression changed from apologetic to astonished. "But I'm twice your size. You can't be worried you could have hurt me!"

"Can't I? Try terrified and maybe you'll get the general idea." Liz squeezed her eyes closed for a couple of long moments, fighting for control. His refusal to take her seriously was absolutely exasperating. "Get out of here, Zack. Please."

Zack stood right where he was. He was beginning to get the message, but he wasn't interpreting it the way Liz would have liked him to. He only knew he'd had one of the best nights of his life with a woman he was already crazy about and didn't want it to end. Maybe she was angry he'd sneaked into her room, but she was also distraught at the thought she might have hurt him. That was laughable, of course, but it also showed she cared.

Fighting the urge to smile indulgently, he asked, "What are you, some kind of female Bruce Lee?"

"Don't tempt me to show you," she muttered.

"I won't," he said. She was so damn beautiful it made his gut ache.

Liz could tell she'd gotten exactly nowhere by the way his eyes traveled up her body. He wasn't checking out her muscles, that was for sure. When he came to her half-open blouse he paused in obvious admiration. She hastily buttoned it up, but her nipples had a will of their own; they hardened into erect little nubs.

"It's hard to believe somebody so soft and slender could inflict so much punishment," he teased, "but I guess I'll have to take your word for it."

"You're damn right you will, if you have even half a brain in that thick head of yours." Liz pointed to the door, at war with her deepest desires. The only way to tip the scale toward logic and common sense was by thinking about what a male chauvinist numskull he was. A female Bruce Lee, indeed! "Out, Zack," she ordered.

When he started toward her instead of heading for the door, she decided he didn't know the meaning of the word no. What else could you expect from a quarterback who never gave up fighting until the clock ran out? Giving him a wide berth, she hurried around him toward the bathroom. Not even Zack could get through a locked door.

Just when she thought she was home free, a firm hand closed around her wrist to stop her. She took another two steps forward, testing whether he really meant to hold on.

He did. His grip tightened insistently. At that point she stopped and waited. It wasn't especially comfortable to stand there with her arm pulled behind her back, but she wasn't about to turn around. She wasn't even going to acknowledge his existence.

He stepped closer to relieve the pressure, then began rubbing his thumb slowly back and forth along the sensitive inner surface of her wrist. The seductive caress made the room feel close and hot, but she didn't respond. He came nearer still, bringing her arm to his lips. She refused to give him the satisfaction of even looking at him, but was still achingly aware of his every action. His mouth settled against the inside of her arm just above her elbow and lazily worked its way down to her hand. Her palm was damp with tension by the time he finally kissed it. A single, gentle nip turned her legs to jelly. She thought she'd go crazy if he didn't stop nibbling her hand. She'd never had a man make love to her that way before.

The momentum was all on his side now. She pictured him lifting her into his arms, carrying her to the bed and slowly but surely undressing her. She didn't have to wonder if he'd take the time to please her, not after the past five minutes. He was obviously a very skillful, patient lover.

Furious with herself, she pushed the thought out of her mind. If she said yes now she'd regret it bitterly later.

He lowered her arm, placed it against her side and released it, coming so close to her she could feel the heat radiating from his body. She was so intent on shutting out what she felt that she gave a startled jerk of alarm when he stepped directly in front of her and took her chin in his hand. She expected to see hot-blooded impatience in his eyes, but his expression was tender and amused. "You look terrified," he said. "Don't be." He gave her a gentle, lingering kiss, added a soft "Good night" and walked away from her.

Every day of the vacation was wonderful and every night Liz paid an agonizing price. She loved watching Zack work out in the mornings. He did everything with such a fascinating mixture of brute strength and athletic grace that it was impossible not to stare. She'd never realized how much power went into the simple act of throwing a football, or how beautiful it could be when form and function combined to create a perfect, poetic whole.

Then there were the afternoons, which even Gladys and her cameraman couldn't spoil. Whether Liz was alone with Zack or part of a foursome with Paul and Jenny, she enjoyed every moment of their sightseeing. Zack had an irreverent sense of humor, but he also had a contagious enthusiasm for anything new or different. He was the first to admit that he and his teammates had spent most of their spare time at beaches and clubs during their previous trips to Hawaii, and he seemed delighted to be able to remedy that. Liz loved to tease him about how docile he was. Give him a fresh can of beer, transport him in a plush limo and there was nowhere Gladys couldn't lead him.

Finally, there were the evenings. The most pleasant meal of all was the one they ate at the Reids', since there were no strangers around to stare or ask for autographs, but even the restaurant dinners were enjoyable. Gladys didn't care a whit about ambience, only about delicious, unusual food. She might have been unmovable when it came to getting her film, but she was also a first-rate tour guide.

The best part of the day came afterward, when Danny and Gladys returned to the hotel and Zack, Liz and the Traverses finally got some time alone. One night they went for a drive along the western coast, finding the scenery glorious and the isolation deeply tranquil. They spent another in the Traverses' suite, playing an increasingly cutthroat game of bridge that the women eventually won. The third night they went club-hopping. A long-haired man in his middle twenties approached them in the last place they stopped into, and at first Liz assumed it was just another request for an autograph. But as soon as the two men had scrawled their names on the menu he held out, the man told them he had some "really great stuff" in his car and asked them if they were interested in buying. They turned him down flat and sent him on his way.

The incident reminded Liz about O'Dwyer's expectations. All but gritting her teeth, she started asking questions. Did this sort of thing happen often? What drugs were usually available? Did the dealers ever offer them for free? Had they ever been with friends who'd said yes instead of no? Paul finally laughed and told her she sounded like an investigative reporter on the scent of a hot scandal. It was enough to shut her up.

They returned to the hotel to find a game of volleyball going on in the pool, and decided to join in. It turned into a laughing, splashing free-for-all that left everyone dog-tired and exhilarated. Liz had led a very serious life up to that point and the idea that she could cut loose and simply enjoy herself was deeply unsettling. It seemed so hedonistic, so irresponsible. She could only handle it by looking on her vacation in Hawaii as a week out of time, not part of her real life at all.

The agony came later, at the end of each day, when she and Zack would walk back to their suite together. After Sunday night she understood the rules perfectly. There weren't going to be any cool, impersonal good-nights. Their relationship was going to be romantic, not platonic. Zack expected her to let him touch her and kiss her. In return, he was willing to keep the embraces light and undemanding until she signaled her readiness to go further.

Liz would stand there suffering while he ran his hands up and down her bare arms, stroked her neck and shoulders and caressed her face. She would permit him to pull her so close she could feel the hard urgency of his body against her belly. He would nuzzle her neck, run his lips along her jaw and press them to her closed eyes. He even brushed them across her mouth at times, but she never allowed herself to give him the response he was waiting for. He never kept her for long, so the torture wasn't unendurable. She suspected he stopped so soon because he didn't trust himself to do otherwise. She could have been blind and still known how much he wanted her. It was obvious from the erratic pattern of his breathing, the dampness of his skin and the reluctance with which he forced himself to leave her each night.

After three nights of it she started wishing he would stop being so damned honorable. He'd never even kissed her again, not the way he had on the airplane, and she lay in bed that night remembering how it had felt and wanting it to happen again. She might have stopped him at first, but her resistance would never have lasted. Both of them knew that. So why didn't he take what he wanted? Why didn't he throw her on the bed and kiss her till she stopped arguing?

She groaned in self-disgust and buried her head in the pillow. If she wanted something to happen, she had to be willing to take responsibility for it. Honest, adult women didn't go around claiming they'd been swept away by passion or seduced against their better judgment. She felt like kicking him for making her choices so painfully, blatantly plain.

The tension got worse and worse as Wednesday went by. Jenny felt under the weather that afternoon, so she and Paul decided to stay in for dinner. The thought of being alone with Zack all evening was enough to give Liz ulcers, but she couldn't ruin Gladys's plans by suddenly backing out of them. They were supposed to go to a luau on the opposite shore of the island, and Gladys had even dragged them out

to shop for Hawaiian outfits to wear. Liz had bought a hal-
ter-topped dress in a bold pink and white print, while Zack
had picked out a shirt bright enough to give the lights on the
Vegas strip a run for their money. It was going to make a
sensational piece of film.

Liz was a nervous wreck even before they left the hotel.
They hadn't been in the car for more than two minutes before Zack was helping himself to a Scotch from the built-in
bar. He looked just as tense as she was. It was the first time
she'd seen him drink anything stronger than beer or wine,
much less gulp it down in five minutes. She knew he found
it hard to walk away from her night after night, but this was
the first time he'd been so obvious about it.

They sat and watched the scenery go by, talking very little. After about ten minutes she asked him to fix her a gin
and tonic. If she didn't calm down a little she was going to
drive herself nuts. The drink was on the weak side, but it still
did the trick. Within twenty minutes of finishing it, the urge
to open the door and jump out of the car had finally less-
ened a bit.

The luau was big, colorful and crowded. Dozens of tables were set out on the beach and hundreds of people were
milling around. Danny filmed Liz and Zack feeding each
other hors d'oeuvres and then followed them over to the bar.
Zack got a beer, while Liz decided to try a tropical concoc-
tion adorned with the toothpick-like handle of a tiny paper
umbrella speared through slices of pineapple and orange. It
was called a Hawaiian Heaven and was evidently mostly
fruit juice. Certainly it tasted that way.

It was Zack's rotten luck that about half the guests would
turn out to be members of a huge tour group operating out
of San Francisco. If these Bay Area natives loved their star
quarterback to pieces when they were sober, they wor-
shipped the ground he walked on once they'd gotten a bit of
a buzz on. Danny filmed him signing autographs and an-

swering questions while Liz stood on the sidelines with Gladys and sipped her second Hawaiian Heaven of the evening. She was beginning to realize the drinks had more rum in them than she'd counted on, but by then she didn't care. It was so nice finally to relax.

Gladys started telling her about the food and entertainment, and she decided the luau was going to be fun. The only problem was Zack's fans. They couldn't keep their hands off him. Despite the smile on his face, he looked like a cornered animal. He did so much better at this sort of thing when Paul was around to help.

Before too long she decided it was her solemn duty to rescue him. She went over to the bar to get him a second can of beer and ordered herself another Hawaiian Heaven at the same time. She drank it down a bit so it wouldn't spill and then, laughing, plunged into the crowd.

"Make way for reinforcements," she called out. "The man needs some sustenance or he'll collapse!"

"You're a mind reader," he said as he took the can out of her hand. "Listen, I'm sorry about all this...."

"Don't be silly. You can't help it if they adore you." Liz flashed a dazzling smile at the people crowding around him and linked her arm through his. "Five more minutes, folks, and then he's all mine. Agreed?"

All the world loved a lover, except perhaps for Zack Delaney. Liz got a raft of indulgent smiles from his fans and a distinctly sour frown from Zack himself. "How many of those things have you drunk?" he demanded.

"Only two. I've barely touched this one."

He eyed her half-empty glass. "You mean two and a half, not to mention the gin and tonic you had in the car."

Liz waved her hand in dismissal. "You barely put any gin in it. It doesn't count."

He gave a skeptical grunt and removed the glass from her hand. "This stuff may taste harmless, but I watched the

bartender mix it. It's loaded with rum. You've had enough."
He poured the rest of it into the dirt and handed her the
empty glass.

Everyone around them was laughing. Liz regarded the
glass in mock dismay, then sighed. "Isn't he impossibly
pushy? He must think he's on the football field, putting the
offense through its paces."

"And here I thought I was signing autographs," he retorted.

"I'll just have to get a refill," Liz said, and started to walk
away.

"The hell you will!" He caught her by her hair, which she
was wearing loose, and gently pulled her backward. "You're
staying right here where I can keep an eye on you."

Liz giggled and curtsied. "Yes, milord."

At that point a teenage girl shoved her cast-covered arm
and a felt-tipped pen under his nose. He scrawled "Heal Up
Fast" and then his name. Liz patiently waited as he continued to sign autographs and chat with his fans. Eventually,
getting a little restless, she trailed a teasing finger up his arm,
across his shoulders and down his spine. He pushed her
hand away and kept on writing. She didn't pay the least bit
of attention to the frown that crossed his face. He was
wearing his shirt Hawaiian-style, outside of his wheat-
colored jeans, and it was too tempting a target to resist. She
slid her hand up his backside and ran it over his bare back.
His skin was smooth and wonderfully muscled.

"Okay, halftime!" she sang out. "Zack gets to take a
break now, but I'll bring him back later."

Far from minding, the crowd broke into whistles, applause and shouts of encouragement. Liz took Zack's arm
to lead him away. He resisted at first, but his fans wanted
him to leave with her and didn't hesitate to say so. Having
little choice, he permitted himself to be dragged away.

"Let's walk along the beach," Liz suggested. The sun was setting over the water and the view was nothing short of spectacular. It promised to be a very romantic night. After five days of being sensible, she was entitled to be a little romantic.

Zack finished up his beer and tossed the can into a trash bin. As they walked away from the crowd, he checked out the terrain in front of them. The area was strikingly desolate compared to the Waikiki side of the island. There were rolling, grass-covered dunes behind a narrow strip of sand and not a soul was in sight. He supposed that was the general idea—to hold the luau as far away from civilization as possible—but it was too far for his peace of mind. Those dunes were easily high enough to shelter them from curious eyes.

Until that moment he would have said there could be no sterner test of his self-control than to kiss Liz good-night each evening and simply walk away. He had the sinking feeling those chaste embraces would be child's play compared to what she was about to put him through.

When they reached the beginning of the dunes he stopped and stared out over the ocean. "It's beautiful, but we really should be getting back."

"But you were the one who suggested this in the first place, on the plane," she answered. "You said we should take a walk along a moonlit beach...."

"The sun is still out."

"A technicality." She tugged at his arm but he wasn't about to budge. People could still see them here. It was the only thing that kept him from grabbing her. The scent of her hair and skin, the feel of her fingers dancing along his back, the glory of the dying sun—he could take only so much of it.

"Don't be so stubborn," she pouted. "I mean, for a man who walks away from me every night like he's just been mercilessly tortured . . ."

"This is different." He decided to lay it on the line and to hell with the risk of insulting her. One of them had to be sensible. "Don't you think I've noticed that you never have more than a glass of wine at a time? You're stinking drunk, Liz, and I'm not about to take advantage of a drunken woman. Now let's get out of here before I change my mind."

Liz would have said she was relaxed and happy, not drunk, but thought Zack was wonderfully courtly to care. "How sweet," she said. "The last of the perfect gentlemen." She started inland, toward the dunes. "I promise not to back you into any corners." She giggled as a stray thought flitted into her mind. "Speaking of backs and corners . . ." She noticed he wasn't following and turned around to motion him over. "Come on, Mr. Quarterback. I have some very important questions to ask you, about football positions." She started walking backward, stumbled over a clump of grass and decided she had to pay more attention to where she was going. "You know what I think? I think they name them just to confuse people. Female people, to be exact. You men have a club and nobody else can get into it."

Zack was afraid she'd either fall and hurt herself or get totally lost if he wasn't around to look after her. He reluctantly started forward, telling himself she'd probably pass out before anything could happen.

Smiling, she bent down to remove her sandals. "Umm. The sand is still warm. Where was I? Oh yes, corners. Why do they call them cornerbacks, Zack? They don't stay in corners. And why is there a free safety but no slave safety? And a tight end but no sober one? It doesn't make the least bit of sense."

He started to say something about the strong safety playing the strong side of the field, where the offense had most of its players, but could tell Liz wasn't listening. "You know my favorite one of all?" she asked dreamily. "Nose tackle. Who would want to tackle anybody's nose? Well, maybe yours. It *is* cute." She playfully grabbed it. "You're gonna get sacked, Delaney. Right down onto the sand."

Zack could think of nothing he wanted more, as long as Liz was doing the sacking. He firmly removed her hand, fighting his baser instincts. The two of them were hidden behind the dunes, it was getting dark out and he wasn't made of dried pigskin. He had to get her out of here while he still had the self-control to be sensible.

No sooner had he gotten rid of her right hand than her left one dived under his shirt and started rubbing his bare chest. He cursed under his breath at how good it felt. Why was God doing this to him? Was it some sort of test? His hands were shaking as he placed them on her shoulders and pushed her away.

"You wouldn't be acting this way if those Hawaiian Heavens hadn't put you into orbit," he said impatiently. "Come on, let's get back to the luau."

She grabbed a fistful of his shirt and started tugging downward. "No way. I didn't entice you out here just to turn around and leave. It's sack city, Delaney."

The next thing Zack knew, she'd mounted a full-scale attack. She was tickling him under his arm with one hand, pulling at his shirt with the other and repeatedly butting him with her hip in an effort to knock him down. She was also reeling off a steady stream of insults, laughing like a crazed hyena in between. "If that shirt were any brighter, I'd need to wear sunglasses.... I'll bet you're a regular cream puff without your offensive line to hide behind.... You call these muscles? I've seen bigger muscles on my grandmother's pet cat.... You can't even handle a woman half your size, so how are you going to handle the Cowboys?''

At first he simply held her at bay, but she was a lot stronger than she looked. The tickling was driving him crazy—making him laugh, turning him on, goading him to retaliate. The insults, although playful, made him itch to shut her up in a time-honored way. When her fingers skittered down his chest and started to attack his stomach, he gave up fighting himself and started to fight *her*.

"So you want to play in the pros, do you?" he growled. "Well, don't say I didn't warn you!"

Liz wasn't the least bit intimidated by the determined look on Zack's face. She was having a wonderful time. It was terrific fun to tease him and unbelievably heady to know she'd win. He was just about to crack, and not a moment too soon. She hadn't known it was possible to want a man so badly.

She braced her feet and pulled his shirt hard, thinking she'd be doing the world a favor if she managed to ruin it. He grabbed her arm and started to drag her down, and since she couldn't match his strength, she had to resort to fouling him. When her hand darted below his waist and started to tickle him mercilessly, he loosened his hold in helpless surprise. He was laughing as she gave him a sudden, hard push, but cursed succinctly when he lost his footing and tumbled onto the sand.

It didn't take him long to turn the tables. She lost her balance almost the moment he wrapped his arms around her legs. She tumbled over his shoulder, then sprawled onto her back, laughing uncontrollably. The situation started to seem less funny when Zack scrambled on top of her and pinned her under his body. He settled himself against her hips, his movements making her keenly aware of how aroused he was.

His eyes were glittering with amusement and self-satisfaction. They never left her face as he brushed her tangled hair away from her mouth and fanned it onto the ground around her head. "Didn't anyone ever tell you there's a penalty for roughing the passer?" he asked.

She swallowed hard, wanting him so much she was dizzy from it. "What penalty?"

"This." His mouth descended onto hers, hard and demanding. She parted her lips and let his tongue exact revenge, shuddering when his hand covered her breast and began to caress it roughly. The raw urgency of his desire for her was in every movement he made, feeding her need like gasoline feeds a fire. She strained against him, giving herself completely. Maybe he'd take her right there on the sand. The thought was almost mindlessly exciting.

She felt his fingers fumbling at the back of her neck, trying to unhook the catch that held her halter top in place, and arched her head to help him. She didn't understand why his hand suddenly stilled, or why he pulled his mouth away from her lips and buried it against her neck.

"Zack?" she murmured.

"No more." His breathing was ragged. "Any more of this and I won't be able to stop."

She threaded her hands through his hair and pulled his head up so she could look him in the eye. "But nobody can see us."

"Unless they decide to come looking." His eyes settled on her mouth. "This is going to be the longest night of my life. One for the road, honey, and then we've got to go." His lips followed his eyes, but his kiss was more restrained this time. Afterward he rolled off her and stood up, looking as if it was the last thing in the world he wanted to do. A moment later he was holding out his hand to her.

Liz allowed him to pull her up, then wrapped her arms around his neck and nuzzled his lips. The world seemed to be spinning around her, but it didn't ease the frustration she felt. "Let's go back to the hotel," she said. "I can't possibly wait all night."

"You'll have to. You probably even deserve to," he teased.

"I'll get Tibbsie's car keys. Danny can drive her back in the van."

He drew her into his arms and held her close. "Be realistic, Liz. She wants to film us at the luau, doing the hula or some other damn fool thing. She's not going to give us her car keys."

Liz got up on tiptoes and began planting soft little kisses all over his neck and ear. "Don't you want to make love to me?"

"That's got to be the dumbest question you ever asked anyone in your life," he answered.

"I take it that's a yes." Satisfied now, Liz backed away and bent down to pick up her sandals. Her voice was a little slurred as she continued, "Just leave everything to me. I'll plead a female emergency."

They walked back to the luau arm-in-arm. Liz wasn't quite steady on her feet, but she didn't let that worry her. She planned to spend the rest of the night in bed.

Chapter Seven

According to Jenny Travers, powerful legs were crucial to a quarterback's ability to throw long, accurate passes. Sitting beside Zack in the front seat of the limo, Liz put her hand on his thigh and gave it an exploratory squeeze. There was no question about it; the man had steel-like muscles buried under that skin of his. She traced a slow, fascinated circle on his knee, then gradually moved higher.

He endured her teasing caresses for about half a minute, then laughed and pushed her hand away. "If you don't cut that out you're going to get us into an accident," he said.

"Then we have a problem here." Liz started massaging the back of his neck. "I can't seem to keep my hands off you. I love touching you. I even love looking at you. You're the most beautiful man I've ever seen."

"I don't suppose I can complain about being a sex object when the feeling is so entirely mutual, but for now..."

He removed her hand again. "Over by the window, honey. Put on your seat belt and behave yourself."

"Oh, all right," Liz grumbled, "but you don't have to look so pleased with yourself." She thought about telling him what that smile of his did to her but decided against it. His head was swelled enough already.

She clicked on the seat belt and snuggled back against the soft, fragrant leather. She felt so light and airy she could easily have floated away. The world seemed fluid and ethereal. Zack turned on the radio and started whistling along with a popular song. He was obviously very happy, and that made Liz happy, too. She was going to make him even happier later, once they got back to the suite.

After a few minutes she put down the window, preferring the natural breeze to air-conditioning. Besides, the car suddenly felt stuffy and warm. She took a deep breath, savoring the cool feel of the wind on her face. The motion of the car was making her sleepy. She yawned and closed her eyes. The world was slowly spinning around her, but it was a pleasant sort of spinning. It matched the tempo of the song on the radio.

She awoke to see the lights of the hotel out the front window, only a couple of hundred yards away. Zack looked over at her and she smiled groggily. "I didn't mean to fall asleep on you," she said. "I'm sorry."

"Don't apologize," he answered. "I'm glad you got some sleep. You'll need all your strength for tonight."

"Is that so!" Liz was conscious of feeling mildly queasy as she straightened up, but put it down to the hors d'oeuvres. God only knew what had been in them, but it was nothing a few antacid tablets wouldn't take care of. "Didn't anyone ever tell you you're not supposed to brag about your performance until after the game is over?" she asked.

He laughed but didn't answer. She knew, of course, that it wasn't a game to him at all. He really cared for her. The thought pleased her, but it also frightened her a little.

He didn't park in the hotel lot, but pulled up by the main entrance to let the valet parking service take care of the car. Liz didn't normally wait around for men to help her out of cars, but when she opened the door and started to get out she suddenly felt so dizzy she had to stop and catch her breath. Zack tossed the keys to the attendant and took her hand to pull her up. She clutched his arm for support, fighting a roiling nausea. Her face felt hot and the ground wouldn't stay where it belonged. She wondered if antacid tablets would be enough to cure her.

The elevator was so crowded it was all she could do not to gag. She felt a little better as they walked down the hall and she told herself the worst was over. But when Zack unlocked the door and swept her up in his arms, it was as if an earthquake had just hit the pit of her stomach. She started coughing violently, realized things had gone from serious to desperate and choked out, "Zack—the bathroom—please..."

Zack hit the light switch, took one look at Liz's face and didn't waste any time asking questions. Her complexion, normally so glowingly healthy, was a sickly gray-white, and her face was beaded with perspiration. His bathroom was closer than hers, so he dashed around the chairs and couches in the lounge and ran into his bedroom, trying not to jostle her too much. He got her to the sink without a moment to spare.

Liz was only dimly aware of him gently holding her as she bent over the sink. She was sure you couldn't feel this rotten and still live. She'd never thrown up this way before. She groped for the water faucet to turn it on, and then, limp with exhaustion once she'd cleaned up, slowly straightened. She was more than willing to lean on Zack and let him support her.

Still holding her, he grabbed a hand towel and held it under the running water. After wringing it out, he ran it over her face. She closed her eyes. The damp terry cloth felt cool and soothing against her skin. Everything would be all right now.

As her nausea faded, embarrassment set in. Zack Delaney had the patience of a saint. The average man would have been cursing her for a fool, not caring for her so tenderly. She started to apologize, but he hushed her up and lifted her into his arms again.

"I'm not exactly inexperienced at this sort of thing," he said as he carried her into her room. "I've taken care of teammates who've celebrated too hard or drowned their sorrows too deeply. I've even done it once or twice myself, with pretty much the same results. I hate to tell you this, honey, but your stomach may not be done protesting."

Liz didn't even want to think about that. Although the nausea had eased off, she was still very dizzy. As careful as Zack had been, the trip into her bedroom had made it worse. When he sat down on the bed with her in his lap, she reached up a hand to caress his cheek. "Thank you. You do have great feet, you know that? You got me around all that furniture and into the bathroom faster than I could have gotten there myself."

Zack fluffed up a couple of pillows and eased Liz onto the bed. She was the first woman he'd ever known who wasn't a royal pain in the neck when she got sick. Allison had usually cursed him out if he came anywhere near her, as if it was somehow all his fault. He smoothed Liz's hair, thinking that she looked like a wrung-out little rag doll.

"Let's get you comfortable," he said. "Where do you keep your nightgowns?"

GET 4 FREE BOOKS, FREE FOLDING UMBRELLA, FREE MYSTERY GIFT!

TO ENTER: Fill out, detach below, and affix postage. See back pages of books for OFFICIAL SWEEPSTAKES INFORMATION and mail your entry before deadline date shown in rules.

S♥I♥L♥H♥O♥U♥E♥T♥T♥E
LUCKY HEARTS
SWEEPSTAKES

Free prizes—you must enter to win. Detach here and mail today!

Sweeps entry—
process immediately!

Silhouette Books®

Prize Headquarters
120 Brighton Road
P.O. Box 5084
Clifton, NJ 07015-5084

Affix
First Class
Stamp Here

She smiled wanly. "In the closet, at home. The only ones I own are gifts I never wear. Go on, go to bed. I'll be fine."

"If you really think that, you've got a lot to learn about alcohol. What do you sleep in? Nothing?"

"Ratty T-shirts. You wouldn't like them at all. I'll manage on my own."

Liz assumed Zack meant to leave when he got off the bed, but he only went as far as her dresser. He rummaged through the drawers, finally holding up a faded UCLA T-shirt. When she nodded, he brought it over to the bed, sat down beside her again and went to work on her halter top. It didn't do any good to tell him she didn't need his help. He pointed out that she was almost too dizzy to move, that he'd already seen her in a bathing suit and that if she'd been ready to go to bed with him only an hour ago she couldn't very well object to letting him undress her now. His logic was irrefutable. She allowed him to do as he pleased.

Zack cursed himself for a pervert as he pulled down Liz's halter top. The woman was miserably sick, so he had no business noticing her full, firm breasts, dusky pink nipples and slender waist, much less getting turned on by them. As he eased the dress down her body he noticed a long straight scar just above her bikini panties, and wondered what it was from. Some kind of surgery, probably. He carefully slid the dress down her legs and tossed it aside. She was so wrenchingly lovely that he didn't waste any time getting her T-shirt over her head. There was no point being masochistic about this whole operation.

By the time the shirt was in place she had the same twisted look on her face as when he'd carried her into his bathroom. She got to the sink on her own this time, but was just as sick as before. There were no embarrassed apologies afterward and no more protests about accepting his help. He carried her back to bed, sponged off her face and brushed her hair. Afterward he got her some ice cubes to suck on, hoping they would ease both her thirst and her nausea. She couldn't even keep the melted water down.

It went on like that for the next two hours. Each time she was sick she would get a little weaker, until she finally fell into an exhausted sleep. Zack left a message for Gladys saying Liz was ill and lay down on the other bed. If Liz woke up again he was going to get her a doctor. He didn't think there was anything wrong with her beyond too much gin and rum, but he was beginning to get worried.

The first thing Liz noticed when she woke up the next morning was that her stomach no longer felt as if it was on its own personal roller coaster ride. She cautiously opened her eyes. The room had finally stopped spinning. She felt headachey, thirsty and rather weak, but otherwise surprisingly normal. Her gaze shifted to the clock on the night table. It was almost eight o'clock.

A soft rustling noise caught her attention. She looked beyond the clock to the other bed and saw Zack lying on top of the covers, turning the pages of the morning paper. He was dressed in shorts and a T-shirt, but his clothes were crisp and dry. Obviously he hadn't gone running yet that morning.

He noticed her watching him as he reached for the glass of juice that was sitting on the night table. "Feeling any better this morning?" he asked.

"Much better," Liz said. Her stomach growled, making her aware of a gnawing hunger. She was actually looking forward to breakfast. "Shouldn't you be out on the golf course?" she asked.

"I spoke to Paul earlier this morning. We agreed to take the day off." He folded up the paper and tossed it aside. "How does breakfast on the balcony sound?"

Liz said it sounded wonderful, providing she had a chance to clean up first. Zack told her to go right ahead—he would wait for her in the bedroom. It was useless to insist she was absolutely fine or to tell him he should leave. He shook his head and ordered her to leave the bathroom door ajar so he could hear her if she called him. Since she could easily picture him answering her arguments by carrying her into the bathroom and standing on the other side of the stall door while she showered, she gave in gracefully. Having taken care of her while she was sick and then spent the night in her room, he seemed to consider her his personal responsibility.

She felt a hundred percent better once she'd showered and washed her hair. She took a couple of aspirins, blew the worst of the wetness out of her hair and opened the door. She'd forgotten to bring in her robe, so she was wearing a bath towel wrapped around her middle. Zack was sitting at the table, drinking a cup of coffee. A room service tray was waiting out on the balcony.

She opened a dresser drawer and pulled out some clothing. "Go ahead and start eating. I'll only be another minute."

Zack looked her up and down. Between her damp, silky hair and the skimpy towel she was wearing, she was a sight for sore eyes. A sharp, painful yearning slashed through his body like a knife, but he tried not to let it show. He had no idea where he stood with her this morning. She'd propositioned him when she was drunk, but she was stone-cold sober now. She'd let him take care of her when she was sick, but she was feeling much better now. He sensed a new intimacy between the two of them, but he also sensed how fragile it was. He smiled and said he would see her outside.

The first words out of her mouth when she joined him on the balcony were a blushing, "About last night—I don't know how to thank you."

He was sorry she felt embarrassed. He didn't want her gratitude, either. He would have preferred her to take his

attentiveness for granted, the way a lover would have. "You
don't need to thank me," he said. "You would have done
the same for me."

Liz was surprised by how very right he was. Rather than
call Paul or a doctor, she would have stayed by his side and
taken care of him herself. She wouldn't have wanted to leave
him, not even for a minute. She was so uncomfortable with
the implications of that that she simply refused to think
about them. "I should have known better than to drink so
much," she said. "Alcohol doesn't agree with me. I've always assumed it was psychological, but maybe my system
just can't tolerate the stuff."

"Psychological?" he repeated. "What do you mean?"

Zack knew very little about Liz's life, nor she about his.
The subject had almost never come up, mostly because
they'd so seldom been alone together. Liz had told him she'd
lived in Denver until her mother's death, and then moved to
Los Angeles to stay with Michelle's parents, but that was
about all. She'd never even mentioned Tommy to him.

She preferred to think of herself as discreet rather than
secretive. She never would have admitted, even to herself,
that she used her job as an excuse to keep people at a distance. For Liz, there was no such thing as keeping too low
a profile or saying too little about her private life. She jus-
tified her reluctance to talk about herself by telling herself
she had a cover identity to protect.

She'd made a minor slip with that admission about
drinking, but there was no reason not to answer Zack's
question honestly. It wasn't as though she was paranoiac or
neurotic about the whole business. "I had a twin brother,"
she began. "His name was Tommy. Moving to California
was a lot harder on him than it was on me. For one thing,
he was a lot closer to my father than I was. Dad was an independent trucker, and that meant long absences from
home. He tried to keep the family together after Mom died,

but there were always problems with finding someone to take care of us when he was gone. So he shipped Tommy and me off to live with my mother's younger sister and her husband. Tommy and Uncle Don were at each other's throats right from the very beginning. Don was a strict disciplinarian, but Tommy was used to a lot of freedom. Each of them wanted his own way. Tommy and I were eleven at the time, Michelle was a toddler and her two brothers, Mark and Josh, were eight and ten. Tommy and the two boys were always getting into fights, which was probably normal for siblings, but Don always seemed to punish Tommy when anything happened and gave Mark and Josh all kinds of sympathy. Naturally I spoke up, but Don never paid any attention to me. It was always, 'Liz is a good girl and a loyal sister, so naturally she takes her brother's side.' I think Aunt Barbara had a very clear idea of what was going on, but she never tried to assert herself. Uncle Don is very much the boss of that family. She may even be a little afraid of him.''

Liz poured herself some juice. No matter how many years went by, she couldn't stop asking herself whether things might have turned out differently. Surely she could have done *something* to change what had happened. ''As time went by we saw less and less of my real father. He sent my uncle a check every month, but there was almost never a letter enclosed. He would call us every few months and visit Los Angeles once or twice a year, but from the time we left Denver until Tommy's death, we only went home once. I made a place for myself in the family by being mature and responsible. I looked after the other kids and took care of the house once Barbara went back to work at Don's construction company. I was valuable to have around. Tommy was always the outcast, though, the hostile problem child. He felt our father had abandoned him and started to hate him for that. Maybe the rest was inevitable. I don't know.''

She gave a pained shake of her head. Her brother had been so sweet as a child, but he'd turned into someone she barely recognized. "Tommy got in with a bad crowd. I suppose it made him feel important to run around with kids he thought of as tough and cool. The two of us had always been close, but even I couldn't talk any sense into him. If he showed up late or had liquor on his breath, my uncle would beat the living daylights out of him and ground him for a week. That only made him more rebellious. The rest is an old story. Drugs, alcohol, a souped-up car..." She brushed away a tear with the back of her hand. She could remember the night the police had come as if it had happened only last week.

"They told us he died on impact," she said softly. "Thank God he didn't suffer. Thank God he was alone and didn't take anyone with him." She took a deep breath, forcing her emotions back under control. "Afterward I had very little use for alcohol and even less use for drugs. Once I was old enough to drink I would take a glass of wine every now and then, but too much more than that and I'd get sick. I blamed that on my memories—on the fear that something terrible would happen to me if I drank too much and lost control, the same way it had happened to Tommy."

The rest of the story wasn't something Liz had ever talked about, except to her family, Gloria Moyers and a very few colleagues at work. Tommy had died at the age of seventeen, during their senior year in high school. Liz hadn't given a thought to her future career until then. She'd assumed she would go to college, experiment with various courses and find a field she liked. But when she started UCLA that fall, it was with a single-minded goal in sight— to work in law enforcement. She would nail the kinds of creeps who'd sold her brother drugs and liquor, because it was the closest she could come to bringing him back to life.

"I'm sorry," Zack said gently. "I can see you have a tough time talking about it. That's only natural."

Liz shrugged and picked up a piece of bacon. "Life is tough. Either you accept that and refuse to let it defeat you, or you wind up like Tommy. It's just . . ." She looked at the table, fighting back tears. "Everything seemed to be against him. He was so sensitive and emotional as a child. If my mother hadn't died, if my father had found us a reliable housekeeper or been willing to change careers, if my uncle had been more understanding or my aunt a little stronger, if only I could have made Tommy listen to me . . . There are so many ifs. It's so damned unfair."

"Unfair and capricious," Zack agreed softly. He'd sensed resiliency and strength in Liz almost from the beginning, and now he knew where they'd come from. She'd needed them in order to survive. One way or another, she'd lost every single member of her immediate family. He came from a close family himself, and couldn't imagine anything more painful than watching someone he loved slowly ruin his life. He would feel so helpless while it was happening and so guilty afterward.

Thoughtful now, he went on quietly, "You know, sometimes I look at my own life and I can't believe how it's turning out. It's like God decided to play a colossal joke on me. He took an average-size string bean of a kid whose fantasies about pro sports ran to visions of being a starting shortstop somewhere, waved His celestial wand, and bingo! One star quarterback."

Liz heard what he was saying, but was so wrapped up in her memories of Tommy that it took her a while to comprehend what he meant. "But every article I've ever read about you goes on and on about what a terrific natural athlete you are," she said. "I assumed you were one of those people who knows from the age of fourteen that he'll have a career in professional football."

"I figured I was too small. It's one thing to be a five-foot ten-inch, one-hundred-forty-pound quarterback in a small rural high school, and another to think you can start for a major college, much less play in the pros. I chose Colgate for its academic reputation. I'd planned on a career in business. I also thought I had a chance to be the starting quarterback there, because it's not in the toughest competitive division."

Liz munched on her bacon, staring at him—all six feet three inches and two hundred ten pounds of him. "Obviously you grew," she said with a smile.

He laughed. "Yeah, obviously I did. Five inches in three years, but my weight and muscle didn't start catching up until I was twenty-two or three. I was the Rushers' third-round draft pick, and I was surprised to be selected that high. It wasn't that I underestimated my own talent, but that I didn't fit the NFL mold. Part of it was lack of strength and part of it was style of play. My biggest assets were mobility and accuracy over short and middle distances, and that wasn't what most teams were looking for at the time. But Ben Halliday was in the process of rebuilding the Rushers during those years, and my talents fit in very well with the type of offense he wanted to establish. I still needed more weight and strength, but he was willing to take a chance and see how I'd develop. I started as number-three quarterback, graduated to backup by the end of my first year and finally started a game near the end of my second year. I came into training camp the following summer determined to win the starting job for good, but it was the middle of the season before I accomplished that. At the time I thought— that's it, I've done it all now, I'm starting and I'm winning. I was pretty naive in those days. I really believed that my only responsibility as the Rushers' starting quarterback would be to win football games."

Zack had told Liz he was the youngest of five children from a small town about fifty miles north of Pittsburgh, but she knew almost nothing else about him. It was obviously a long way from rural Pennsylvania to the California fast track—perhaps even longer than she'd imagined. "I suppose you're talking about charity work, personal appearances and media attention," she remarked. "Did the demands on your time really come as that much of a shock to you?" *Haven't you ever looked in the mirror?* she silently added. When a professional athlete was as handsome as Zack Delaney and a winner in the bargain, of course the public was going to want a big chunk of his hide.

"Not so much the demands themselves, but the nature and extent of them," he answered. "In my first few years with the Rushers we were still rebuilding. We were doing well to win as many games as we lost, so nobody paid any attention to a backup quarterback. I didn't even live in San Francisco during the off-season. I would make the family circuit each winter and spring—travel back home to Yorkeville to see my parents, go up to Boston to visit my sister, go to Pittsburgh, Houston and Los Angeles to see my brothers. All that changed when the Rushers started winning with me as first-string quarterback. Yorkeville was the kind of place where everyone knew everyone else. You could shake hands on a deal and it was as good as signing a contract. People were absolutely straight with each other. And here I was, the one-time runt of the family, the baby brother who everyone protected whether he wanted them to or not, coming up against people who flattered and lied and promised me the world just to get what they wanted. Hell yes, it came as a shock to learn they were full of bull. There's nothing like being played for a sucker, especially by someone who claims to love you." He pushed away his plate, looking annoyed with himself. "File that one under the heading Past Romantic History. I shouldn't have brought it up."

Zack might just as well have ordered Liz not to think of the word "elephant." It was only human to wonder whom he was talking about and what she'd done. The name "Allison Chase" came to mind, mostly because Michelle had said Zack had decided not to marry her. He wasn't the type to break up with a woman just because he was afraid of commitments, so what had really happened?

The confession that followed owed a lot to feminine curiosity, since Liz hoped it would encourage Zack to open up. It was also an entirely natural response to a conversation that was growing more and more serious, more and more intimate. For some reason, Zack was unusually easy for Liz to talk to. She was also interested in him as a person. The more he told her about himself, the more she wanted to know about him. Choosing her words carefully so as not to give too much away, she said, "I guess we all carry around our share of emotional baggage. In my case it was a man I once worked with. He wanted someone to cook, clean, bear his children and carry out his orders, but it was two years before he finally admitted it to either of us. I needed to be independent, especially after all those years of watching Aunt Barbara jump to do Uncle Don's bidding in the office and then constantly knuckle under to him at home. I haven't been involved with anyone in a very long time now."

Zack sat there wondering how the serious, almost wounded woman sharing breakfast with him could possibly be so different from the one he'd first met on the set of *Main Attraction*. "Some free spirit," he teased. "You sound like you're dedicated to your career—whatever your career *is*. I don't think I've figured it out yet."

"Private security," Liz said. She'd been prepared for that question, although she'd hoped it wouldn't come up. She didn't enjoy lying to Zack, but orders were orders. O'Dwyer said she couldn't tell him who she was, so she wouldn't tell him. Neither would she explain that the man she'd wasted two years on had been a fellow agent who'd expected her to give up her career to be his wife. She would talk in generalities, knowing that the fundamentals were true even if specific incidents weren't.

"I was never really a buyer when I lived in San Francisco," she said. "I was a store detective. Gloria knows all about my various jobs, and that's how I got on the show. One of the roles I play is the dizzy dumb blonde. It puts people off their guard. They'll do all sorts of stupid things in front of me because they think I'll never notice. Gloria was desperate for women who could act that part on the show, and she really leaned on me to help out."

"And that business about loving sports?"

"It's true. Don't forget, I grew up near Denver. I started skiing as a toddler and I love it. I also water-ski, sail, hike and play tennis." That much, at least, was accurate, but the rest of what Liz was about to say was pure fiction. "I took the job at Diamond's because they agreed to let me work an evening shift. It leaves me plenty of time to enjoy myself during the day. I guess there's a little hedonist in me after all."

"So you're not so mysterious after all," Zack said.

"No, I'm not." Liz paused, then hit him with the question she'd been leading up to for the past five minutes. "But you are. That past you mentioned a few minutes ago—would the woman be Allison Chase? Michelle mentioned you'd dated for several years and then broken up."

The question put a moody frown on his face, or maybe it was just the mention of Allison Chase's name. "Michelle is a regular expert on my private life," he muttered.

"Absolutely. She follows it religiously." Liz grinned at him, totally unrepentant. "Come on, Zack. I told you about my mistake. The least you can do is tell me about yours."

"True enough." He filled up his cup with coffee, looking nettled but resigned. "Did Michelle happen to mention Allison's pretensions as a designer?"

Liz searched her memory. "I think there was something about sports clothes."

"Sports clothes with my name on them," Zack amended. "I had two problems with that. First of all, Allison knew nothing about designing comfortable, well-made clothing that would hold up under tough conditions. When it comes to clothes, her major talent is walking into a store, grabbing half a dozen items and putting them together in a way that looks unbelievably sexy. Second, I didn't *want* my name on a line of sports clothes. If I'm going to endorse something, I want to know enough about it to be sure of what I'm doing. That's easy with soft drinks or shoes, but not so easy with clothing. In the end, Allison gave me an ultimatum. Either we were a team or we weren't. Either I let her use my name for the business she wanted to establish or we were through. It made me recognize some things I'd always ignored about her."

"Such as?" Liz asked.

He sighed and leaned back in his chair, picking up his cup. Taking a sip, he said, "We met at a charity dinner near the end of my third season with the Rushers. She'd used her father's connections to arrange to get me there and have me seated next to her, but I didn't know that at the time. When I eventually found out, I was flattered. She was beautiful, rich and smart, and I was very attracted to her. I thought of her as being part of another world, a world that was somehow far above me. It took every ounce of courage I had just to ask her out. It never occurred to me that I was much more important than she was at that point. I was the Rushers' regular quarterback by then, we'd won all but one of the games I'd started, and the local sportswriters were billing me as the next Bart Starr or Johnny Unitas." He gave Liz a self-deprecating smile. "I told you I was naive."

"You're saying she wouldn't have bothered with you if you'd still been playing backup on a losing team?"

"That's what I'm saying. She wasn't about to get involved with a nobody when she could have a star. She was very definite about what kind of man she wanted and God knows I was prime material for her to mold. She was always telling me what to do—what charities to support, what appearances to make, what reporters to cultivate, even where to invest my money. At first I was so impressed with her background and connections that I listened to every word. I was a rather young twenty-four and a half at the time. The problems began when I grew up enough to take control of my own life. Allison had it all figured out for me. When I retired I'd become a jock media star, like O.J. Simpson. I'd still be in the public eye and she'd be in it with me. Announcing is an option I've considered—I did color commentary for the NFC play-offs the year before last—but I'm not sure it's what I want. I own some commercial real estate and a couple of fast-food franchises, and I may decide to stay with my original plans and go with a business career. In any event, Allison's ultimatum about the clothing company wasn't what ended our relationship. It was the realization that she would only love me, if love is the proper word, as long as I was a celebrity. After a while you get a bellyful of people trying to use you, even well-intentioned people who want you to lend your name to good causes. You certainly don't need it from your friends or the woman in your life."

Liz's heart went out to him. She'd grown up knowing she had to protect herself, but Zack obviously hadn't. As tough as he was on a football field, he was gentle, sweet and vulnerable off one. He'd learned the hard way that people took advantage of you if you allowed them to, and the lesson had obviously carried a high emotional price. It had to be difficult to be wary when you'd always trusted people, or to be selfish with your time and talent when your natural inclination was to give of them unstintingly.

She didn't know what to say, so she picked up the last piece of toast and took a halfhearted bite out of it. It was cold and chewy by then. Zack leaned forward and rested his elbows on the table. One look at the expression on his face and she knew exactly what he was thinking. The conversation had drawn them much too close. They'd shared too much pain to keep playing games with one another.

"You're as far from that sort of person as anyone I've ever met," he said, and reached out to smooth her hair. "The man you told me about was a fool to ever let you go."

Liz nervously dropped her eyes. Why did he have to say things like that? Why did he have to make it even harder than it had been all week? She stared at her plate, hoping the moment would pass if she simply didn't respond.

Zack being Zack, he refused to back off. "At least look at me," he said.

She sighed and gave in. "Zack, please..."

"Please what? Please drop it? I'm not going to drop it. Do you know what it does to me to leave you every night? Right at this moment, I want you so much I can hardly sit still. I'd like to throw you on the bed and touch you until you're so crazy with frustration you're tearing at my clothes and begging me to put you out of your misery. And don't try to tell me it wouldn't happen. After last night, I know better than that."

So did Liz. Blushing hotly, she mumbled, "Last night I was drunk."

"Exactly. You were drunk, so you finally did what you've been dying to do for days and offered yourself on a silver platter. Dammit, Liz, what's the problem here? We like each other. We care about each other. We're attracted to each other. Why not let things happen naturally?"

The answers were clear enough. Things hadn't changed. Zack was a part of Liz's job, not that she'd done that job particularly well. He was so well-known that a close relationship with him would make her well-known, too. That was fine for the immediate future, but it would destroy her ability to take on a new undercover assignment later on, at least in California, where his life was an open book. The relationship had no future. If she allowed it to become intimate, ending it would only be more painful for both of them.

Since she couldn't say any of that, she shook her head and did her best to look confused. "I'm not ready for what you want. Please don't keep asking me to—"

"For what I want?" he interrupted angrily. "You make it sound unreasonable or selfish. All I want is to make love to you, to take the emotions we both feel and express them physically. I'm not your goddamn ex-boyfriend. I don't want to run your life or keep you barefoot and pregnant. What does it take before you're ready? A proposal? Because if that's the price tag, I'm willing to discuss it."

"Don't be ridiculous." Liz's features tightened with tension. Zack was offering her so very much, but she simply couldn't accept it—not if it was going to cost her her life's work. She was perilously close to tears, but she couldn't afford such a disastrous show of emotion. It would land her smack in his arms.

"I don't see why I should have to explain myself," she said curtly. "I have the right to say no and I'm saying it."

Football is a very physical game. Zack couldn't have played it if he hadn't enjoyed that aspect of it, but every now and then the ritualized violence of the football field threatened to spill out into his real life. Right at that moment, he was so furious with Liz and life in general that he wanted to bring his fist down on the glass-topped table and smash it to pieces. Liz wasn't making sense. He couldn't escape the feeling she was lying to him. A dozen arguments went through his mind, but he didn't give voice to a single one of them. She looked implacable, even angry with him. He could drag her into bed and see that she enjoyed it, but he needed her to give herself freely, not just allow herself to be taken.

He got up from the table, mumbling that he was going to go find Paul. He'd decided to work out that morning after all.

Chapter Eight

Liz knew she'd made the right decision. After all, what was the point of complicating her life? Her career had always been deeply satisfying. The work she did was tremendously important. She would pick up exactly where she'd left off the moment she was back in California, and before too long, Zack Delaney would be nothing but a bittersweet memory. She told herself as much at least a dozen times a day.

There was only one thing wrong with her logic. Her heart refused to listen. Her heart insisted that Zack Delaney was the best thing ever to come into her life. It told her that only a fool would let him go. Hearts, of course, were notorious for ignoring the practicalities of a situation and rushing headlong into disaster. Liz told herself *that* at least a dozen times a day, too.

She felt like the rope in a violent tug-of-war, pulled in opposite directions. She'd had a lot of experience in dealing with heartache, though. All other things being equal, she would have managed to cope. What she couldn't cope with was watching Zack's reaction.

Outwardly, nothing changed. He had far too much class to try to pressure her into changing her mind or to go off into a corner somewhere and sulk. He still made wry comments in museums and told entertaining stories at dinner. He was still a gracious escort. Yet Liz couldn't escape the feeling that he was only going through the motions of enjoying himself. It was as though somebody had pulled the plug and drained the joy and zest right out of him. She hated being the cause of that.

Paul and Jenny Travers flew back to the mainland on Friday morning, as scheduled. They'd continued to be warm and cordial to Liz, but they'd also closed ranks behind their dearest friend. Quite naturally, they'd wanted to take the pressure off him, so they'd stuck by his side for two straight days and kept the conversation on unthreatening shop talk. Liz became the outsider, and maybe even the villain of the piece. It wasn't particularly pleasant for her.

Gladys had scheduled a full day's activities that Friday. Liz would have preferred to stay in her room, but was too emotionally drained to protest. They were leaving Saturday afternoon, and she felt she could endure anything so long as it was for only thirty-six hours.

The afternoon went fine. She and Zack spent it walking around the Polynesian Cultural Center, looking at native crafts and life-styles. They did a lot of smiling for Danny's camera but very little talking. With only a final dinner to get through, Liz was sure the worst was over.

She didn't count on how awful that dinner would be. Jenny and Paul were no longer around to keep up the conversation and act as a buffer, and their absence made the meal an ordeal. Liz tried talking to Zack about the food, but he barely even answered her. He didn't seem so much angry as subdued and remote. After a while she gave up trying to make conversation and concentrated on her food. She wasn't hungry, but eating gave her something to do. Autograph seekers had never been so welcome. They broke up the awkward silences.

By the time they walked out of the restaurant, Liz was a nervous wreck. They still had to drive all the way back to the hotel. The thought of sitting only inches away from a tense, withdrawn companion was enough to make her shrivel up inside. Obviously it was her fault. She should never have encouraged him. She should have never gotten drunk and propositioned him. She should never have talked so freely to him. She'd accomplished only one thing by letting him get so close—she'd hurt him badly.

Gladys had dragged them through the last three days of their schedule with such bracing efficiency that it came as a total surprise to Liz when she suggested to Zack that he drive. Liz didn't think Gladys had even noticed anything was wrong, but obviously she had. She slid in next to Liz in the back, and then, a few minutes after they'd gotten underway, took her hand and gave it a sympathetic squeeze. Liz's eyes filled with tears. She didn't feel she deserved such kindness.

When they got back to the hotel, Zack mumbled that he was going for a walk and would see Liz in the morning. She should have been relieved to be alone, but she only felt anxious and depressed. She took a long, hot shower before getting into bed, hoping it would relax her and help her sleep. It didn't. She was still wide awake when Zack came in. He stopped at the refrigerator, then continued on to his room, shutting the door behind him. It was something he'd finally learned—to shut the door to his bedroom.

Liz lay in bed another ten or fifteen minutes, then gave up trying to sleep and went outside to the balcony. It was a warm, lazy night with a glorious full moon shining over the ocean. She leaned over the railing, looking down at the beach. Maybe Zack had gone walking there. The two of them had never gotten around to taking that moonlit stroll he'd suggested on the plane.

She was deeply torn and miserably confused. Tomorrow she would leave Hawaii. She would never see Zack again, except on a television screen. She swallowed hard, finding the thought unbearable. Why did life have to be so painful? Why did it constantly confront her with traumatic losses and horrible choices? And dammit, where was it written that Elizabeth Reynolds Pittman always had to be strong, sensible and practical?

She took a deep, shuddering breath and turned away from the railing. Self-pity wasn't her style. Neither was all this raging emotion. She'd get back into bed and she'd damn well lie there until she fell asleep. The confusion and pain couldn't last forever.

Somehow, though, it wasn't her bed she headed for once she'd let herself back into her room, but the closed door. She opened it, crossing the lounge like a woman in a trance. She was shaking like a leaf as she opened Zack's door. It was probably the first time in her life that her heart had ruled her head, but she didn't want to think about that. She didn't want to think at all.

He was sitting up in bed with a magazine in front of him, but followed Liz with his eyes as she slowly crossed the room. She was suddenly painfully aware of the faded T-shirt and cotton panties she was wearing. It wasn't exactly an attractive outfit. He tossed aside the magazine, a blank, almost bored expression on his face. Whatever he felt, if anything, was buried deep inside him.

She stopped by the side of the bed, her mouth so dry with tension it was hard to get a single word out. "I couldn't sleep," she finally said.

"Oh," he replied.

She coughed several times, wishing she had a glass of water. "I'm not sure what I'm doing here. I know I shouldn't have come but I just couldn't help it. I wish I knew what I wanted."

His expression went from blank to cool, pushing her farther away than ever. He opened the night-table drawer, took out a pen and a sheet of hotel stationery and scrawled something across the page. Then he handed it to Liz. Her face reddened when she saw what it was—a San Francisco phone number. "If you ever figure it out," he said, "call me. Until then, we don't have anything to talk about."

He hadn't raised his voice, but Liz could still hear the cold disapproval in it. It was so unlike Zack to be cruel or sarcastic that for a few moments she simply stared at the piece of paper, stunned by his hostility. "I was just..." she began, and then had to stop, because her eyes had filled with tears. She took a moment to compose herself, then tried again. "I wanted to tell you how I felt. You might at least try to understand."

His expression got even colder. It was the look Liz had read about, the one she remembered from the airport, and she cringed just as surely as his teammates did to find herself the target of it. "Dammit, Liz, you drag your way in here with all the enthusiasm of a condemned prisoner walking her last twenty feet to the gas chamber, and I'm supposed to be understanding? I'm not your psychiatrist. I don't want any favors from you. If you want to sleep with me, just say so, but for God's sake make a decision and stick to it."

"Don't you think I'm trying?" she asked hoarsely. "It's not that easy."

"Thanks for the vote of confidence," he muttered.

"Zack, please listen...."

"No, *you* listen! Nobody can decide what you want but you, so give us both a break and do it. Trying's just not good enough." He picked up his magazine and stuck his nose in it, ignoring her.

Liz was too wrought up to think straight. She only knew she wanted Zack, and at that moment it was all that mattered. The future could take care of itself. As she'd said on *Main Attraction*, she could get hit by a truck next week or killed in an avalanche next month. Why worry?

She sat down on the edge of the bed and removed the magazine from Zack's hands. His only response was to give her a wary look.

"Do you want me to stay?" she asked softly.

"We were talking about what *you* want," he reminded her.

She pulled off her T-shirt with shaking hands. Her breasts were aching for the warmth of his caress, the nipples sensuously aroused. He stared at them as if he was dying to touch them, but didn't move an inch. Tension throbbed through the room.

"I'm staying," she finally murmured.

If the smile that flickered across his face was anything to go by, it was apparently the right thing to say. He covered her breast with a gentle palm, then moved his hand downward to her belly. "All night?"

"Yes."

"And you won't be sorry in the morning?"

She stroked his chest with light, teasing fingers, following the mat of blondish-brown hair to the point where it disappeared under the covers. "I won't be sorry." She gave him a smile of her own. "If I moved my hand lower, what kind of clothing would I feel?"

"I'll let you find that out for yourself." He ran his finger along the fine white line of her scar. "What's this from? It looks fairly recent."

"I had surgery six months ago," Liz said. "I was, uh, attacked. He had a knife."

He paled a little. "You mean he stabbed you?"

"Yes. I came out on top, though." She winked at him. "I'm a female Bruce Lee, remember?"

"Dear God, how can you joke about it?" He took her in his arms and held her tightly, comforting both of them. Liz snuggled against him, loving his warmth and strength. Her arms went around his back, then slowly slid lower. It answered her question about what he slept in. He was delightfully naked under the covers, a state she took full advantage of.

Tenderness gave way to passion as her fingers explored the contours of his hip and then slipped between his thighs. He brought her lips to his mouth and hungrily took his fill, plundering the sweetness inside. It seemed as if she'd waited forever to reexperience the taste and feel of him. His kiss was quintessentially male—restless, bold, dominating. She parried it with feminine coyness, deliberately provoking him with teasing nips and maddening little withdrawals. She wanted to drive him crazy. She wanted to tantalize and excite him until Allison Chase and every other woman he'd ever been with went straight out of his mind.

Her strategy backfired. She was the one who was tantalized and excited as Zack took her breasts in his hands and gently lifted them to his mouth. She trembled when his teeth closed over a vulnerable nipple and began to work their magic. Her body was on fire, its core like molten lava. As he nibbled and sucked first one nipple and then the other, she thought hazily that she'd been a fool to wait so long. She should have known he'd be perfect. Everything he did was perfect, and if it wasn't, he practiced it till it was.

Practiced, she thought. She hated the implications of that. Frowning, she put a hand on each side of his face and forced his head up. "Zack . . ."

He gave a low grunt and trailed his lips along her collarbone. "Hmm?"

"You know too much about women. I don't think I like that." She was only half-serious. It wasn't the sort of thing you could complain about.

He cocked an eyebrow at her. "Oh yeah?"

"Yeah." His lips were against her mouth now; she took a spiteful little nip and giggled. "Who taught you? Allison?"

"Who taught *you*? That male chauvinist creep you dated?" He slid an arm under her knees and another under her back, lifting her up as he eased himself off the bed. "I need to shave. You can keep me company."

Liz ran her finger down his cheek. "It's not so bad. It won't bother me."

"It will by the time I'm through with you," he informed her. "I plan to keep you up all night."

"Bragger!" she teased.

"Wait and see," he answered.

There was something very intimate about sitting and watching a man while he performed the ritual of shaving. Liz imagined that old married couples must share such moments, although she felt anything but old and wifely to see him standing there without a stitch of clothing on. In the end his naked body was too much to resist. She slid her toe up his leg to his thigh, only to earn herself a ferocious glare in response. When she blithely persisted, he swatted away her foot and told her not to fidget. Shaving was serious business and she wasn't to distract him. He held up the can of shaving cream as a warning about what would happen if she didn't behave herself.

As they walked back into the bedroom, he mentioned stopping into a drugstore earlier in the week and asked if he'd needed to bother. She smiled at the shyness in his voice and shook her head. "You could set a calendar by me. It's the wrong time of the month."

He frowned at that. "I've heard that one before, usually with the tag line, 'Famous last words.'"

"Not in my case. Believe me, it's okay."

He didn't ask any more questions. Switching off the bedside lamp, he tumbled onto the bed and pulled her down on top of him, fitting her intimately against his body. At first only a thin layer of cotton separated the two of them, and then, as he slowly slid down her panties, nothing at all. Hot flesh strained against hot flesh. She groped for his mouth, still night-blind in the moonlit room. She was suddenly desperate for him, desperate to feel him inside of her, desperate to know the pleasure she'd denied herself all these years—but only with this particular man. She couldn't conceive of letting anyone else touch her, ever again.

She parted her thighs and arched her back in invitation, but he teased instead of taking, stubbornly resisting her. Finally, pushing her onto her back, he rocked up onto his knees and straddled her thighs. He hooked his fingers around her panties and slowly inched backward, gradually working them down her legs. When they were finally past her ankles and off, he started back in the other direction. His fingers grazed the insides of her legs and thighs, arousing and tormenting her as they moved higher and higher. Her whole body seemed to be melting. She felt the hot intimacy of his fingers and moaned his name. He delicately stroked her until every ounce of consciousness was focused on the need for release. She wanted to touch him back, but she couldn't seem to reach him. Eventually she stopped even trying. It was impossible to do anything but writhe against his hand and let herself drown in the pleasure he was giving her.

When he finally eased himself on top of her, she wrapped her legs around his thighs and tried to hurry his pace. He was going too slowly. She was going to explode before they even joined together. She groaned, "Please, Zack. I can't stop. . ." just as his mouth came down to claim hers. There was a little pain when he first entered her—it had been so long—but it passed almost at once. She tried to hold back as he teased his way deeper and deeper, but it was impossible. She was crying out her pleasure after the first few unbridled thrusts.

He went rigid for a moment, then let go. The waves of ecstasy seemed to go on forever, crashing over them like a violently erotic storm. Afterward they clung to each other, cooling off and catching their breaths. When they finally separated, Liz began to apologize. "I'm sorry I couldn't wait. . . ."

"I'm not," he murmured, and kissed her shoulder. "It was terrific. I especially liked the part where you started begging."

She realized he was laughing at her. "I did not beg," she insisted, "and anyway, I'd like to see how well you do if I touch you till you're half crazy with frustration."

"You've got yourself a deal. How soon are you going to start?"

"Very soon." Liz wanted to bask in the afterglow first. She felt so relaxed, so wonderful. After so long, her body should have been feeling the aftereffects, but there was no discomfort, no soreness. She suddenly realized why there wasn't, and, loving Zack for his thoughtfulness, sprawled on top of him and gave him a big hug. "You're so sweet. You took your time because you didn't want to hurt me."

His arms closed around her back. "It was entirely self-serving. I told you, I'm going to keep you up all night."

"What a delightful prospect," Liz said, and hungrily sought his mouth.

Liz wasn't up all night, but she didn't sleep the usual eight hours, either. Either she or Zack would always wake up after a while and arouse the other into wanting to make love again. When she finally woke for good, he was sitting outside with the morning paper and a cup of coffee. There was a room-service tray on the balcony table, the platters still covered with silver lids. She slipped into his bathrobe and went outside to join him.

"I'm starved," she announced, and kissed him good-morning. She hadn't eaten a decent meal in days. She hadn't been able to. "What did you order?"

"Bacon and eggs, a side order of sausage, some Danish, a waffle with strawberries and whipped cream, and some banana and nut pancakes. I didn't know what you'd want."

Liz laughed and sat down. "Just wait till Gladys sees the bill."

"She won't complain," Zack said, "I think she's a closet romantic. She's probably been dying to get us together."

"You just might be right." Liz started removing lids. They ate entirely too much, then went into the bathroom to shower together. Zack was deliciously thorough about soaping her up, but their lovemaking never got beyond the preliminaries. Their schedule was clear that day and their plane didn't leave until three. There would be time to enjoy each other later, when they weren't so sated with food and pleasure.

Zack tried to talk her into going running with him, but she felt much too lazy to exercise. Her muscles, she pointed out, had received a thorough workout during the night. He finally gave up coaxing her and slapped her lightly on the backside as a reminder of the one place where she needed to lose weight. She retorted that he hadn't seemed to mind it in bed.

She sent him on his way with a kiss that promised more and went into her room to pack. The light on her phone was blinking, and, wondering who could have called her, she walked over to pick it up. "This is 1505," she said. "Do you have a message for me?"

"One moment please." There was a short wait while the clerk checked her mailbox. "Your boss would like you to call him at home, Miss Reynolds. He said you would know the number."

Liz thanked her and hung up, feeling distinctly uneasy. The message had been worded so that if Zack or Gladys had happened to intercept it, they would have assumed someone from the casino had phoned. The "boss" in question was obviously Jack O'Dwyer, but Liz couldn't imagine what he wanted.

She fished her address book and telephone credit card out of her purse and picked up the receiver again. She didn't want the call listed on the hotel bill. Her heart was beating erratically as she punched the buttons. The real world had intruded into her life with a bang, and she would just as soon have kept it at bay.

Jack's wife Nina answered the phone. It seemed to take forever for her to call him in from the backyard. Liz drummed her fingers on the night-table and told herself something critical must have happened on the case. Otherwise Jack would have called her tonight or tomorrow, when she was back in California again.

"So how's the vacation going?" he asked when he finally took the line.

Liz's guard went up a little higher. Jack sounded much too casual for a man who almost never wasted time on small talk. "All right," she answered.

"You don't sound too enthusiastic. Are you bored with lazing around on the beach all day?"

"I haven't been lazing around," Liz said. "Gladys—the tour guide—has been dragging me all over Oahu. How are things going back there?"

"Very well. Hoag finally asked Bill to deliver something more than shampoo last Wednesday. We've identified two of Hoag's associates already, one at the Diamond Plaza

Hotel in Los Angeles and the other at the Diamond Plaza in Seattle. There's still no lead as to who's actually running the show, but we're looking into Hoag's background and finances. It's doubtful he could have bankrolled the operation himself."

He wasn't telling Liz anything she hadn't suspected. Hoag was using his legitimate business as a cover for an illegal drug distribution system, and Diamond's was directly involved. Her task now would be to identify and gather evidence against everyone else involved, especially the men on top. She told Jack she was looking forward to getting back to work and waited for him to get to the point.

He didn't, at least not right away. First there was some uncharacteristic chitchat about what she'd done in Hawaii and whether she'd had a good time. The warning lights in her brain were flashing faster than ever now, but it was mostly a matter of instinct. Jack's questions were totally innocuous. Maybe that was what worried her.

"And Zack Delaney?" he finally said.

Liz had barely mentioned Zack or the Traverses. It was always "*I* did such-and-such" rather than "*We* did such-and-such."

"What did you find out about him?"

"He's clean. Both he and Travers apparently believe that nobody on the team is involved with drugs. Certainly they aren't. We were in a club one night and some man came up to them and offered them some 'good stuff.' They told him to get lost."

"I see." Jack paused. "Tell me, Liz—what was your impression of Delaney?"

She stalled for time, wanting to feel her way carefully. "My impression of him? In what way? As an athlete? Intellectually?"

"As a person," Jack answered. "You had a positive opinion of him before you left. Did it hold up?"

The question took Liz's amorphous suspicions and brought them into sharp, disturbing focus. Jack O'Dwyer was a fine man, an honest, hardworking agent and an understanding boss. She had a tremendous amount of admiration and respect for him. But she didn't deceive herself about his willingness to use other people to accomplish his ends.

She had to be very, very cautious about how to proceed. She had to put Jack off, but he was no pushover when it came to believing evasions and lies. "Let's just say I'm glad the vacation is over," she answered.

"Why?"

She sighed. "Jack, do I really need to go into this? Isn't it enough that I'll be back on the job on Monday?"

"In a word, no." He sounded impatient with her. "Let's have it, Liz. What in hell's going on there?"

"Delaney is a very dedicated athlete."

"Dammit, Liz..."

"All right, all right." She forced a note of hard annoyance into her voice. "It's not very pleasant to talk about, okay? From the stuff reporters write, you'd think Delaney was a saint, but let me tell you, he's anything but. On first impression he's shy and self-effacing, but if you want to know the truth, I've spent the whole week fighting him off. He seems to assume it's his God-given right to go to bed with me. Maybe he started off as a nice kid from Pennsylvania, but he's been spoiled rotten by all the attention he gets. His first priority seems to be football and his second is his public image. He can be incredibly obnoxious in private, but in public he's Mr. Wonderful. He's damn careful about how he comes across on television and how he treats his fans."

"So you don't plan to see him again once you're back in California?"

"Are you kidding me?" Liz was miserably tense by then. She was so terrified of slipping up that the muscles in the back of her neck were as tight as bowstrings. Somehow she had to nail her point home without laying it on so thick that Jack would get suspicious. "Oh, God, Jack, maybe I'm overreacting. Zack is a good-looking guy. Maybe he's so used to having women fall all over him he can't believe I really mean it when I say no. It's just that I go out there and risk my life day after day to try to do a little good in this world, and it infuriates me to come across someone like Delaney who could probably make a hell of a lot more difference than I could if he only cared enough to try. He never will, though. He's totally out for himself."

"And his friend Travers?"

"Another real gem. He propositioned me the moment his pregnant wife was out of earshot. I can see why he and Delaney get along so well. Look, Jack, I'm not stupid. I can see what you're getting at, but I think you'd be wasting your time and possibly even compromising the case. If you want to ask them to help you, go ahead, but leave me out of it. I don't want anything to do with either of them. Some other agent will have to take over."

"Okay, Liz—just settle down." Jack was using his most placating voice, the one he resorted to when he'd pushed his agents too hard. "I understand it's been a tough week for you. Monday's your day off at the restaurant, right?"

"Yes."

"Then don't bother checking in with Bill until Tuesday. Take some time to relax. I'll speak to you again next week, okay?"

"Yeah. Sure. Thanks, Jack." Liz hung up the phone, then slumped over in relief. She would have liked to stay that way all day, just blocking out the world, but Zack could come back at any time. She left him a curt note—"I need to do some thinking. I'm going downtown"—and hurried out of her room. She was so afraid of running into him in one of the hallways that she dashed down a flight of stairs, rode the elevator to the second floor, and left the hotel through the back entrance. She hitched a ride into town with one of the other guests. She spent the next couple of hours walking aimlessly around Waikiki. No matter how many ways she looked at it, the situation didn't change. There was no way on earth she was going to allow Zack Delaney to get mixed up with a federal drug investigation. She had no doubts at all that that was what Jack O'Dwyer was pushing for, and she simply wasn't going to permit it.

Even during the spring and summer, Zack had precious little privacy. Once the football season started he was like a goldfish on display in a tank. If they used him as bait to hook the biggest fish, those nameless men who controlled Johnny Hoag, it would inevitably find its way into the papers. A man like Zack couldn't rub elbows with the shadowy figures of the underworld without people finding out about it.

Liz didn't even want to think about what that would do to his reputation. There would always be doubts about him, even after arrests were made. People would speculate that he'd been caught red-handed and only agreed to cooperate in return for sweeping his involvement with drugs under the rug. She couldn't let that happen.

Then there were his teammates. He didn't know it, but some of them were involved and might eventually be named. His loyalty to the men he played with was obviously very strong. Liz couldn't ask him to choose between helping her and knifing his friends in the back. She was afraid he would choose her and never stop regretting it.

She was almost calm by the time she returned to the hotel. She wasn't going to let herself think or feel. There was only one course of action open to her, and that was to break off her relationship with Zack Delaney so coldly and firmly that he'd never.come around again.

Chapter Nine

In Ben Halliday's opinion, Marshal College was the ideal place to hold a football training camp. The campus was both beautiful and isolated and the facilities were excellent. The nearest town, the mountain village of Marshalton, wasn't much more than a few streets' worth of shops and places to eat. The area was sparsely populated, so there weren't many groupies around to distract his players from the job at hand. True, the temptations of South Lake Tahoe were only forty-five minutes away, but that wasn't enough time for his players to get back and forth and still raise any hell unless they were willing to miss curfew. Ben wasn't much for bed checks—he preferred to pretend that even the most imma-ture of his boys were grown men—but he did send an assis-tant coach around to check for curfew violations at unpredictable intervals. A couple of heavy, well-publicized fines and there was seldom any problem about obeying his rules.

There had been summers when Zack Delaney had bridled under Halliday's Spartan regimen, but this particular summer wasn't one of them. Zack looked forward to the bone-grinding workouts. He was eager for the evenings of high-stakes poker in the dorm, or beer and laughter at the local pizza joint. In other words, he was angry and hurt, and welcomed any activity that would distract him from how he felt.

Almost the first person he ran into after arriving on campus was his roommate, Paul Travers. Paul was still unpacking when Zack walked into their room, but paused to find out how things had gone with Liz after he and Jenny had left Hawaii. Zack wasn't one to broadcast the intimate details of his relationships, but he and Paul were exceptionally close. He found himself repeating most of what had happened during the final Friday and Saturday. He'd been confused, frustrated and angry when Liz had broken things off, and now he felt those same emotions all over again.

"She was like a robot," he said. "There wasn't even a trace of real emotion, much less any human warmth. She just kept repeating the same thing over and over again, like a broken record. She'd thought it over carefully and decided not to see me anymore. We had no future together. She was sorry, but there was no room in her life for a man right now. Eventually I gave up trying to talk to her and kept out of her way. We sat on opposite sides of the plane going home. She didn't even say goodbye to me when we reached San Francisco."

Paul knew that Zack wasn't so much asking for advice as looking for a sympathetic ear. When Zack was finished talking, Paul led him into the lounge to get him a drink. The room, which was shared by the four bedrooms on the left side of the stairwell, was furnished with the basic necessities—a refrigerator stocked with beer and a table and chairs for playing cards.

Paul took out a couple of cans, opened them up and handed one to Zack. "Personally I think you'll hear from her," he remarked. "She really seemed to like you."

"Maybe." Zack tipped back his head and gulped down half the can. It was hot as the blazes in California, even way up in the mountains, and the dorms had no air conditioning. "She doesn't seem to know what the hell she wants. I can't figure out why it's so complicated for her. We were great together, Paul. In bed, out of bed, you name it."

Paul put a hand on his shoulder. "Give it a little time. She had a lousy childhood and a love affair where everything went wrong. It sounds like she's had a run of bad luck with the people closest to her. She's probably scared to try again, but if you were great together, she must know it, too."

Zack did give it time, but it didn't do him any good. Liz neither wrote him nor phoned him. She never showed up to watch any of the team's practice sessions, either. He saw her cousin Michelle at every single meal, working behind the counter in the cafeteria, and constantly felt an urge to ask her how Liz was doing. He always resisted it. The next move, if there was one, would have to come from her.

His job, he continually reminded himself, was football. He attacked it with an enthusiasm that was rare even for him. The soothing rhythms of training camp gradually took over his life. You worked till you were ready to drop and cursed the heat till the hot spell snapped, and then you started griping about how windy it was. You hazed the rookies in the dining hall by making them sing their college fight songs and cut them down to size on the field by making them look inept if they tried to impress the coaches by playing too rough. When the first cut came, you pretended that the guys who didn't show up for breakfast the next morning had never been there at all. For entertainment, there were card games, the local bars and oversize radios that blasted out the latest hits. There were also women, but Zack wasn't interested in them.

The first preseason game was a real confidence-builder. Zack came out after the half, with the score 21 to 3. Both their other quarterbacks got in some playing time, too, and both played well. The next morning Ben gave the team a lecture about getting too cocky just because they'd won big. He reeled off all the mistakes they'd made, but Zack still felt good about his performance. Almost everything he'd tried had worked.

He'd never been able to separate football from the rest of his life, and the high from the game carried over into his mood the next day. It seemed to him that nothing could possibly go wrong with his life, not after such a perfect game. The team had only a light workout that day, a mid-morning session to practice the plays they'd made mistakes on during the game. The afternoon was open.

When Zack walked into the cafeteria for lunch and saw Michelle Pittman standing behind the counter, he made a snap decision about how to spend his free time. Pointing to a bowl of fruit, he said casually, "I thought I'd go up to the lake later. What's your cousin's phone number?"

She put the fruit on the counter, not meeting his eyes. "It's unlisted, Zack."

"Are you saying she told you not to give it to me?" He could hardly believe she would go that far.

Michelle looked miserably uncomfortable. "I'm sorry."

Zack didn't press her. She had enough problems already without getting mixed up in his relationship with Liz, and he didn't want to add to them. Most of her troubles were concentrated in the person of one Kenneth James Brandenburg, a running back out of the University of Alabama and the Rushers' number-one draft pick. The kid was blazingly talented and would have been selected early in the first round if he hadn't been such a major head case. An erratic senior year hadn't helped matters. Despite all that, he acted as if he was God's gift to the team. Zack suspected that underneath the arrogance he was painfully insecure, but Zack had never really talked to him. Rookies and veterans didn't generally mix.

He'd seen Michelle with Brandenburg four or five times, walking hand-in-hand around the campus, and thought to himself that if Kenny gave her even half the grief he was giving the coaches, she would dump him before the middle of August rolled around. Of course, at the rate Kenny was going, he'd probably be cut from the team by then.

Zack should probably have forgotten about Liz on the spot, but his stubbornness took over. Who did she think she was? She couldn't make love with him all night long, smile at him the next morning as if he was a ray of sunshine in a dark and gloomy world, and then flatly refuse to see him. So okay, she'd had a tough time of it in life. She was frightened and confused. He understood that. He was willing to be patient with her, if only she'd stop stonewalling him and talk things through.

He had neither her phone number nor her address, but he did know where she worked—Diamond's Hotel and Casino. About an hour later he was walking through the lobby door. He went up to the first uniformed security man he saw, intending to ask for help. The man did a double take, then smiled and greeted him by name.

"Great game last night, Zack. What can we do for you?"

"I was looking for one of your employees," Zack said. "Her name is Liz Reynolds. She's blond . . ."

"Sure, sure." The man was nodding to show he knew her. "You mean the girl you went to Hawaii with. She works upstairs in the Marquise Room, but they don't open till four-fifteen."

"The Marquise Room?" Zack repeated. He was puzzled by that. He'd pictured her serving drinks in the main casino.

How else did you keep your eye on the dealers to make sure they weren't pocketing chips?

"That's right. In the cocktail lounge. Look, why don't you try her at home?"

Zack decided she must have been assigned to watch one of the cashiers and told the security man he hadn't seen her since Hawaii. "To tell the truth, I never got her phone number and address," he admitted. "I figured we wouldn't be seeing each other again."

"Changed your mind about her, huh?" The security man started toward a house phone and motioned for Zack to follow. Picking up the receiver, he went on, "I can't blame you. She's one hell of a looker. Let me see what I can find out."

A minute later he handed Zack a slip of paper with a phone number and address written on it. Zack immediately tried to call, but there was no answer. Since the address was a post office box number, he'd apparently reached a dead end.

He went into the coffee shop for a cup of coffee, signed some autographs as he drank it and then tried the number again. There was still no answer. Since he didn't want to hang around Diamond's for the next couple of hours, there was only one option. He would have to find out where she lived.

There were several possibilities—the police, the local utility companies, the post office. It was a Sunday, though, so that narrowed down his choices to one. Ten minutes later he was giving the female officer on duty at the police station his most winning smile and explaining what he wanted. He could tell she'd recognized him but she kept her answer polite and professional. The information he wanted wasn't on record, but even if it had been she couldn't have helped him out.

He threw himself on her mercy, appealing to the romantic in her. Hadn't she seen *Main Attraction*? Yes, of course she had. Everyone had. Then she knew he'd gone to Hawaii with Liz Reynolds? Yes, she had to admit she did. He leaned closer and confided he'd acted like a total jerk on the last day of their vacation together. He'd gotten Liz angry and now he wanted to apologize, but he didn't know where to find her. Couldn't she see her way clear to help him?

She melted like an ice cube on a desert rock. The address read "Elizabeth Reynolds c/o N. Thorne," and she admitted she knew who "N. Thorne" was. "That must be Nicholas Thorne, the one who writes the spy thrillers. I think he lives somewhere off Pioneer Trail. Somebody may know the exact address. Wait here and I'll see if I can track it down for you."

She returned five minutes later with a street name but no house number. "But don't worry," she said. "One of the guys gave me a description of the house, and he says you can't miss it. It's a two-story, green A-frame with some aspens out in front." She lowered her voice and gave him an encouraging smile. "Good luck. I hope things work out for you."

Zack thanked her, thinking the story would be all over town by Tuesday. He had no problem finding the correct street, but the house was a different story. There were three green A-frames on the street, and two of them had aspens in front. He had just turned around in order to take another look when he noticed a car approaching from the opposite direction. There were two people in front, a male driver with shaggy dark hair and his blond female companion—Liz. They pulled into a driveway several houses down from him and got out of the car. He stopped by the side of the road to watch them. He wanted to know what Liz was doing with such a good-looking guy, and smack in the middle of the day to boot.

All his worst fears were confirmed when they reached the front porch. Liz laughed and put her arms around the man's neck. A long, passionate kiss followed. Zack had absolutely no doubts about what would happen once the two of them got inside.

He put the car in reverse and slowly backed up. He was sorely tempted to floor it, but one didn't want to wreck one's brand-new Mercedes. He now understood Liz's behavior. There was obviously another man in the picture, a man who'd been there all along. He wondered bitterly why she hadn't had the decency to level with him about it in Hawaii.

Bill Genaro didn't mind kissing Liz Reynolds, but he did recognize that passion had nothing to do with her sudden affection toward him. For all the enthusiasm she displayed, she might as well have been kissing an old dust mop. She fumbled with her key before she managed to get it into the lock, making him realize how upset she was. Once they were both inside she leaned against the door to close it, her shoulders slumped in dejection and her face twisted into a mask of pain. He'd never seen her look so awful, and God knew she hadn't exactly been herself for the past couple of weeks.

He put a comforting arm around her shoulders and led her to the living-room couch. He'd been in the house many times, so he knew where she kept the liquor. He only wished she drank the stuff, because she looked as though she needed it badly.

He sat down beside her and took her hand. "Liz, you've got to tell me what's going on. You can't keep dismissing the subject of Hawaii or claiming nothing important happened there. I can see that it did."

She took back her hand, her expression icing over. "I don't want to talk about it."

"Fine." He hated to threaten her, but she wasn't giving him any choice. "You want me to go to O'Dwyer? You want me to tell him how edgy you've been lately? You want me to explain that you do crazy things like laugh for no reason at all and then ask me to kiss you?"

Liz knew Bill was right. It was one thing to hold out on O'Dwyer, but Bill was her partner and he had to be able to trust her. She didn't think she'd fallen down on the job but she *had* been tense and moody. She owed him the truth, not the same cock-and-bull story she'd given him and everyone else for the past two weeks.

She only wished it weren't so hard to talk about. She didn't know why it hurt so badly to think about Zack, only that it did. And idiot that she was, just when she'd gotten herself halfway back on track she'd gone and made it worse by watching the Rushers on the bar's television set on Saturday night. It had brought back too many memories of practice sessions at Cooke Field, of Zack's smile when he was happy, of breathless dancing and wild games of water volleyball and the sweetest, most exciting lovemaking she'd ever known in her life.

At first she said none of this. The subject was so painful that she could only bring herself to raise it by easing into it. "Did you happen to see the car parked down the street?"

"There were lots of cars," Bill answered.

"The blue Mercedes. The little sports car."

He nodded. "Yeah, I remember it. Why?"

"Did you see the driver? Or notice the license plate?"

"What is this? Twenty questions?" His smile was gentle and reassuring. "It's all right, Liz. You can level with me. Anything you say will stay in this room."

Liz briefly closed her eyes, feeling very tired. Thank God she knew she could trust him. "The plate was RUSHR 14."

"Delaney." Bill gave a short, disgusted snort. "You mean the guy's still hitting on you? No wonder you've been such a wreck lately! Just leave him to me. I guarantee you, there won't be any more problems.''

The promise was so absurd that Liz didn't know whether to laugh or cry. She found she was doing both, giggling a little hysterically while tears spilled out of her eyes. ''Zack Delaney wouldn't hit on a woman if the two of them had been stranded on a desert island for six months and she looked like Bo Derek,'' she said. ''Between O'Dwyer and Whittaker I think I may go crazy. O'Dwyer wants Zack to flush out Hoag's bosses and Whittaker wants him to show up at his stupid golf tournament. I'll be damned if either of them is going to have his way. I won't have Zack involved in my work.''

Bill waved his hand back and forth to cut her off. She'd never seen him look so confused. ''Wait a minute, Liz. You're going too fast for me. The last I heard, Delaney was out of this. Jack said neither of you would cooperate, Delaney because he wasn't the type to want to help and you because you think he's a first-class jerk. For two weeks now you've been telling me what an arrogant bastard he is.'' He frowned and took out a cigarette. He had a habit of lighting up when he was trying to reason something out. ''You were protecting him,'' he finally said. ''You don't hate the guy at all. You're so hung up on him you decided to put him first, even before the case.''

Liz bristled at the critical tone he'd used. ''There are more important things in the world than this particular investigation,'' she snapped. ''I happen to consider Zack Delaney's reputation one of them. Don't start in on me about it! It's bad enough I have to put up with Jack calling me every few days to find out if I've cooled down yet. If I didn't know him better I'd think he wants me to prance into training camp and seduce Zack into cooperating. In the meantime, Whittaker has called me into his office twice in the past two weeks to talk about the golf tournament. He wants

Zack at the wrap-up party Sunday night, and you don't have to be Albert Einstein to figure out why."

"To offer him drugs," Bill said slowly. "I'll be damned. Has it ever occurred to you that it could be a big break for us if Zack went along?"

Liz glared at him. "Maybe for you, but not for Zack. I won't have anything to do with it, and frankly I don't think Zack will either, unless I'm the one to ask him. He's much too loyal to his teammates to take part in something that could get some of them indicted. He probably wouldn't even believe you if you told him they'd been implicated in the course of an investigation, especially if I deny it."

Bill sat there smoking his cigarette, a resigned look on his face. "I think," he said, "that you'd better begin at the beginning.

Liz knew better than to make the same mistake twice. When Saturday night rolled around she spent every spare moment talking to her customers and stayed as far away from the TV as she could get. She wasn't about to stand by the bar again, staring at Zack Delaney and torturing herself with memories.

That left her fellow workers to contend with. News traveled fast around the hotel, so all of them knew Zack had come looking for her the Sunday before. It was easiest to let them think he'd found her, just as it was easiest to say on Saturday night that she wasn't watching the game because it made her too nervous. People were only too happy to tell her what was happening.

For the first time in more than a year, the Rushers lost a game. Zack threw two interceptions in two quarters of play and had problems getting away from the pass rush. The team as a whole looked sloppy and careless, but as the first-string quarterback, Zack got most of the blame. The more generous among Liz's friends said he'd had a lousy day. The rest of them were blunter and less forgiving. They grumbled that he'd stunk. *How quickly they forget,* Liz thought.

She wondered how the players' wives and parents stood it. Even the best athletes occasionally had off days. How could their loved ones bear to watch, and what did they say afterward? At least when *she* made a mistake in her work, the whole world didn't have to know about it.

On Monday morning, Sy Whittaker called her at home for the third time in as many weeks and told her to stop by his office before she reported in at the restaurant. She expected some hard-nosed pressure, but he'd apparently decided to be subtle for a change. After telling her how great she was with the customers and how much people liked her, he offered her a part-time job as his assistant. He claimed he needed extra help with the golf tournament, which was only a week and a half away now. After all, there were all those celebrity golfers to keep happy, not to mention the reporters and television personnel who would be coming up to cover the event. The stick hadn't worked on Liz, so now he was trying the carrot.

Naturally she agreed. It was the opening she'd been waiting for. She knew it wasn't going to be easy to satisfy him unless she produced Zack or another major star, but she didn't let herself worry about that. She'd simply have to improvise. Maybe the team would play so poorly over the next two weeks that she could claim Halliday had refused to allow anyone to leave camp.

The job might have been a plum to gain her cooperation, but there was also real work to be done. Liz was on the phone all day, making a series of special arrangements. A rock star wanted a certain brand of imported chocolates in his suite, so she ordered them flown in from Paris. The network televising the final two days of play needed eight extra hotel rooms, but Diamond's was booked solid. She found them space elsewhere. People were clamoring for invitations to Sunday night's party, which was being held at the lakefront estate of a local millionaire, and Liz had to sort out the "yeses" from the "nos." She was hoarse by the time she finally left the office.

The days ahead promised to be very hectic, but at least there had been no phone call from Jack O'Dwyer that week. Bill had been an absolute angel the previous Sunday, listening to her explanation of what had happened in Hawaii, letting her cry on his shoulder until she finally ran out of tears and promising he would get O'Dwyer off her back. She had no idea what he'd said, only that it had worked.

Later that evening, unwinding in her landlord's spa, she told herself that the worst was surely behind her. In another couple of weeks the regular football season would begin. Zack would be back in San Francisco. The golf tournament would come and go, and Whittaker would finally stop pressuring her. Maybe he would even start confiding in her. Between her and Bill, maybe they could learn who the bosses really were and put them in jail where they belonged. For the first time in more than ten weeks, she felt as though she finally had some control over her life.

She turned on the air jets and closed her eyes. The telephone rang but she ignored it. If it were really that important, the caller would phone her back.

Chapter Ten

The phone *did* ring again. Liz was up in the bedroom by then, watching a favorite movie on TV, and cursed under her breath as she reached for the receiver. If it had been Bill or somebody from the casino, she would have asked him to call back at ten, but it turned out to be her cousin Michelle. The two hadn't spoken in weeks now and Liz was relieved to hear from her.

"It's about time you finally called me," she scolded. "Don't the people there give you your messages?" Michelle was living in the dorm and sharing the floor's single pay telephone with more than a dozen other girls.

"I got them. It's just that I didn't know what to say." Michelle took a deep breath. Her voice had sounded rushed and unnaturally high. "I need to talk to you, Lizzie. Please come see me."

Liz got the impression she was fighting back tears. "What's wrong?" she asked. "Are you feeling all right?

You're not in any trouble, are you?'' Her aunt and uncle would have hysterics if she'd gotten herself into serious trouble.

"No, I'm fine. Just a minute.'' There was a long pause. Liz heard chatter and giggling in the background. She was beginning to get alarmed. "I can't talk now. Please Liz.'' Michelle began to sob, and not all that quietly, either.

At that point Liz stopped asking questions and told Michelle she would be at the college within an hour. All she would need were directions to the dorm.

Michelle sniffed and gave a deep, shuddering sigh. "No, not tonight. I want you to spend the day with me. There's someone I want you to meet.''

She sounded slightly calmer now, but Liz wasn't reassured. The girl was obviously involved with some man, and whoever he was, he was giving her a very hard time. "If you want me to come tomorrow, I'll come tomorrow,'' she said, "but I've just started a new job working for one of the hotel's assistant managers. I'm supposed to be in his office for the next three days. I still work in the restaurant Thursday through Sunday, but it's a shorter shift. I could come Thursday and stay until three. Is that too long for you to wait? Be honest, now.''

"It's fine. Really, I'm doing okay. It's just that I've been going so crazy. There was nobody here to talk to, nobody I could trust.''

"Man troubles, huh?'' Liz asked sympathetically.

Michelle gave a nervous giggle. "Promise you'll keep an open mind about him.''

"You know I will.''

"Do you think you could come Wednesday night, then? It would give you a chance to talk to him. It's the only time they have to themselves—after the team meeting at night. They're through about nine.''

Liz said she would be there and jotted down the necessary directions. The knowledge that she was coming seemed to settle Michelle down, but there was still a part of Liz that felt she should climb into the car that very moment and head west. She only hung up once she was sure that Michelle could handle the three-day delay.

She went back to watching the movie and was soon as engrossed as ever. It was only when a commercial came on that Michelle's remark about the "team meeting" hit home. Her boyfriend was someone on the Rushers. He was one of Zack's teammates. If Liz spent an entire day at Marshal College, she would inevitably run into Zack. He would look at her in that ice-cold way of his and she'd want to die. There were very few people in the world she would have endured that for, but Michelle was one of them.

She finished work at six on Wednesday, ate dinner in the hotel coffee shop and drove directly out to the college. Although it wasn't a long drive between South Lake Tahoe and Marshalton, she saw little point in returning home only to drive back to the college in the morning. She planned to stay at a local motel.

Michelle was sitting on the steps leading up to her dorm, looking tanned and fit but thinner than Liz liked to see her. It was only after Michelle had gotten into the car that Liz noticed the dark circles under her eyes and the tension in her every movement and word. They drove to the motel so Liz could check in and spent the next hour in her room, talking.

Michelle's boyfriend was named Kenny Brandenburg. He was twenty-two years old and had grown up in Alabama. Liz immediately realized he was the one reporters had asked Zack about at the airport. She could recall some of the phrases they'd used—"quick-tempered, hard to coach, a loner"—and also Zack's reply: "Brandenburg's problems in the past don't concern us. All we're interested in is what happens when he shows up in camp."

Michelle was painfully frank about what *had* happened. Kenny had continued to act in the same self-defeating way as he had when he was in college.

"He doesn't seem to realize he's his own worst enemy," she said. "He's got as much natural talent as anyone in the league but he's terrified he won't make the team. He goes all out and his teammates resent it. Every team has its own way of doing things, and the Rushers have a tradition of holding back a little on the hits they make during practice sessions. Kenny ignores that. He's afraid to let up."

"And the guys give him a hard time about it?"

"The other rookies do. The veterans pretty much ignore him, even when he makes a good play in a game. So he plays even harder to force them to notice, and when they still don't, he pretends he doesn't care. He also has a habit of acting like he knows everything. He'll even argue with the coaches when they tell him what to do. He can go on and on about how he knows his own strengths and weaknesses better than anybody else and doesn't need their help. I've told Kenny that if Ben Halliday didn't have the patience of a saint, he'd be back in Mobile, Alabama, by now."

"And what did he say?" Liz asked.

"He changed the subject. He won't discuss football with me. He says women don't understand the way men think. I met him the first day of camp, before the veterans got here. He was polite and sweet and much more open than the boys I'd met at school. We talked about everything that first night—our families, what books and movies we like, even our dreams for the future." She looked into her lap, her voice growing softer. "He reminded me of Tommy, Lizzie. He had a horrible childhood. He's so desperate to succeed—and so terrified to fail."

Over the next half hour Liz heard more of the details. Kenny Brandenburg's mother had run off with another man when Kenny was seven. He'd been raised by a taciturn father who had demanded perfection from the first time his only child had picked up a football and shown how fast he could run with it. Anything less had been punished with cold ridicule. The portrait Michelle painted was that of a troubled young man. She claimed Kenny had never been violent or abusive toward her—quite the opposite, in fact—but Liz was still worried about his self-control. She wanted a firsthand look at him.

Michelle had told him to meet them at the entrance to the campus around nine o'clock. They'd been waiting for only a few minutes when he trotted up to the car. Michelle slid out to kiss him hello and then made the introductions. As he and Liz shook hands, he murmured in a slow, Southern drawl, "It's an honor to meet you, ma'am. Michelle talks about you a lot."

During the drive into Marshalton she got called "ma'am" so many times she finally ordered him to call her Liz. He was nothing if not polite and respectful. In fact, Liz had trouble picturing him as the obnoxious spoiled brat she'd heard about.

Michelle directed her to a chain restaurant on the town's main drag, explaining that it was the rookies' traditional watering hole. The veterans usually congregated at a pizza place down the road a ways, and it was an unspoken rule that rookies never went in there without a specific invitation. So far this season, none had received one.

A casual observer would have seen nothing in the next hour to cause her concern, but Liz was well-trained when it came to human behavior. The booth Kenny chose was far away from the restaurant's main traffic pattern. His teammates straggled in in groups of two or three, but they never came over to say hello to him and he never waved to them to get their attention. Although he treated Michelle in a way that demonstrated his love and respect for her, he was also disturbingly isolated from his teammates.

Liz could see why Michelle was smitten. Women had always been suckers for men who needed them, and Kenny was handsome into the bargain. He was also a member of the team she adored. Liz had promised to keep an open mind, but it wasn't going to be easy. Between his looks and his problems, Kenny Brandenburg was a dangerous package, especially for a woman as young and inexperienced as Michelle was.

Liz drove them back to campus and then returned to her motel for the night. Practice began at eight-thirty the next morning. Having watched Paul and Zack at Cooke Field, Liz found the exercises and drills to be very familiar. After the preliminaries were over the team broke into smaller groups. Kenny was practicing blocking, hitting his targets so hard that Liz could hear the crunch of colliding equipment. She didn't know whether he was using an unreasonable amount of force, but his teammates seemed to think so. She could see their annoyed expressions even behind the face masks of their helmets.

Every now and then her eyes would stray to Zack's section of the field, but only because she kept forgetting herself. Padded or not, his uniform fit him like a second skin. She could remember exactly how it had felt to caress the warm flesh and sinewy muscle underneath. He threw and ran with a fluid grace that reminded her of the way he made love. She would stare at him with blind yearning, then catch herself and hastily look away. At one point in the practice Paul Travers noticed her standing on the sidelines and waved to her. She forced a smile onto her face and waved back.

About midway through the practice there was a scrimmage to go through some plays for Saturday's game. Players came in and out of the scrimmage according to the particular series of plays involved. First they walked through their assignments in slow motion to make sure they had them right and then they practiced at regular speed. Liz could see absolutely no difference between the intensity of play during the scrimmage and what might happen in a real game, with one exception—when an offensive lineman missed his block and allowed a defensive tackle to get to Zack. The man roared out, "You're dead meat, Delaney!" but the hit wouldn't have stopped a high school second-stringer. Liz had the feeling the lineman would have veered away if he could have, but when you were moving that fast and weighed that much, sheer momentum took over.

Michelle nudged her when Kenny joined the game, telling her to watch carefully. He reminded Liz of a coiled snake, full of tension and eager to bite. So much was happening on the field at any given time that it was impossible to follow it all, but she found it relatively easy to keep track of a single player. At one point she watched Kenny crash into another player, saw the man tumble down and caught the fury in his eyes as he peeled himself off the turf. He said something to Kenny afterward, but Liz couldn't hear what it was. Kenny answered with a time-honored gesture of disdain and strolled back to the huddle.

He passed right by Michelle, but he didn't seem to see her. There was no response at all to her hesitant smile. When the huddle broke, he ran back to his position, all charged up now. They walked through several more plays, then lined up again to do them for real.

Ben Halliday was standing on the sidelines about ten feet in front of Liz and Michelle, watching the team work out. Liz felt the blood drain from her face when Zack looked straight in her direction, but then she realized he was looking at Halliday, not at her. One of the other coaches whispered something in Halliday's ear and then both of them turned away, facing each other rather than the field.

Zack looked from his right to his left to his right, in the timeless way of quarterbacks everywhere. He took the snap and started his pivot. Kenny came running across the field to take the handoff.

The rest of the play seemed to happen in even slower motion than the earlier walk-throughs. The offense simply opted out. The blocks were halfhearted at best, nonexistent at worst. The defensive players came barreling across the line of scrimmage, headed straight for Kenny Brandenburg. Liz had never seen anyone hit so brutally. She was openly shocked by the scene. When the dust finally settled and the pileup dispersed, Kenny was lying curled up on the ground, still clutching the football. Michelle started forward, but Liz grabbed her arm. Outsiders had no business getting involved in something like this.

He sat up slowly, then shook his head as if to clear it. The other players were already walking back to the huddle, ignoring him. Halliday called out his name, asking him if he was all right, and he nodded. But when he stood and tried to walk, he staggered and fell down before he'd taken even two steps. The trainer told him to stay where he was and trotted over to take a look at him. He wasn't seriously hurt, just badly shaken up. He remained at the practice, but didn't get into the scrimmage again.

Michelle led Liz away from the field a short time later. "So what do you think?" she asked as they walked toward her dorm. The expression on her face was chiseled out of stone. Liz knew she was dying inside.

Liz sighed and shook her head. "Sometimes I think Kenny might be right—men live in a whole different world than we do. An eye for an eye and all that. Maybe Kenny deserved it, but he could have been seriously injured. I don't know whether they were right or wrong."

"I wasn't talking about that," Michelle answered. "He was playing too rough, and they played rough right back."

"But four against one..."

"Even four against one. Halliday knew about it in advance. I could tell." Her voice was shaking so badly she had to stop for a moment to get a grip on herself. "I meant before. The way he acted."

Liz assumed she meant the way Kenny had looked right through her when he'd passed her on the sidelines. She was about to say that Michelle shouldn't be hurt by it. After all, Kenny had probably been too wrapped up in the game to acknowledge her. Then a picture of his face flashed through her mind. She saw him making blocks, first one-on-one and then during the scrimmage. The violence and rage on the one hand and the blankness on the other—it wasn't normal. Paul had once remarked that some of his teammates were first-class flakes, but Kenny didn't strike her as a cutup or a jokester. He'd been soft-spoken and polite the night before.

She finally understood why Michelle had asked her to come. "You're telling me you think he's taking something," she said.

Michelle closed her eyes, squeezing out two tears. "Yes."

Liz gathered the girl into her arms and gently stroked her back. "Just try to take it easy, honey. First of all, have you asked him about it?"

"Yes."

"And?"

"He denied it." Between choked-back sobs Michelle added that the man she watched in workouts every day was not the same man she spent her evenings with. Every time she'd tried to discuss his behavior with him, he'd either clammed up or changed the subject. She didn't know what to do.

Liz waited until Michelle had calmed down enough to contain her tears and then gently suggested that perhaps she and Kenny should stop seeing each other. Her reaction was so violent that Liz backed off immediately. She didn't want to close down the lines of communication. Michelle had trusted her enough to call her, and if she destroyed that trust by taking too firm a position, the girl would have no one to turn to.

She'd asked for Liz's opinion, but Liz was a law enforcement officer, not a physician. "I can stand here and tell you it sounds like drugs," she said, "but frankly it doesn't fit any pattern I know of. It would have to last three hours or more but then wear off unusually quickly. The only thing I know for sure is that Kenny could use professional help. No matter how much you care for him, there's only so much you can do."

"I thought maybe—I know you're working on an investigation that has something to do with football, and I thought maybe you'd found out who was behind it."

"I'm afraid not."

"But if you do find out, if you could stop them—maybe all Kenny needs is a good scare."

"We've got no leads, Michelle. If you can talk to Kenny and get him to cooperate, we'd certainly follow up on whatever he tells us. There shouldn't be any problem in getting him immunity from prosecution if all he's doing is buying some stuff occasionally. At this point, though, the sports angle is only a sidelight. I'm afraid that's as much as I can say."

"I'll do what I can," Michelle said. "I'll mention about going to a counselor, too, but he probably won't listen to me. He thinks 'real men' can work out their problems by themselves."

It was all Liz could really hope for. She walked Michelle to the dining hall, telling her she would call in a day or two to see how things were going. There was no point in hanging around. She'd seen what Michelle had asked her there to see.

Zack couldn't get Liz's face out of his mind. He knew that her visit to the training camp had had nothing to do with him and everything to do with her cousin, so why had she kept staring at him that way? What did she want from him? Wasn't one lover enough for her?

As he walked into the cafeteria with his lunch, he saw Kenny Brandenburg sitting all alone at a table in the back. It reminded him of the look on Liz's face just after they'd torpedoed the guy. She'd been appalled. She probably thought they were a bunch of bastards to hit him so hard, but it wasn't a kindergarten romper room out there. There were people who insisted on learning things the hard way, and Kenny was obviously one of them.

He slid his tray onto a table and turned to Paul, who had followed him through the line. "I'll just be a minute," he said. "I want to have a word with Kenny."

Brandenburg happened to look up as Zack was crossing the room and jumped to his feet as soon as he realized Zack meant to talk to him. Zack didn't know quite what he was doing there, only that it had something to do with Liz. He had to prove he wasn't as much of a bastard as she thought. It didn't seem to matter that she'd never find out about it.

"How are you feeling, Brandenburg?" he asked.

"All right, sir."

Zack had the feeling that the "sir" was automatic. The kid had probably been raised to address his superiors that way. It was just too bad that a little of his politeness toward Zack didn't carry over to his general behavior.

The cafeteria was suddenly as quiet as a morgue. A quick look around told Zack that everyone in the room was watching them. Brandenburg, who was usually so cocky you wanted to kill him, was standing there like a raw recruit in front of a leathery drill sergeant.

Zack permitted himself a small smile as he held out his hand. "Welcome to the NFL," he drawled. The men who were close enough to hear his comment burst out laughing.

Brandenburg reddened, but he also accepted the handshake. "Thanks," he mumbled.

Zack almost walked away at that point, but something held him back. At least the kid was trying. He hadn't given Zack a snot-nosed answer or dismissed him with a throwaway curse. The Rushers needed a big, strong back who could dance around the defense like a man fifty pounds lighter, and maybe Zack could help.

Forget it, he thought. If Halliday and the guy's girlfriend couldn't get through to him, what made him think he could? On the other hand, he silently argued, what did he have to lose? He picked up the kid's tray and told him to follow. For once in his argumentative young life, Kenny kept his mouth shut and obeyed.

Paul reacted to this unprecedented turn of events with his usual aplomb. For the next twenty minutes the three of them talked over Saturday's preliminary game plan, just as if it was the most ordinary thing in the world for a rookie who gave people fits to sit and chat with the team's two biggest stars. Zack finally decided to give the kid a little friendly advice. Certainly subtlety wasn't going to get them anywhere.

"You've got a hell of a lot of talent," he said. "As much speed and mobility as I've ever seen in a guy your size. But all the talent in the world isn't worth a bucket of spit unless you listen to the coaches and learn our offense. You don't have to prove you're good. We already know that. You have to prove you can fit in. We're a team here, not just a collection of individual cannons firing in forty-five different directions. If you want to talk, you know where my room is." He picked up his tray and walked away from the table. Paul followed a moment later.

There were times during the next week when Zack wondered why he'd bothered with the kid, but then Kenny would dazzle them with one of his incredibly agile moves or apologize to one of the coaches for being difficult, and he'd tell himself the kid was making a little progress. He'd learned to take something off his hits so at least he wasn't constantly antagonizing people. He even went out with some of the other rookies one night, leaving Michelle behind for a change. Zack had nothing against women, but if Brandenburg spent all his spare time with Michelle, he was never going to become part of the team.

He was walking back from morning practice the next day when Michelle ran up to him, threw her arms around his neck and burst out, "Thank you, thank you, thank you!" She kissed him on the mouth. "There! I actually did it. I told myself I was going to."

She was so exuberant that Zack had to laugh. "I take it that had something to do with your boyfriend?"

"Of course it did. You're the first one he's ever listened to. He was really flying after Saturday's game and do you know why? Not because he rushed for a hundred yards, but because you told him what a great job he'd done. I've been nagging him to go to this therapist I know, and yesterday he finally called her up. They spoke for over an hour. The next thing I know, he's going out with some of his teammates." She stared at the ground, suddenly shy and embarrassed. "It wouldn't have happened without you, Zack. I think you're wonderful."

Zack gave a wave of his hand, dismissing his contribution. "The timing was right, that's all. People listen when they're ready to."

Michelle was shaking her head. "You're wrong. I know Kenny. After the way you creamed him in practice he would have withdrawn even more. But you shook his hand in front of everyone on the team and made him understand there wouldn't be any hard feelings if he started to shape up. He's really trying, Zack, and your encouragement means the world to him. He idolizes you."

Zack stood there thinking about how ironic life was. He'd done the right thing, okay, but for the wrong reason. "You want the truth?" he asked. "If it hadn't been for your cousin I might never have gone over to talk to him. When he was lying on the ground, she looked at us like we were a bunch of criminals. Maybe I wanted to prove I wasn't the creep she thinks I am."

"But she doesn't think that at all!" Michelle reddened even more, bit her lip and buried her face in her hands. "Oh, damn. Forget I ever said that. I've got to go, Zack." She took off toward the dining hall, running almost as fast as her boyfriend might have.

Zack wanted to call her back, but realized he'd be wasting his time. Her reference to Liz had been an uncharacteristic slip. She was usually very closemouthed.

Over the next day or so he tried to get her comment off his mind, but it always came back to haunt him. He knew there was something between him and Liz. Maybe there was another guy in the picture, but she couldn't have been in love with him. Otherwise she would never have stared so much in practice.

Maybe he was a glutton for punishment, but by Thursday afternoon he'd decided to make one last stab at talking some sense into her. The team was leaving for Southern California after practice on Friday, so it would have to be Thursday night. He didn't want to wait until after they got back.

He resigned himself to paying a heavy fine as he climbed into his car that night. It was ten o'clock, curfew was in half an hour and Liz probably wouldn't get off work till one or two. It would be the middle of the night before he got back, and something told him he was going to get caught. He didn't care.

He drove straight to her house and parked his car in her driveway. Nobody was home and the doors were locked, but that didn't discourage him. One way or another he'd manage to get inside. He had second thoughts about how easy it was going to be when he noticed the wrought-iron bars across the first-story windows, but a couple of second-story windows were open a crack. He analyzed the possibilities as he stood on the redwood deck in back. Maybe if he stood on the railing, he could shimmy up the side of the house and grab hold of a sill. It wouldn't be hard to lever his way up. Certainly it was better than spending the next two or three hours in the car.

He'd just hopped up on the railing when he heard the sound of a rifle being cocked. He grabbed the corner of the house to steady himself and then froze. Whoever was holding the rifle was moving toward him, his feet crushing dead leaves and twigs as he approached.

"Turn around nice and slow," the man said. "You'd better be Zack Delaney, because if you aren't, you're going to get charged with grand theft auto along with attempted burglary."

"I am," he said, and cautiously turned around. The man smiled and lowered his rifle as soon as he got a look at Zack's face. At that point Zack breathed a sigh of relief and hopped down from the railing. "Miss Reynolds is a friend of mine. I, uh, I thought I'd wait for her inside, but everything was locked."

"Ever heard of keys?" the man asked laconically. "Thorne—the fellow who owns the house—is a real security nut. If you'd tried to open one of those top windows even a little more, an alarm would have gone off in the police station. In five minutes the place would have been crawling with cops. It all goes back to the time some kids broke in and messed up his stuff, including a book he was working on. He's a writer—spy stories. It's made him into a paranoid, if you want my opinion.''

The neighbor, whose name was Harvey Quill, was nothing if not friendly. Zack spent the next hour in his living room, talking about football and Nicholas Thorne. According to Quill, Liz had rented the house for six months while Thorne was in Europe researching a book. Thorne had told Quill she seemed like a nice, quiet lady who wouldn't cause problems, but he'd asked him to keep an eye on things just in case. In the end Quill gave Zack a key chain with seven different keys on it. After explaining what each one unlocked, he told him to go ahead and let himself into the house. He could drop the keys in the mail slot before he left.

Zack had read a number of Thorne's books and was frankly curious about the man. The place was furnished with beautifully restored antiques, and had a lot of World War II memorabilia on display. The only modern piece of equipment in the whole house other than the security system and appliances was the computer in Thorne's office.

Quill had mentioned an office safe while showing Zack the keys, and he was just curious enough about Thorne to try and find it. The man evidently had a sense of humor, because he'd installed it in a very traditional place—behind a sliding panel in the bookshelf.

Within ten seconds Zack gave in to temptation and unlocked it. He expected to find some manuscripts in there, or maybe some valuable World War collectibles, but all he saw was a gun, a small notebook and a billfold of some sort. The gun didn't surprise him, given Thorne's mania about security.

He gingerly took it out and then picked up the slim black billfold underneath. It seemed to be an ID case, the kind a detective might carry. The first thing that hit him when he opened it up was Liz's picture, and the second was her name—Elizabeth Reynolds Pittman. His mind reached the obvious conclusion. Her uncle and aunt must have legally adopted her, and the black billfold identified her as a member of the Diamond Corporation's security staff.

Then he took a closer look, and frowned in bewilderment. The badge didn't belong to the Diamond Corporation, but to the Drug Enforcement Administration. What the hell was she doing with a DEA shield?

He picked up the notebook and started to thumb through it. There was no mistaking what it was—a record of a case someone was working on. There were dates, times, names or initials and notes going back to early March. An entry dated June 9th caught his eye because the names Slama, White and Johnson were listed. There was also the notation, "Mtg. with O'Dwyer, Luft and Angelo in Sac. Played tape. Delaney—knowledge of drug use?"

As he rifled the pages he saw his name or his initials several more times. One of the most recent entries read, "8/18, 10 A.M.—Conv. with W re: ZD & PT. Stalled him." PT was Paul Travers. Zack knew that from the entries made while Liz was in Hawaii.

The final entry was dated the day before. It read, "Call from M. KB seems better. Still denies drug use." M as in Michelle. KB as in Kenny Brandenburg. What was going on here?

He started to do a slow burn. It was obvious what was going on. Elizabeth Reynolds, also known as Elizabeth Pittman, was investigating the San Francisco Gold Rushers. With all the big-time scum running around operating major drug networks, she had nothing better to do than harass a bunch of innocent football players. He gathered up her badge, notebook and revolver and went downstairs to wait for her.

Chapter Eleven

Sy Whittaker, Liz thought to herself, had to be the cheapest little worm who'd ever crawled the face of the earth. Thursday was supposed to be one of her days off, but she'd spent every hour of it in his office. And then the creep had told her to work her usual shift in the cocktail lounge, to help with the extra business from the golf tournament. She wanted to nail him so much she could taste it.

When she saw Zack's car sitting in her driveway, she put her head down on the steering wheel and moaned aloud. Of all the times for him to show up, this had to be the worst. She sighed and silently corrected herself. It would have been worse if he'd shown up a couple of hours before, at the hotel. She'd finally given up arguing with Whittaker and told him Zack would be at the party Sunday night. When he didn't actually show she'd do her best to act surprised and annoyed, but in the meantime, Whittaker was telling half the world about it. If Zack had come looking for her at the hotel, somebody would surely have mentioned something about it.

She could see lights shining through the closed blinds on the living-room windows and realized that Harvey must have let Zack inside to wait for her. She didn't like the idea that Harvey had keys to the front and back doors, but Thorne had insisted. Harvey had assured her he would only use the keys in an emergency, but he was also a fanatical Rushers fan. If Zack Delaney wanted access to Liz's house, that probably constituted the most urgent emergency he could imagine.

Bracing herself for the worst, Liz got out of her car and dragged herself up the front path. She was so damn tired. Why did Zack have to be so bloody persistent?

She unlocked the door and went into the living room. He looked so entirely at home sitting on her couch that a painful lump rose in her throat. In a different world maybe they could have been together. Maybe they could have come home to each other every night and talked about how their days had gone, like other happy couples did.

Nobody had to tell her how wonderful he was. There weren't many men who would have taken the time to help a kid like Kenny Brandenburg or who could have made such a difference in his life. Zack was special, and it killed Liz to have to keep rejecting him.

She faltered for a moment when she got a good look at his face, then forced herself to keep walking. She'd never seen him look so furious. Never. She understood why as soon as she got far enough into the room to see what was sitting on the couch beside him. Harvey hadn't just let him in—he'd given him a whole damn set of keys, including keys to the safe, the window bars and several curio cabinets. Harvey wasn't even supposed to have those, much less give them to someone else. This had to be the worst day of her life.

She sat down on the chair across from Zack, waiting for him to say something. Her cool composure was strictly an act. Her stomach felt as if it was on a trampoline and her heart was beating so fast her chest felt ready to burst. She told herself it was just as well he was angry. He'd obviously reached some harsh conclusions, but she wasn't going to disabuse him of his misconceptions. This weekend of all weekends, she wanted him far away. She didn't care what she had to do to accomplish that.

He gave her a long, contemptuous stare, then said "You're a federal drug agent."

Liz crossed her legs, trying to seem nonchalant. "Yes."

"You're investigating my team."

"Among other things, yes."

"Based on what?" He picked up her notebook, gave it a shake and then slapped it against the coffee table—hard. She was intimidated by all that pent-up fury but didn't let it show. "A hot anonymous tip from some doped-up junkie?" he demanded. "Gossip on one of your illegal wiretaps?"

Liz gave him a bland stare. She knew how to deal with questions and accusations because she'd watched Jack O'Dwyer do it so many times. "I'm not at liberty to discuss the specifics—"

"Oh, for God's sake, don't give me that!" he exploded. "Don't you people have better things to do than go on fishing expeditions looking for athletes to send to jail? I've been sitting here for the last hour thinking about how much trouble you went to to meet me. Your friend Gloria was obviously very cooperative about helping to arrange it. Hell, you must have started salivating when that guy came up to Paul and me in Waikiki and offered to sell us some drugs. What would you have done if we'd said yes? Arrested us on the spot?"

It was all Liz could do not to cringe and look away. It hurt to be attacked so viciously, especially by a man she cared for so deeply. She was amazed by how calm she managed to sound when she finally answered him. "Probably not. Our usual procedure is to try to trace drugs back to their source. I would have observed the buy and tried to get information on the seller. I would also have wanted to know who else on the team was using drugs."

He brought his fist down on the table in a violent show of frustration. Liz couldn't help but flinch. She was making her answers as provocative as she could, and only hoped he'd leave the house in one piece when he decided he'd heard enough.

"I told you in Hawaii," he said. "Nobody on the Rushers uses drugs."

"If you don't mind, I'll withhold judgment on that until we finish our investigation."

"Right." He gestured toward the notebook. "Including your intimate surveillance of Michelle's boyfriend. I suppose she's another one of your little helpers."

"She's always been very cooperative," Liz agreed.

"I'll bet she has. You're lethal, lady. Nobody would dare cross you, even your own cousin. But get it through your head that you're wasting your time. Brandenburg may be a mixed-up kid, but he's not a junkie. Go fish in somebody else's pond."

"I'll certainly convey your suggestions to my boss," Liz said. "And now, if you're quite finished yelling at me..."

"Christ, you're cool!" He jerked himself up from the couch, looking as if it was all he could do not to wring her neck. "Give my regards to your boyfriend. I'm sorry you couldn't get more information out of me. Or was the one-night stand just for fun?"

Since Liz had never asked him a single question that night, she could hardly claim she'd been after information.

A part of her was bitterly hurt that he could even think he motive for making love with him had been anything but rea caring, but she knew it was better this way.

She gave a casual shrug. "There was a strong physical at traction between us. Bill was very understanding about it.'

"Well, I'm sure as hell not!" He picked up the keys and the items he'd taken from the safe. At first Liz thought he was going to throw them at her, but he merely walked over to her chair and disdainfully dropped them into her lap, one by one. "The tools of your trade, Miss Reynolds. As of right this moment, you're out of business. If I see you around camp again, I'll start talking to reporters."

The implications of that were chilling. Liz could handle his anger and even his insults, but she was terrified about what could happen to her if he shot off his mouth about who she was. "Your team is only one aspect of the investigation," she said. "If the people here found out I was a federal agent, they might very well kill me. If you're going to talk, even to your teammates, I'd appreciate a little advance notice."

"Not only cool, but melodramatic, too." He gave a disbelieving shake of his head. "Relax, Liz. You've got nothing to worry about. I make enough mistakes on the field without broadcasting the ones I make in my private life."

He stalked out of the room and left the house, slamming the front door with such force that the chandelier in the hallway shook. Liz slumped down in her chair as his car roared down the street, her face wet with tears.

Zack knew it was pointless to abuse both his car and the local roads by driving like a suicidal maniac, so it wasn't too long before he'd slowed to somewhere near the legal limit. Unfortunately, driving more slowly only heightened his frustration. He needed a water cooler to kick or a bench to mangle. He'd never been so angry in his life, and the lack of a physical outlet was driving him crazy.

He replayed his conversation with Liz over and over again as he drove back to camp, getting madder by the minute. She hadn't been the least bit apologetic. She didn't give a damn about him or his feelings. She was the coldest, most manipulative bitch he'd ever had the misfortune to meet.

The capper to the whole night came when he ran into Halliday in the parking lot. Zack didn't even give his coach a chance to get a word in.

"Ben, if you want to fine me, fine me. Two grand, three grand, five grand—I don't give a damn how much. But don't start lecturing me. I'm not in the mood."

"Tough night, huh?"

Ben had sounded more or less sympathetic, so Zack allowed himself to hope he'd get off easy. "Very tough," he said.

Halliday gave a thoughtful nod. "Okay then, no lecture. Check with me Sunday morning and I'll let you know if you're starting against the Titans. And be at practice half an hour early tomorrow morning. We'll see if we can get your mind back on football."

Not start? Zack was so irate he didn't even trust himself to answer. He turned away and headed toward the dorm, jogging at first and then running at top speed. He also ran up the two flights of stairs to his room, but it didn't help dissipate his anger. He still felt like a walking time bomb.

He tried to be as quiet as he could, but he still woke Paul up. Paul sat up slowly, yawning and rubbing his eyes. "What time is it?" he asked groggily.

"I don't know. Maybe two o'clock."

"You don't sound too happy. What happened?"

"She wasn't home yet. A neighbor let me into her house. I started looking around. The guy who owns it has a safe in his office, and I had the key—" Zack abruptly shut his mouth.

"So what did you find?" Paul prodded.

"Nothing." Zack could hardly believe he was standing there refusing to talk, but he'd promised. The sheer stupidity of the situation enraged him. Did Liz really think Paul Travers was going to order a hit on her? Or knew the type of person who would?

At the end of his tether now, he grabbed the nearest inanimate object to vent his fury on. It happened to be Paul's radio. He hurled it to the floor as hard as he could, taking rare satisfaction in the loud crash it made and the way the pieces scattered all over the room. It felt so good to wreck the radio that he looked around for something else to destroy. His eyes lit on a potted fern.

Paul jumped out of bed and leaped between Zack and the plant. "Oh, no, you don't! That fern was a present from Jenny. You and I are going for a walk and you're going to do some talking. I've never seen you like this before. I intend to find out what happened."

"I can't tell you. I promised her I wouldn't talk about it." He pounded a fist into the opposite palm. "Damn, I feel frustrated!"

"That's nothing compared to how my radio feels," Paul said mildly.

Zack looked at the floor, suddenly repentant. The radio was a lost cause. "I'm sorry about that. I'll buy you a new one."

"Never mind about the radio. Come on, let's go outside."

"I told you . . ."

"I know. You promised her you wouldn't talk about it. So call her up and tell her you changed your mind."

Now that Zack thought about it, she hadn't exactly asked him not to talk. She'd only wanted some notice beforehand. He didn't really want to hear her voice, but he dug out her number from his wallet and walked into the lounge to make the call.

He didn't identify himself when she answered, but said curtly, "I need to talk to Paul. Maybe you should dust off your bulletproof vest."

There was a long pause. Her voice was noticeably shaky when she finally answered him. It made him feel like a total heel. "Of course you can talk to Paul. Goodbye, Zack."

There were still some undeveloped areas on campus, far from any of the buildings, and that was where Paul took Zack to talk. As they walked through the brisk night air, Zack told himself he was a sucker to care about Liz's feelings. The woman had lied to him from the word go. She had ice water in her veins instead of blood. All she cared about was making her monthly quota of arrests.

They stopped by a quiet stand of trees, Paul leaning against a tree trunk while Zack paced restlessly back and forth. It wasn't hard to remember the conversation he'd had with Liz. He managed to repeat it almost word for word.

"Are you looking for an opinion?" Paul asked him afterward.

Zack stopped directly in front of him. "Why else would I tell you about it?"

"Because you want me to agree with whatever you think."

"I take it you don't."

"I didn't say that. But at least I can be objective about it. Your emotions are so involved you can't look at it logically."

"How logical do you have to be . . . ?"

Paul cut him off. "Do you want to listen or do you want to argue?"

"Listen." Zack had expected Paul to be as outraged as he was and was irritated that he wasn't. What had ever happened to friendship and loyalty? "So I'm illogical, huh? How do you figure that?"

"You're making everything into a giant conspiracy, starting with the last-minute switch that got Liz on as a contestant in your segment of *Main Attraction*. Don't forget, I saw the show. I'd say she did everything she could to turn you off. If she'd wanted to go with you, she wouldn't have resorted to some convoluted strategy to catch your attention. The woman I met in Hawaii was beautiful, intelligent and giving. All she had to do was show those same qualities during the interview and you wouldn't have had to think twice about picking her. So okay. You're in Hawaii together now. Granted she asked questions about drug use on the team, but she also tried to keep you at a distance. She didn't worm her way into your confidence and try to wangle information out of you."

"There was no information to wangle," Zack said. "She'd probably figured that out."

"So what would her next logical step be? She happens to win the trip so they assign her to check you out. She sees you refuse to buy drugs and realizes you're clean. Now what?"

"How the hell should I know?" Zack was in no mood for guessing games. "Do I look like a DEA agent?"

Paul ignored Zack's sarcasm. "I can think of two possibilities. One, she can write you off as a source of information. If her only interest is professional, she's going to ignore you from that point on. Two, she can try to get you to cooperate with their investigation. She can ask you to buy drugs if they're offered in order to track them back to their source. In that case, she'd probably try to manipulate you by coming on to you. So what does she actually do? She gets tanked, makes a pass, changes her mind and then turns into a nervous wreck. In the end she shows up in your bedroom and more or less throws herself at you. She makes love to you all night, and then, for no reason you can understand, walks out of your life forever. And you think any of that adds up? Suppose she'd asked for your help that morning? Would you have turned her down?"

Zack was a little calmer now, and he had to admit Paul's questions made sense. Liz's behavior *was* baffling. He'd been so infatuated after they'd made love that he probably wouldn't have refused her a thing. So why hadn't she asked?

"I don't know," he finally said. "There would have had to be guarantees. I don't believe anyone from the team is involved with drugs, but if they were, I wouldn't help send them to jail. Not unless they were actually dealing."

"And if she gave you those guarantees?"

He shrugged. "Maybe. I suppose so. Hell, I thought I was falling in love with her. I probably would have jumped through hoops if she'd asked me to."

"So we come back to the same exact question," Paul said. "Here's this cold, manipulative woman who's got you wrapped around her little finger. Maybe you could bust her case wide open for her, but she never even asks you to try. When I ask myself why, I have to start wondering about those other aspects of the investigation she mentioned. Have you thought about what they might be?"

"Not really," Zack admitted. "I was too burned up." He wasn't angry anymore, just puzzled and confused. He began to think out loud. "They placed her in a casino. Most of them are probably clean, but maybe—maybe Diamond's isn't. Maybe there's a tie-in to organized crime there. God knows the Mafia has its fingers into the drug trade."

"And would love to have its fingers into professional sports. Think of the money they could make by taking bets on fixed games. With a team like the Rushers, you wouldn't even have to arrange a loss. All you'd have to do is tamper with the point spread on games where we're a big favorite to win."

Zack could accept Paul's logic, but couldn't see how it applied to the Rushers. "I've played with this team for six years. If any of the guys ever deliberately blew a play, I never saw it."

Paul conceded the truth of that, but insisted it didn't matter. The DEA seemed to think there was a problem, so why hadn't Liz asked Zack to offer himself as bait? This time, though, he suggested a possible answer. "Maybe she was worried about your reputation. Let's assume they know something we don't. If Liz continues to see you, the people above her might pressure her to get you involved, or even approach you themselves. You're crazy about her so you agree. You buy drugs and somebody sees you. It winds up in the papers. She doesn't want any of that to happen so she tells you to get lost."

"Are you saying she was trying to protect me?" Zack asked incredulously.

"Why should she be different from all the other women in the world? I don't know what it is about you, but even Jenny isn't immune to it. Didn't you ever notice how she behaves when the three of us go out together and reporters come around? Like a tigress whose cub is in danger. And *she* was the one who insisted we should go to Hawaii to save you, not me."

Zack felt himself redden. "Oh, come on," he mumbled.

"You think I'm making it up?" Paul demanded.

"I think it's crazy. I'm a grown man, not a kid. I can take care of myself."

"You know that and I know that, but *they* don't know that." Smiling now, Paul began to needle him playfully. "Yes ladies, it's the one and only Zack Delaney. You want grace under pressure? You got it. You want coolness under fire? You got it. You want the biggest dimples and the cutest smile this side of Shirley Temple? You got those too. It's a heck of a package, ladies, a heck of a package."

"Go to hell," Zack said, laughing. "You know something, Travers? You must be the only guy in the world who could make me laugh after some woman lies to me, two-times me and then dumps me."

"I'm always glad to help," Paul said with a grin. After a few moments, he sobered and added quietly, "Frankly, I don't know what the truth is. If you start with the woman you talked to tonight and work backward, you reach one conclusion, and if you start with the woman you got to know in Hawaii and work forward, you reach a different conclusion. You'll have to decide which you believe."

It was sound advice, but easier to give than to take. By the time the team left for Los Angeles the next day, Zack was sick of the whole subject. There was too much conflicting evidence. Which did he believe? Liz's smile after they'd made love, or her icy calm on Thursday night? Her quiet emotion as she'd told him about her brother, or her oh-so-innocent questions about whether anyone on the team used drugs? Her fiery passion every time she'd touched him or the eager way she'd embraced another man? It was too much to sort out, especially with a football game to win.

He was glad when Sunday came, glad to concentrate on nothing but his job. Ben let him start, and he was grateful for that because the game was being shown on national television and sitting on the bench during the first quarter would have been painfully embarrassing. It was the kind of contest broadcasters love—well-played, hard-fought and close. The Titans had a tough defense, especially against the passing game, so the Rushers relied on rushing to get them the yards they needed. The running backs, including Kenny Brandenburg, got a real workout. The only major mistake anyone made was a fumble by Brandenburg in the third quarter. At the time, Zack put Kenny's clumsiness down to rookie nerves in a tight spot. The Titans recovered the ball for an eventual touchdown, but it hadn't affected the outcome. The Rushers won by three points.

It was only later, in the plane going home, that the incident began to bother him. He'd tucked that football right into the kid's arms and the kid had taken off like greased lightning. Then a linebacker had more or less bounced off him and the ball had gone flying out of his hands. Why had he lost control of it? This wasn't a kid who normally fumbled. On the contrary, he'd managed to hold on to the ball when four huge Rushers had barreled into him during a scrimmage.

The more Zack thought about it, the less he liked it. The Rushers had been on the Titans' twenty-yard line. If Kenny hadn't fumbled, they would have scored at least a field goal and probably a touchdown. Instead the Titans had eventually scored. The Rushers had been favored to win by six points. They'd won by only three.

He walked to the back of the plane where Kenny was sitting with one of the other rookies. "Tough luck in the third quarter," he said.

Kenny glanced at him, then looked down. He could see the kid was uncomfortable. Was he embarrassed—or guilty? "I shouldn't have let it get away from me," he said. "I wasn't hit that hard."

You're damn right you weren't! Zack thought. "I want to talk to you about that," he said aloud. "In private."

Kenny's seatmate picked up a magazine and tried to pretend he was invisible. Everyone knew that Zack's usual response to glaring errors was a cool stare. "Talking it over" was his personal equivalent of anyone else's raging tantrum.

There was only one place they could really be alone, in one of the plane's rest rooms. Under other circumstances Zack might have seen the humor in trying to squeeze two big football players into a space that even an average-size woman might have found cramped, but he wasn't in any mood to laugh. He *hated* closed-in places. He pointed to the john and Kenny sat down. The kid was a lot bigger than he was. Standing and glaring down at him gave Zack a psychological advantage.

"I'm going to lay it on the line," he said. "I think the fumble was deliberate. I think you're mixed up in something very, very dangerous. I want the details."

Naturally Kenny denied it. He claimed his hands were sweating from the heat. He said he hadn't seen the linebacker coming. The hit had startled him and affected his concentration. The next thing he knew, the ball was gone. He was so convincing Zack almost believed him. Almost.

"I've got to tell you," he said, "I'm getting impatient with all this bull. When I make a handoff I make it right. You had the ball solidly under your control. It didn't just fly off by itself; it was given a deliberate push."

There was another round of denials, more heated than the first. Zack waited till Kenny was through, then increased the pressure. If he was wrong, he'd eat crow later. "I'll paint you a picture, Kenny. You've been taking drugs. You think you need them to play, to win. But now your supplier is asking for more than money. He wants you to throw games. You're desperate so you agree to fumble during a crucial play. How many times do you think you can get away with something like that? The first time it happens, people will believe it's accidental, but after a while they start getting suspicious. And what do you suppose your contact will do when he decides you aren't useful to him anymore? Remember, you can identify him."

Zack didn't miss the flicker of terror in the kid's eyes. He waited, but Kenny didn't say a word. His suspicions had just been confirmed, but a part of him could hardly believe it. How could a kid with such blazing talent also be so stupid?

Was he self-destructive? Incredibly insecure? Or just monumentally foolish?

Zack continued to pressure him, but a little less harshly now. "I have a friend who might be able to help you, but you have to be straight with me first. I'll need the details."

Kenny looked up at him, his eyes full of fear. "You mean you're not going to tell Halliday?"

"Not at this point, no."

The kid was so relieved he actually started to shake. "Thanks. Oh, God, I don't know where to begin. I feel so sick...."

"Take your time," Zack said gently. "It's going to be okay. We'll get you the help you need." He only prayed he was right. Although outwardly calm, he was pretty shaken up himself.

The story came out in fits and starts. Kenny was a young man who simply couldn't cope with everyone else's expectations of him. He was supposed to lead his team to a national championship. He didn't. He was supposed to win the Heisman Trophy. He didn't. He was supposed to be one of the top three picks in the NFL draft. He wasn't. During his senior year the pressure had been so intense that he'd eventually turned to drugs for help. The drugs had added a pressure all their own—the fear of getting caught. Then, just after the end of the regular season, he'd met a man who'd offered him something new. It was a so-called "designer drug," tailored in the laboratory to have certain specific effects and undetectable by the usual tests. It was a yellow powder, packaged in clear capsules, and the man had referred to it as "Dynamite." Kenny had first used it just before the Cotton Bowl. It had made him feel invincible, as if there was nothing he couldn't do on a football field. Zack remembered the game well. Although Alabama had lost, Kenny had been like a battering ram, gaining three to four yards or more on almost every carry.

His supplier had contacted him again a few weeks after the draft, giving him a bottle of pills to take to California with him. Kenny claimed he'd finally stopped taking them after the incident during the scrimmage, largely because Michelle had kept telling him he was a different man on the field, brutal and almost amoral. He finally began to realize it was true, and then to get scared about what was happening to him. Next, just after the team arrived in Los Angeles, he received a call from somebody who said he was a friend of Kenny's contact in Alabama. The man, who had a pronounced Boston accent, had identified himself only as "Norm."

Norm told him they wanted one key fumble out of him, to prevent a Rushers score. When Kenny refused, Norm threatened to withhold the drug from him in the future. Kenny said he was no longer using it, and Norm threatened him with public exposure. All they wanted, he claimed, was this one play. Then they'd leave him alone.

Kenny wasn't naive enough to believe it, so he refused to go along. Inevitably, perhaps, they upped the ante. If he ever wanted to see Michelle Pittman alive again, he would stop arguing.

"I was terrified," he told Zack. "It never occurred to me they knew anything about my personal life. Michelle was up in Marshalton, I was down in Los Angeles and there was no way to protect her. I was afraid they would get to her even if I went to the police. Even though I knew better, I convinced myself it would only be this once. But it won't be."

Kenny was right. They would bide their time so as not to arouse too many suspicions, but then, when the right game came along, he would get another phone call. Once guys like Norm got their hooks into you, they didn't let go easily.

"For the moment," Zack said, "let's forget this conversation ever took place. I'll talk to my friend and see what I can arrange. Then I'll get back to you."

Kenny looked almost pitifully relieved to have someone else take over. Zack's emotions were a lot more complicated. He was ashamed of the accusations he'd flung at Liz and angry she'd let him believe the worst. He was embarrassed he'd been naive enough to insist the team was one hundred percent simon-pure but happy she cared for him enough to worry about involving him.

Most of all, though, he was glad the interrogation was over. Twenty minutes in a tiny rest room was enough to make him sweat. He unlocked the door and pushed it open. He'd never been so happy to get out of a bathroom in all his life.

Chapter Twelve

The Rushers' charter touched down in South Lake Tahoe shortly after seven o'clock. Zack had to take the team bus back to camp and pick up his Mercedes, so it was close to nine before he finally pulled up in front of Diamond's. He handed his keys and a ten-dollar bill to a parking attendant, saying he'd only be a few minutes, and then went inside to find Liz.

He hadn't gotten more than ten feet into the lobby before a desk clerk came trotting up to intercept him. The man greeted him by name, told him how glad they were he'd made it and started reeling off directions to some sort of party.

Zack stood there in baffled silence, trying to make sense of the whole thing. Apparently he'd been expected here. The party seemed to be connected to the golf tournament Diamond's sponsored every year. A couple of the guys had been talking about it on the plane, saying it had been won by a Canadian who was new to the tour.

His instincts told him to act as if he knew what was going on. "I thought I'd stop in and pick up a friend of mine first," he said. "I hope there's no problem with her leaving work."

"You mean Liz Reynolds?" The man waited for Zack's nod, then went on, "She's already over there. You two must have gotten your signals crossed."

Zack smiled and agreed. As he doubled back toward the lake, he tried to fit the pieces into place. Since nobody from the hotel had contacted him about the party, Liz must have promised to bring him. Why hadn't she mentioned it? Because she didn't have the guts to ask a favor after the way she'd thrown him out of her life? Or because she didn't want him there but was afraid to say as much to her boss? And if she didn't want him there, was it because she was determined to keep him away from somebody?

The house was built into a gentle hillside that sloped down toward the waters of Lake Tahoe. Expensive cars lined the driveway and spilled out onto the main road. Zack parked behind the last of them and started walking. A light breeze had come up, but it was still warm and pleasant outside. He could see the lights of the house and patio blinking through the waving trees, and he could hear people talking and laughing.

Two huge men were stationed at the bottom of the driveway—bouncers, obviously. Zack spent a few minutes discussing the game with them and then continued on to the house. It was surrounded on all four sides by a redwood deck holding wall-to-wall people. A lot of them recognized him and called out greetings and congratulations. He answered with friendly smiles and polite thank-yous but didn't allow himself to be drawn into any conversations. He wanted to locate Liz.

He hadn't been looking for her for more than five minutes before a man he'd never seen in his life came up to him and greeted him like a long lost friend. The badge clipped to the pocket of his golf shirt identified him as Sy Whittaker, an assistant manager of the hotel. Zack recognized the name immediately. It had been in Liz's notes.

Whittaker pumped his hand, beaming at him. "Great game, Zack. Great game. We're thrilled to have you here. I've got to admit, after that sack in the third quarter, I wondered if you'd make it."

"I collected a few extra bruises today," Zack agreed. "The Titans have a tough defense."

"Right, right," Whittaker said. "I saw the game on tape. They're showing it inside if you want another look, but I hope you'll circulate a bit, too. It's like I was telling Liz. A lot of the people here will get a real thrill out of meeting you. If we show them a good time and introduce them to a few people such as yourself, they'll give us even bigger donations. And that's what it's all about, Zack—raising money for charity."

"I'll be glad to do what I can," Zack said. A man who'd had a little too much to drink backed into his bruised right hip, making him wince in pain. He hadn't realized how tender it was.

Whittaker noticed his grimace and gave him a sympathetic look. "It must be tough. I mean the physical grind, year after year. A star like you, with a reputation for being the best scrambler in the game—he gets to be a target for the other team. Every lineman in the league wants to sack him."

It was hardly a new observation but Zack's antennae went up all the same. Whittaker had evidently been pressing Liz to get him to this party. What did the man really want out of him? A few handshakes with wealthy contributors, or something less altruistic?

Zack decided to make a leading statement or two and see what developed. "You're right," he said with a shrug, "but it's all part of the game." He took a glass of champagne from a passing waitress and took a healthy swallow. "That's good stuff you're serving here. It eases some of the aches and pains." He smiled. "I guess I must be getting older, because every year I seem to feel it more and more. Maybe I should have been a golfer."

Whittaker laughed. "Don't ever let the fans hear you say that. They want you to go on forever."

"I will if they can find me the fountain of youth. I'll never get bored with playing football. I love the game."

"That's part of what makes you such a great player. Your mental attitude." Whittaker put his arm around Zack's shoulders and led him toward the house. "As far as the physical part goes, there's a friend I want you to meet. He's very interested in the whole question of helping athletes get the most out of their bodies."

Zack was more suspicious than ever, but he continued to play dumb. "You mean conditioning and nutrition?"

"Among other things, yes." They made their way through the crowd, stopping every now and then so Whittaker could introduce Zack to one of the other guests. They entered the house through a sliding-glass door, coming into a game room where a dozen or so men were watching the tape Whittaker had mentioned.

Zack saw himself take the snap, drop back to pass and come up empty on open receivers. He scrambled to his right and picked up a few yards, but he couldn't make it out of bounds before the defense got to him.

He laughed at Whittaker's expression. "It looked a lot worse than it felt, Sy."

Half a dozen heads turned at the sound of his voice. There was some talk about the game—most of the men watching had been playing in the tournament and hadn't seen it live—and then a round of introductions. One of the men had a pronounced Boston accent. Zack wasn't particularly surprised when his name turned out to be Norm. He was even less surprised when Whittaker told him Norm was the friend he'd wanted Zack to meet. It was probably no accident that Whittaker hadn't mentioned the man's last name.

After a few minutes Norm got up to join Zack and Whittaker in the center of the room. He took the champagne glass out of Zack's hand and walked over to the bar. "How about something decent to drink? Whiskey? A beer? A Berry's Natural Cola?"

Zack smiled and asked for a beer. Norm opened a can and brought it over, but instead of returning to his chair, he motioned the other two men toward the hallway. Whittaker started to repeat the conversation he'd had with Zack as they all walked away, but Norm didn't seem to be paying any attention.

He opened a bedroom door, clicked on the light and gave Whittaker the kind of dismissive look that told Zack exactly who was in charge. "I'd better get back to the party," Whittaker said hurriedly. "I'll see you later, okay, Zack?"

"Sure," Zack answered. He watched Norm close the door, wondering how the man would proceed. After all, Zack's reputation was spotless. You couldn't throw drugs at him and expect him to do anything but walk out.

Not surprisingly, Norm turned out to be smooth as glass. He claimed he'd been a Rushers fan all his life. To hear him tell it, last year's Super Bowl win had been one of the high points of his existence. It just so happened that a friend of his, a chemist with a big drug company, had been experimenting on the side with a painkiller and found a related formula with some pretty amazing properties. Not only did it help block pain; it allowed you to exercise harder and longer with no dangerous side effects.

Zack wasn't about to snap at the bait. Norm was going to have to talk him into this—or think that he was. "Sounds like great stuff," he remarked. "When it comes on the market, I'll probably be first in line to try it."

Norm screwed up his face in disgust. "You know how the government is. They want so many tests it takes five or ten years just to approve a new flavor of kids' cough syrup. If you want to try it, I have some in my dresser.''

"I appreciate the offer, but I don't mess around with illegal drugs," Zack said.

"Who said anything about illegal? The stuff is brand-new. It's not against the law." Norm put a hand on his shoulder. "I told you, I've loved your team since I was a kid. I've been watching you for six years now, and I'd rank you right up there with Unitas. If I can help you play better, it would be a real privilege. Take a bunch of capsules. If you want to try them, fine. If you don't, that's fine too. I'll give you my number. You want some more, you give me a call."

Zack hemmed and hawed for another five minutes before allowing himself to be persuaded. The capsules Norm gave him were clear with a yellow powder inside. Their chemical name was a polysyllabic head spinner, but their nickname was a lot easier to remember: Norm called them "Dynamite."

Liz was doing her best to avoid Sy Whittaker. If he couldn't find her, he couldn't keep asking her when Zack Delaney was going to show up. She'd even watched the game that afternoon in the hope of seeing either a loss or a few rough sacks, but nothing had happened to keep Zack away. As a result, she'd been reduced to mumbling that maybe that tackle in the third quarter had been worse than it looked.

In the meantime, she'd been busy helping in the kitchen. Somebody handed her a tray of hors d'oeuvres, and she made her way to the deck to pass them around. Just as she stepped outside, somebody shouted her name. She turned toward the sound of the voice, saw Zack standing a few yards away and almost dropped the tray on her feet. She could feel herself go pale. What in the hell was he doing here? She had to get rid of him, and fast.

She slid the tray onto the nearest table and elbowed her way through the crowd. She didn't waste time on niceties when she finally reached him, but demanded to know what he was doing there. Her tone made it clear how unwelcome he was.

"Looking for you," he answered. "Frankly, you're not giving me a very friendly greeting. I thought you liked having big football stars at this sort of thing."

Liz ignored his sarcasm. "How long have you been here?"

"I don't know. Maybe thirty minutes."

Thirty minutes? My God, if he'd been here thirty minutes, Whittaker must already have seen him. He was probably biding his time, waiting for the right moment to make his move. She took Zack by the arm. "Come on. You're leaving."

He paid absolutely no attention to her gentle tug. Beginning to panic, she pulled as hard as she could. It didn't do a lick of good. She might as well have tried to move a brick wall. "Come on, Zack," she repeated. "You've got to go."

"I'll go all right, but first we talk," he said.

Liz would have agreed to anything by then, just to get him out of sight. "All right," she said. "We can use my car."

"We'll talk down by the lake," he corrected, and started toward the steps leading down to the woods. Liz, who was still holding his arm, found herself being dragged through the crowd. She released her hold, then scrambled after him.

The staircase led to a dirt pathway that meandered through the foliage. It was very dark out, and Zack was walking so briskly that Liz was afraid of tripping. The nearest lights were by a private dock down by where the path emerged from the trees, about ten feet shy of the water.

They were nearly at the end of the trail when Zack grabbed her by the wrist and hauled her into the woods. Her confused protest was cut off with a drawled, "You sure are eager to get rid of me. Why?"

Liz couldn't think of an answer. Her brain, normally so fertile, wasn't working at its usual efficiency. "Never mind why. Just take my word for it, it's not a good idea for you to be here."

"Take your word for it, huh?" She could just make out Zack's features, which were twisted into an expression of total incredulity. "Listen, lady, if I'd made a habit of taking your word for things, I'd still think you were a cocktail waitress with the brains of a canary. Answer the question."

"I can't." She gave him a pleading look. "Please, Zack. Do what I say."

Instead of listening to her, he started toward her. She took a step backward, and then a second and a third. He followed suit, hunting her like a well-fed cat in search of a little entertainment hunts a helpless mouse. Her retreat came to a sudden halt when her back collided with a tree trunk. Zack's hands came up to trap her, one on either side of her body.

He kept on moving until his chest was flush against her breasts. His hands moved down to her hips, lifting her and pulling her against him. He was treating her like his personal property, as though he had the right to do whatever he pleased to her. She stiffened, her heart pounding, and told herself he had no business holding her so intimately. Unfortunately, the hard feel of him made her burn wherever their bodies touched.

Torn between giving him hell and giving in, she managed to do the first. "Look, Zack, I don't have time for games...."

"Neither do I. If you think this is a game, you're crazy."

Liz tried again. "I don't know what you want...."

"Sure you do." He started to nuzzle her neck. "At least you know part of what I want. It's the same thing you want."

Liz couldn't convincingly deny it. His lips were wreaking havoc on her blood pressure. He slid his hand under her black silk top and caressed the bare flesh underneath. She felt dizzy and weak as he worked at the sensitive nipple. She might have blamed it on the altitude, except that he always had that effect on her.

"This is just physical," she insisted. "An empty physical attraction."

"The hell it is." He began teasing her lips, lightly nipping and sucking. "Keep saying that and you'll wind up flat on your back with your clothes off. I've taken as much from you as I plan to take. From here on in, I call the shots."

Liz didn't let anyone boss her around that way, not even a man she was crazy about. "Dammit, Zack, if you don't get your hands off me..."

"Why don't you shut up and kiss me? Both of us know you're dying to."

"Because you're an arrogant, pushy, conceited—"

"Oh, hell!" He cut her off with a hard kiss, his mouth possessive and insistent but also hotly persuasive. Liz could fight her own feelings, but she couldn't resist the temptation of his lips. She'd missed him so much, thought about him so much and wanted him so much, and even if he was being impossibly provocative at the moment she couldn't deny the truth of what he'd said. She *was* dying to kiss him. As his tongue probed and caressed her mouth, she put her arms around his waist and did exactly that. For a few wonderful moments the two of them were alone in an isolated, impenetrable forest.

She would gladly have kept kissing him forever, but he pulled away and gave her a knowing stare. She was too dazed by the force of her own emotions to say a word, but *he* looked smugly self-confident. In fact, she'd never seen him look so sure of himself, except on a football field.

"Just physical, huh?" he said. "Next you'll be telling me you're really a female impersonator. That guy I saw you kissing. Bill. Who is he?"

It took Liz a moment to manage an answer. "My boy-friend." It wasn't exactly a lie. Bill *was* playing the role of her boyfriend.

Zack looked upward in exasperation, then shook his head. "Really? Is that why you made love with me all night in Hawaii? Is that why you came to Marshalton and stared at me all morning? Is that why you're so worried about me tonight? Because you care about somebody else?"

Liz couldn't meet his eyes. The situation was already out of hand. Anything she said, any claim she made, was only going to make it worse.

"You know what I think?" he went on. "I think you saw my car that day. I think the kiss was strictly an act. I think you wanted to get rid of me because you were worried about involving me in your work." He took her chin in his hand, forcing her to look at him. "I *know* I'm damn tired of being lied to. Let's have it, Liz. I want some answers."

Liz told herself he was only speculating. He couldn't be a hundred percent sure of anything. "You have a very vivid imagination," she said.

"Not as vivid as yours." He paused a moment. "Okay, you win. Give me your hand."

Before she could really give it, he had grabbed it and was pulling it toward his body. He pushed it into his right front pocket. "Go ahead, feel what's in there. Take my word for it, they didn't come from the local drugstore."

What she felt, besides the curve of his hipbone and the firmness of his flesh, were capsules—pill capsules. "Where did you get those?" she demanded.

He shook his head. "No way, lady. You don't get a drop of information out of me until you start telling me the truth. Why did you try to get rid of me before?"

Liz pressed her lips together, desperately trying to reason things out. Why had he come? How much did he really know? Had Whittaker given him the pills, and if so, what had he asked in return? Her head was spinning so fast she couldn't come up with any answers.

Zack's expression softened. He put his hands on her shoulders and gently massaged them, as though he couldn't stop himself from touching her. "I'll make it easy for you, honey. You didn't want me to meet Sy Whittaker. You didn't want to put me in a position where I'd get offered the stuff in my pocket. They call it Dynamite, by the way, and somebody named Norm gave them to me. Now who was the guy you were kissing?"

Liz looked into his eyes, saw the intense emotion there and gave up. He already knew the answer. He probably knew how much she cared for him, too. "His name is Bill Genaro. He's working this case with me."

"And that's all? He's just a colleague?"

"Yes," she admitted. "You were right. I did see your car. It's not exactly a low-profile automobile."

"True." He smiled at her, that same overpowering smile that had already gotten her into enough hot water to drown a dinosaur. "In that case, you won't have any problem about spending the night with me tonight."

"Zack, I don't want you mixed up in this."

"It's a little late for that." He patted his pocket. "These capsules have already gotten your cousin's boyfriend into a heap of trouble, but I'll get to that later. The bottom line is that something is going on and I don't like it any better than you do. I'm willing to help you end it."

Liz put her arms around his neck, thinking he was the sweetest, most decent man in the world. "Darling, listen to me. You don't understand what you'd be getting yourself into. You're just too famous for this. You can't go anywhere without being spotted. Your name could be dragged through the mud...."

"I've had a bellyful of you treating me like a naive little kid," he interrupted. He put her arms at her sides and took a few steps backward, removing himself from her reach. She

could see how much she'd annoyed him. "I said I was willing to help, but only on my terms. First you're going to start
leveling with me. I expect to be kept fully informed from
here on in. And second, nobody on my team gets prose-
cuted unless they're dealing. I can either talk to you or I can
go to your boss. Which is it going to be?"

The man might be sweet and decent, but he was also as
pushy as hell. "You seem to hold all the aces," Liz said irritably.

"You bet I do. Now which is it going to be? You or
O'Dwyer?"

"How do you know—Oh. The notebook." Liz sighed
deeply. She didn't seem to have much choice. Not only did
Zack have the capsules; he was the only one who could trace
them back to their source. He also seemed to have important information about Kenny Brandenburg.

Her heart skipped a beat as a play from the game flashed
into her mind—Kenny's fumble in the third quarter. She'd
paid very little attention to it at the time, but maybe she
should have watched the instant replay more carefully. What
was it Jenny had said? That Zack never made bad hand-
offs? If Kenny had had the ball solidly under his control,
why had he lost it?

"You mentioned Kenny before," she said. "What kind of
trouble did you mean? That fumble he made . . ."

"Forget it, Liz. You get zero information until we come
to terms."

She stood there battling her frustration. She had to be
logical about this. There wasn't a chance in the world that
Jack O'Dwyer would turn down Zack's offer of help. The
only way to give him any protection was to set herself up as
a middleman.

"Okay, you win," she said. "Your conditions shouldn't
be a problem. I'll talk to O'Dwyer in the morning. Now
about Kenny . . ."

"Later." He took her in his arms and brushed his mouth across her lips. "About tonight . . ."

"Is that another of your conditions?"

"Yes. Tonight, next week, next month . . ." His lips were soft and seductive against her mouth. "I snap my fingers and you come running. That's the arrangement I want."

"Since when did you get so bossy?" Liz grumbled.

"Since I realized it was the only way to handle you," he answered with a grin.

Liz surrendered and allowed herself to be teased. She *had* given Zack a miserable time, so maybe she even deserved it. "Like I said, you seem to hold all the aces," she murmured against his mouth. She put her arms around him and slid her tongue between his parted lips. She didn't want to think about tomorrow, only about tonight. She finally had what she'd been wanting for weeks, and she couldn't bear to give it up.

The kiss was tender at first, then raw with need and desire. They separated by unspoken agreement, knowing that if they didn't stop soon they wouldn't stop at all.

They drove home in separate cars. After so many weeks apart neither had the self-control for love play. Zack pulled Liz into his arms the moment they were inside and the door was closed. They left a trail of clothing on the steps, tumbled onto the bed in her bedroom and took each other with a frenzied passion meant to ease all the frustrations, fears and doubts of the past month.

Afterward Zack traced lazy circles on Liz's belly and thought to himself that no yellow powder on earth could possibly be as potent as his feelings for the woman by his side. Although he was still annoyed whenever he thought about her misguided efforts to protect him, he also recognized that she'd put her concern for him above both the dictates of the investigation and her own personal desires.

His finger stopped at the low, straight scar on her abdomen. In Hawaii, he'd automatically assumed it was the result of a chance encounter with a mugger, but now he wasn't so sure. "How did you really get this?" he asked. "Was it connected to one of your cases?"

Liz had been lazily content, sure that she'd never felt so wonderful in all her life. Making love with Zack was a trip all its own, from heart-stopping excitement to feverish pleasure to utter relaxation. His question took that relaxation and brought it to a nerve-racking end. Her first instinct was to lie, but she knew she'd lied too much already. She had to start being honest some time.

"Promise me you won't go around the bend if I tell you the truth," she said.

"I take it that's a 'yes.'"

She smoothed his hair, soothing him in advance. "It happened in San Diego. The man's name was Higgins. He owned a clothing company. They had a couple of factories south of the border, and he was smuggling in drugs along with the clothing. I got a job inside the company, as a secretary. I was told to be in his office when they came to arrest him, to be sure nobody else got in the way. When he realized what was about to happen, he grabbed me and pulled out a knife. He meant to use me as a hostage, to escape. I managed to get away, but not before he stabbed me." She could feel Zack getting tenser and tenser with every word, but he never said a thing. "It wasn't so bad," she assured him. "We got Higgins on attempted kidnapping and assault in addition to the drug charges. It's part of my job, just like this is part of yours." She ran her hand over his bruised right hip.

Zack thought the comparison was ludicrous. A minor injury or two was child's play compared to putting your life on the line every day. Remembering the things he'd said on Thursday night was enough to turn his stomach inside out. Liz hadn't been kidding about people deciding to kill her. It scared the hell out of him.

There was no way he wanted her to continue to expose herself to that kind of danger once the case was wrapped up, but he knew better than to say so. Their relationship was far too new and fragile for him to start offering up his opinions. She would only tell him to mind his own business.

He took the coward's way out and changed the subject to the investigation. They exchanged information so that each would have as complete a picture as possible, then speculated on what would happen next. Zack was a little overwhelmed by the complexity and importance of the case. They weren't just after small fry, but hoped to indict and convict men at the highest reaches of organized crime.

His team, however, was of more immediate concern to him. In addition to him, two players and a coach might eventually be asked to testify. He told Liz that Ben Halliday would have to be informed. She answered that she didn't think O'Dwyer would have a problem with that, but would check with him to make sure.

She was acting the part of the seasoned professional, but deep down she was frightened and unsettled. Zack's actions had taken matters out of her hands. He was a grown man and he'd made his own choices, but she was uneasy about what he'd gotten himself into. She was also worried about Kenny and Michelle.

She bent her lips to his chest, pushing the fear out of her mind. He gave a low grunt of pleasure as her mouth moved lower and her tongue began to delicately tease him. He twined his fingers into her hair and arched his hips. His desire set her blood on fire, burning away everything but the need to give and receive. They didn't waste any more time talking.

Chapter Thirteen

They tracked down Norm's identity using phone-company and government records. His full name was Norm Pinella and he worked for Hoag Enterprises, as an executive assistant to Johnny Hoag himself. Liz wasn't surprised by the tie-in. After all, Hoag's company was at the hub of a drug distribution network that extended across seven Western states.

Zack made his first phone call to Norm about two weeks after the party. The regular football season had started by then and the Rushers were back in San Francisco. Norm readily agreed to supply Zack with more pills, saying he would get them to Liz in the next day or two. There was no mention of payment.

Liz's involvement in the exchange reflected the fact that Whittaker and his cronies had come to trust her. She'd gotten Zack to the party, after all. She knew he was using Dynamite, she knew Bill Genaro was transporting drugs for Hoag's company and she knew Whittaker was supplying drugs to hotel guests, yet she'd never questioned a single one of those things.

It wasn't too long before she was working for Whittaker full-time as his personal assistant. Her duties were strictly legal at first, but they didn't stay that way. Not only did she get a close-up view of the local drug-distribution operation Whittaker was running; she also came across snatches of information about his counterparts in other hotels. Only one thing continued to elude both her and everyone else—the identities of Hoag's superiors, if indeed such men existed.

In the meantime, her relationship with Zack had become public knowledge. She got used to seeing their names linked together in the gossip columns and on the sports pages. There was even a front-page article about their trip to Los Angeles in mid-September to tape a follow-up segment for *Main Attraction*. They denied Denning's claim that a wedding was in the works, but admitted they saw as much of each other as their schedules permitted.

If the Rushers were playing at home, Liz would drive to San Francisco on Thursday or Friday and return to Lake Tahoe after the weekend. If they were going on the road, she would visit Zack in the middle of the week, before they left town. Not surprisingly, Whittaker was always very accommodating about giving her time off.

The hours she spent with Zack were the happiest of her life. He was the first man she'd trusted completely, the first one she'd ever confided in. She told him about everything—her childhood, her feelings about her dead brother and now-remarried father, details of previous cases, progress on the current case. He was equally open with her, sharing problems that came up at work as well as his concerns about the future. At times he worried that nothing could ever replace the cheers of the fans and the camaraderie of the locker room. He would retire a wealthy man, without the need ever to work again, so what did he do with

the rest of his life? They spent a lot of time talking over his
options.

Their lovemaking had a passion and a fulfillment that
only come when two people care deeply for one another.
The words "I love you," whether moaned in the breathless
excitement of erotic intimacy or whispered in the sweet
contentment that followed, became a regular part of their
lives.

Only a single subject was taboo—the future of their relationship. Each had good reason to avoid it. Zack could see
that Liz's work meant a great deal to her. He was afraid she
would refuse to give it up. He told himself that time was on
his side. The closer he got to her, the more important and
even essential he would become. He decided not to raise the
issue until he absolutely had to.

As for Liz, she knew she couldn't have both Zack and her
current type of work. The choice was so difficult and painful that she decided to put it out of her mind until the case
was over and it was time to move on. That was impossible,
of course, and she often found herself wishing they could go
on forever, just exactly as they were.

The two of them seldom went out, because if reporters
didn't find them, the fans did. Instead they spent their time
alone in Zack's home or over at the Traverses' place, talking and playing bridge. Liz got accustomed to being photographed entering and leaving Zack's house and learned to
respond to reporters' questions with smiles and noncom-
mittal answers. She was painfully aware that her associa-
tion with him wasn't doing much for his reputation, so she
tried to keep a low profile.

Stories about her always seemed to identify her as "casino
executive Sy Whittaker's personal assistant." It was never
"hotel executive," always "casino executive." There was no
getting around the fact that gambling, even legal gambling,
had unsavory overtones. Inevitably, her job began to tar-
nish Zack's perfect public image. He kept telling her not to

worry about it, but she knew that it bothered him. It bothered her, too.

Zack made his second call to Norm Pinella about a month after the first one, on a Sunday night after the Rushers' sixth game and first loss of the season. He hadn't played particularly well that day, but there was no mystical reason for that. Things just hadn't broken his way. A lot of NFL quarterbacks would have been satisfied to equal his performance, but Zack expected more out of himself. So did everyone else.

Zack told Norm he'd run out of Dynamite and let him draw his own conclusions about the Rushers' loss that day. Norm, smelling the opening he'd been waiting for, replied that there was no such thing as a free lunch. Dynamite was expensive stuff, in short supply. He could get Zack another batch of pills, but Zack would have to do them a favor in return.

The demand didn't throw Zack in the slightest. He was beginning to understand why Liz enjoyed undercover work so much. Norm and his pals were the lowest kind of scum, and he relished the idea of nailing them to the wall. It went without saying that he wasn't too crazy about some of the stuff being printed in the paper these days, but it was a price he was willing to pay. His reputation could survive a few potshots.

He looked at Liz, who was listening to the conversation on a set of headphones connected to wiretapping and taping equipment. She seemed a little worried, so he smiled at her and gave her a confident wink.

"I'm willing to negotiate," he said to Norm, "but not with errand boys. You need to remember who you're dealing with. I don't need your stuff to be a winner. I've always been a winner." He paused. "Then again, you can always do business with Kenny Brandenburg in two months. I do know about that, Norm. Don't forget, he dates my girlfriend's cousin."

Liz sat there thinking that Zack had the makings of a professional narc. It was the perfect stand to take. Kenny had done all of them a favor and injured himself in the second game of the season. He'd be lucky to return by December. As long as he couldn't play, he was safe from the likes of Norm Pinella.

In the meantime, he was continuing to see Michelle, but less often now that she was back in school. He was also getting the help he needed and had made some good friends on the team. Liz had the feeling he had a bright future, providing he stayed clean and kept seeing his counselor.

Assuming Norm had no other contacts on the Rushers, his back was against the wall. Norm needed Zack more than Zack needed drugs. When Zack insisted that, Dynamite or no Dynamite, he was only going to deal with the boss, Norm quickly gave in. He said he would set up a meeting with Johnny Hoag in Las Vegas. They agreed to make it on Tuesday, which was the Rushers' day off.

The following day at work, Liz told Sy Whittaker about the upcoming meeting and offered to go along. She explained that Zack was edgy about the whole thing and pointed out that she would be able to keep him calm and under control if she stuck by his side.

Whittaker gave her an approving smile and picked up the phone to call Hoag. "You're a smart girl," he said. "You're going to go a long way." Hoag didn't need any convincing. He thought it was an excellent idea.

Liz drove back to San Francisco that same night. Early the next morning one of O'Dwyer's technicians stopped by Zack's house to fit her out with a tiny electronic transmitter. The bug would pick up any nearby conversations and relay them to a team of agents working out of an unmarked car.

Hoag sent a limousine to the Las Vegas airport to bring them out to his home. He and his wife were waiting there with three other couples. Outwardly the afternoon was a purely social one. The men were local businessmen who wanted to meet Zack, so they talked about football and other sports over a leisurely lunch.

It was only afterward, when the other couples had left, that Hoag invited Zack into his office to talk business. He also directed his wife Maria to show Liz around the garden. Much to her chagrin, her fellow agents got nothing more to tape than a discussion of desert landscaping.

Still, Zack would be able to give verbal testimony about what had gone on in the meeting. Liz dearly hoped that Hoag would turn out to be the man on top, because then Zack's role in the case would be finished.

He filled her in on what had happened as soon as they were back in San Francisco and nobody was around to overhear them. Hoag had given him the pills, and in return, he'd agreed to blow a touchdown opportunity sometime during Monday night's game. The easiest way to do that was by throwing an interception.

Liz was openly horrified. "But you can't do that," she said.

Zack thought to himself that Liz still didn't seem to realize he could take care of himself perfectly well. "I have no intention of doing it. It was the obvious demand to make. I could see it coming. Paul and I have been working on a play for the past couple of weeks, early in the morning at a high school field near his home. I'll send the ball in high, with a little something on it to make it tail away. It will look like I'm throwing to the man covering him. If things go the way we plan, Paul will make what appears to be a great save. But if he can't catch it, he'll knock it out of the way."

Liz only hoped it would work. She put her arms around Zack's waist and snuggled against his chest. "I'll be glad when this is over. Thank God you're finally out of it."

Zack stroked her hair. "But I'm not. Hoag isn't the one you want, honey. He made a phone call while we were in his office, to tell someone to check things out with 'the boss.'"

It took about five minutes for Hoag to get an okay. Next time I call for pills, I'll insist on dealing with whoever gave that 'okay.' And *I'll* have to wear the transmitter.''

Liz didn't like that at all, but as long as Zack wanted to cooperate, O'Dwyer was going to accept his help. Her mood, which was somber to begin with, got even worse when she opened the sports section of the San Francisco *Times* the following afternoon. Somebody had seen Zack get on the plane to Las Vegas the day before and had phoned the paper in a fit of righteous indignation. The reporter who had taken the call had promptly called the airline to confirm the allegation, and now he was asking some pointed questions.

Why was Zack Delaney running off with his girlfriend when he'd had such a lousy game on Sunday? After all, his team had lost. Maybe Tuesday was the Rushers' day off, but he should have been meeting with the coaches to discuss strategy for next week's game or studying game films of their next opponent.

And why Las Vegas of all places? Didn't he know how that looked? Nobody seriously thought Delaney was a crook, but he should have had more brains than to go visiting the local gambling towns. Somebody, either Ben Halliday or the team's owner, needed to have a talk with him.

The reporter asked Zack those same questions at practice the next day. Zack knew they weren't entirely unfair, but he still felt impatient and irritated. After six spotless years, he should have built up some trust with these people. Maybe he had, but apparently not enough of it to avoid criticism and questions.

He answered that he'd gone to Las Vegas to have lunch with one of his girlfriend's business associates and some of the man's friends. The reporter immediately demanded names. Zack hesitated, then declined to give them. He pointed out that his fellow guests were entitled to a little privacy. They'd come because they were Rushers fans, not to take part in some kind of sinister conspiracy. The reporter kept after him, first about the game and then about why he was flitting around the country instead of working at football these days. In the end Zack got so fed up with being badgered that he lost his temper and walked away in disgust. The story in the paper the next day made it look as if he'd *run* away from questions he couldn't answer.

Liz, who was asked a similar series of questions by reporters who phoned her office, gave very similar answers. Ben Halliday, who had supported the investigation as long as the team was winning but was getting impatient now that they'd lost, said that Zack Delaney's private life was nobody's business but his own, and then refused further comment. The league commissioner suggested that perhaps Mr. Delaney should pay more careful attention to the people he associated with and the places he went.

The speculation died down over the next several days, especially after Maria Hoag called the *Times* with her guest list, but Monday night's game stirred things up all over again. Watching the game on television, Liz thought the pass looked like one of the strangest Zack had ever thrown. In reality, it was a work of art. It went exactly where it was supposed to, catching the cornerback covering Paul so off guard that he missed whatever chance he might have had to intercept it. Paul made a diving catch, staggered and took off toward the end zone. Although he was stopped at the sixteen, the Rushers eventually scored a field goal on the possession.

The play, and the pass itself, monopolized the postgame interview session. A dozen different reporters wanted to know why Zack had thrown to Paul Travers when Paul wasn't open and other receivers were. Zack said he'd had a gut feeling that Paul would manage to *get* open. They asked why the pass was so off-target when Zack had had all the time in the world to throw. He shrugged and admitted it was a lousy pass that probably should have been intercepted. He added that he was taking Paul to dinner the next night to thank him for saving his hide.

In one form or another those same questions were asked over and over and over again. Zack patiently gave the same answers over and over again, struggling to keep his temper in check. It was damn unpleasant to be attacked that way, especially when you'd always been as straight as they came. It offended his sense of justice.

Liz came to think of it as the pass that wouldn't die. Reporters kept asking questions, not only about the pass, but about the businessmen Zack had met in Las Vegas. Were they really as legitimate as they'd seemed at first glance? Halliday got so fed up with the endless speculation that he threatened to bar the press from practice sessions. Zack bought himself an answering machine and left it turned on, just to avoid the constant phone calls.

By Friday Liz had taken all she could take. Instead of driving directly to Zack's house that morning, she stopped in at O'Dwyer's office. Marching in with the newspaper held high, she slapped it onto his desk and pointed to a column on the front page of the sports section.

"How much longer are we going to let this go on?" she demanded. "They're crucifying him, Jack. Every time I turn around there's another disgusting little innuendo about Zack Delaney's Las Vegas connections and inexplicable passes. It's horrible."

"I know. I've been following it." Jack ran a hand through his hair and gave a tired sigh. "I'm sorry about all the publicity, Lizzie. It must be difficult for both of you."

"Then call the papers. Set them straight."

"Don't you think I've considered it? I can't take the chance. Let's say I level with them about Zack's role in all this—that I tell them they're interfering with a federal investigation by continuing to raise questions about him. They might go along, but they're just as likely to decide that what

I've told them is news and has to be printed. Even if I make it off-the-record, there still could be a leak.''

Liz knew that as well as Jack did. She sat down in the chair opposite his desk and rubbed her temples. Her head had begun to throb.

"I can't get around the fact that Zack is our only lead to whoever is in charge," Jack said quietly. "I've been fighting battles of my own here. Did you know that Paul and Zack never told Halliday what they planned to do?"

Liz stared at him in disbelief. "It never even occurred to me to ask. I just assumed Ben had okayed it."

"You assumed wrong. Halliday finally got the truth out of them and stormed in here in a bloody rage, threatening to pull Zack off the case. I can't blame him for being furious. It's beginning to affect his team. I told him we had over fifty agents in eleven states working this case, all of whom have come up empty about who's on top. I stressed the importance of identifying and arresting those men. I reminded him that Zack is the only one who can help us do that. I appealed to his sense of patriotism. Hell, Liz, I practically got down on my knees and begged. In the end he agreed to give us a few more weeks." O'Dwyer gave Liz a gentle smile. "Hang in there a little longer, honey. If Halliday can, you can."

Liz nodded slowly, but it was hard to be calm and objective when she went to another game that Sunday. People stared at her and whispered behind her back. Zack was actually booed when he first ran out on the field. The opposing team had a mediocre defense and the game turned into a blowout, but even the cheers at the end of it couldn't make up for those initial boos.

The worst part of all was the waiting. Hoag had given Zack a two-to-three-week supply of pills, so he had to let two more games go by before he could call for a refill. The Rushers won both, but any mistake by their quarterback had become grist for reporters' mills. Even the best quarterbacks occasionally misread the defense, missed open receivers and threw interceptions, but when Zack did any of those things he was bombarded with a hundred suspicious questions.

Zack had never had a problem handling pressure on the field, but he was finding that attacks from the media in the locker room were a whole different story. The endless questions and negative publicity were hurting him a lot more deeply than boos ever had. When the fans had booed him in the past, they were criticizing his performance on the field. They weren't questioning his morality and decency.

He tried to keep his answers polite and to the point, but it was impossible to stay cool and professional when reporters were doing their level best to taunt him and trap him. He wouldn't let Ben throw them out and he never again made the mistake of walking away, but the postgame interview session became an exhausting, painful ordeal. He found himself withdrawing from everyone but Liz and the Traverses. He also began to worry that the furor would eventually affect both his own play and that of the team.

As the person closest to him, Liz was well aware of his anger and his hurt. For all his legendary coolness on the field, he was anything but unemotional. She gave him as much support as she could, but it could never be enough. No matter how tenderly she made love to him, no matter how many hours they spent talking, it could never make up for watching his name and reputation relentlessly ripped to shreds. She'd never felt so helpless in her life—or so enraged.

Despite all of it, he was nothing short of brilliant when he finally called Johnny Hoag. His tough, hard voice set the tone for the conversation that followed. It said he wasn't some insecure rookie to be pushed around, but an equal. Each of them had something the other wanted and they would proceed on that basis. He told Hoag he'd already taken enough heat about the pass to Travers to fill Death

Valley and was thoroughly sick of the subject. It wasn't *his* fault Travers had made a brilliant catch. He'd upheld his end of the bargain and he wasn't going to put up with them dangling their Dynamite in front of him like cops promising dope to a junkie in order to make him talk. There would be one final deal to cover the rest of the season and he would make it with the man on top.

Hoag said he would have to get back to him and hung up. Liz was a nervous wreck as Zack put down the phone, but Zack was smiling confidently. He'd always been a fierce competitor, and she had the feeling he was enjoying the contest of wills. "Don't worry," he said. "They'll bite. I could smell it."

He was right. Hoag called back that same night, telling him the meeting would take place the following Tuesday in Palm Springs. Zack jotted down the details—SFO/9 A.M./Air Cal/white limo—and then said to Hoag, "Yeah, she's here. You want to speak to her?"

He held out the phone. "For you."

Hoag was chillingly direct. "See that you keep him in line, Liz. Make him understand that we expect results this time. The boss has a strong personal interest in this, and if there's another screwup, people are going to get hurt." There was a click, and then the line went dead.

Liz's hand was shaking as she hung up the phone. Zack asked her if Hoag had told her whom they'd be meeting, and she shook her head. Then she repeated what he'd said. Whoever the man was, he was cautious, powerful and very, very dangerous.

As they left the house the following Tuesday to drive to the airport, a reporter darted into their path to block their way. Zack stiffened, but he also stopped to let the man ask his questions. "Where are you going? Las Vegas again?"

"Palm Springs," Zack answered.

"What for?"

Liz had heard enough. "It's personal," she said. "Why don't you leave him the hell alone?" She took Zack's arm and dragged him to the car as the reporter followed and shot questions at them. When Zack pulled into traffic, the reporter did the same.

After a few silent moments, Zack looked at her and smiled. "I appreciate the rescue, but it's the wrong way to handle those guys. It's better to dig in your heels and outlast them."

"I know." Liz was suddenly close to tears. "It's just that I can't stand what they're doing to you. It's all my fault. If you'd never met me..."

"I'm not sorry I met you. I love you. I was a volunteer, honey, not a draftee." He brushed a tear off her cheek. "It'll be okay. It's almost over."

Liz sat there thinking that she should be comforting and reassuring *him*, not the other way around. The reporter was right behind them as they pulled into the short-term parking lot. He followed them into the terminal, firing out more questions. Zack gave him polite but terse answers and kept on walking. Liz had never been so glad to get on a plane in all her life.

The white limousine they'd been told to expect was waiting for them in front of the terminal in Palm Springs. The driver, who never said a single word to them, took them to a Spanish-style mansion and escorted them inside. Then he left the house.

Liz and Zack sat down in the empty living room to wait. Liz had never been so edgy in her life, but it wasn't herself she was worried about. It was Zack.

He was the one with the bug taped to his chest. Suppose he was searched? Suppose the agents assigned to trail them from the airport had lost the white limo? Suppose they hadn't lost it but were spotted hanging around outside? They wouldn't suspect Liz of anything, only Zack.

A uniformed maid finally walked in and told them to follow her. They climbed a flight of steps and walked down a long hallway. All the doors were closed. She knocked on the last of them, waited a moment and then opened it up. A formal library lay beyond, its walls lined with floor-to-ceiling bookshelves.

The room was large enough to hold several couches and tables but was furnished with only a single leather chair, in the farthest corner. Liz didn't recognize the man sitting in it. He looked to be in his late sixties and was eccentrically dressed—a white suit and shirt, white cotton gloves, black and white sneakers, a turquoise string tie, a leather cowboy hat. He spoke with a noticeable drawl.

"Just what is it you want, Mr. Delaney?"

Zack hesitated. "I didn't catch your name."

"I didn't throw it to you."

"That's true." Zack casually shifted his weight from one foot to the other. Liz knew he wasn't as relaxed as he looked, but admired the way he was carrying things off. "I like what you supply. Notice I said 'like,' not 'need.' In return for a three-month supply, I'll give you one game. Just one. Our opponents will beat the point spread. That's a guarantee."

"Dallas," the man stated. "November 16th."

Zack shook his head. "We won't be favored by more than a few points. I'll need a bigger point spread to work with."

"New York. November 23rd."

"All right. And the pills?"

The man coughed into his gloved hand and then straightened his string tie. "I understood you owed us a favor, Mr. Delaney. I don't know anything about any pills."

"I think you do," Zack said. "They're called Dynamite. They're clear capsules..."

"Good day, Mr. Delaney," the man interrupted.

Zack went right on talking. "With a yellow powder inside, and I have no intention of leaving here without them."

The man looked at Liz, his expression icy. "Explain the meaning of 'good day' to your friend, Miss Reynolds."

She took Zack's arm. The man hadn't directly implicated himself, but they'd probably gotten enough for a legal wiretap. "Let's go. I'm sure we can trust them to hold up their end of the bargain."

"In a minute, honey." Zack took back his arm and walked over to the man's chair. As Zack held out his hand, the man visibly shrank back, yanking his own hand out of reach. He wasn't quite as fast as Zack, though. Zack caught him by the wrist, forced the handshake on him and gave him a cool smile. "It's been a pleasure doing business with you. I'll see you around." He strolled back to Liz, put his arm around her waist and led her out of the room.

The part of her that wasn't appalled wanted to burst out laughing. She didn't dare. Only the Zack Delaneys of the world could get away with behavior like that. He was the most amazing mixture of shyness and arrogance, of sensitivity and self-confidence, that she'd ever come across.

They were back in San Francisco by midafternoon and spent the rest of the day in O'Dwyer's office working with a local police artist. They came up with a very good likeness of the man in Palm Springs, but nobody knew who he was. They did identify the house, however. It belonged to a Hollywood actor. According to his agent, he was filming in Europe and couldn't be reached for questioning.

O'Dwyer put the house under twenty-four-hour surveillance. When the man finally left three days later, he was followed to Dallas. By the time Liz checked with O'Dwyer the following week, they finally had some answers.

"His name is Hugo Crenshaw," O'Dwyer told her. "Does it ring a bell?"

"Crenshaw," Liz murmured. She remembered the name from the business pages of the paper. "Isn't the family into oil or minerals?"

"Both. Hugo is allegedly worth around half a billion dollars. He's reclusive to the point of neurosis and very secretive about his business affairs. Nobody has seen him in years, except for his closest associates. We're finding out as much as we can."

Liz reminded him they had a deadline. "The Giants game is a week from Sunday. If Zack goes in there and plays his best..." She took a deep breath, fighting to control her fears. "I'm worried about him, Jack. Those people don't fool around."

"I've already spoken to Washington. They understand we'll have to move in before Sunday regardless of what we have or haven't found out. Thank Zack for his help and tell him everything's under control."

"And is it?" Liz asked pointedly.

O'Dwyer didn't meet her eyes. "I hope so. God knows I hope so."

Chapter Fourteen

Liz had no intention of leveling with Zack. He'd held up very well for more than two difficult months now, but the unceasing pressures on him were finally taking their toll. Another round of speculative articles had followed the trip to Palm Springs. The reporters were hounding him as much as ever and even his teammates were starting to ask questions. He wasn't sleeping well at night, he looked tired most of the time and Paul Travers was the only one who could get a laugh out of him anymore.

She gave him a fierce hug as soon as he'd let her into his house and then told him his role in the case was finished. Hugo Crenshaw was definitely the man at the top. It was just a question of tying up a few loose ends in regard to Crenshaw's business interests. Arrests would be made the following week.

Zack didn't bother to hide his relief. Liz had been right in August—he'd had no idea what he was getting himself into. He didn't regret his decision to cooperate because he felt it was essential to keep sports honest, but he was at the end of his tether by now.

He wanted his regular life back. He wanted to be a hero again, not a villain. He wanted to concentrate on football again, not on drug deals. And most of all, he wanted to be with Liz.

Maybe he was taking things too fast, but he'd waited as long as he could. The two of them belonged together, not just two or three days out of seven but all week long. It was about time the people in this city realized that she was a first-class heroine and not some sleazy trollop who'd corrupted his morals. There was life after football, all right, but he was ready to start living it now, while he was still playing. It included the woman he loved, the family they would have and the home they would share.

He took Liz's hand and led her into the living room. "I have something for you," he said.

They sat down on the couch together. Liz watched him take a small package out of his pocket, knowing what it was before she even opened it up. She felt miserably guilty. Not only had she just lied to him—she was afraid she was about to hurt him deeply.

The ring inside was beautiful, a large sapphire surrounded by eight diamonds. "I want you to marry me as soon as this is over," he said. "It drives me crazy to think of you taking on people like Whittaker and Hoag. Every time I touch the scar on your stomach and remember how it got there, I start feeling physically sick. Come live with me. Transfer to a desk job. Let's spend the rest of our lives making each other happy."

Liz took the ring out of its velvet box and slowly twirled it around, studying the way the facets of the gemstones reflected back individual rays of light. She wished Zack had waited a little longer. She wasn't ready to make impossible decisions just yet.

When she finally answered him, her voice was hoarse with emotion. "I love you very much. But you're asking me to give up something I've dedicated my life to."

She expected a show of anger or frustration, but all he did was put his arm around her shoulders and kiss her temple. "You've given them seven years. During all that time you've had no real life of your own. I understand about Tommy, but even Tommy wouldn't have wanted you to make that kind of sacrifice. It's time to think about *you*—about us."

"But my life has been fulfilling. I've enjoyed it. I've gotten immense satisfaction from it." Liz paused, finding the next words the hardest of all. "I don't know if I could be happy without it."

Zack gave her a tender smile. "And could you be happy without me?"

She looked at him, her eyes filling with tears. "No."

"So?"

"I don't know." The tears spilled down her cheeks. He gathered her into his arms and held her close. She cried until she'd run out of tears and his shirt was thoroughly soaked, but it didn't help. She still felt as if she was standing at the edge of a precipice.

"Try to understand," she pleaded as she straightened up. "This is all I've wanted to do, ever since I was seventeen and my brother died. I hate bastards like Hoag and Higgins. After Higgins stabbed me, when I had to work a desk job, I was so frustrated I wanted to explode." She started to sob again, but more quietly now. "I wasn't cut out to be a professional football wife. And to be Mrs. Zack Delaney— to have to say the right thing, and look the right way and wear the right clothes..." She couldn't go on.

"The hell with those things," Zack said. "Nobody's telling you not to have a life of your own. Jenny Travers always has."

"But Jenny is a model, not an undercover drug agent." Liz took a final, regretful look at the ring, then forced herself to place it back in its box. "Here. I can't accept this. If I leave my job to marry you I'd only be restless and bored. I'd only make you unhappy. I don't want to do that."

Zack pushed the box back into her hand and closed her fingers around it. She didn't know it yet, but she *was* going to marry him. She loved him too much to do anything else. If he hadn't believed that, he would have gone crazy.

"Keep it for now," he said. "Think it over. I'm not asking for an immediate decision. I just want you to keep one thing in mind. Maybe you were frustrated working a desk job because there was nothing in your life to replace the excitement of working undercover. Your job was the only thing that mattered to you, but that's not true anymore. *I* matter. The kids we're going to have some day matter. We'll talk this over again after the arrests are made, but in the meantime I've got to warn you—I don't give up easily."

Liz might have told him that she wasn't going to change her mind, but she wasn't absolutely certain of that, especially after he began kissing away her tears. His lips moved lower, his tongue teasing its way into her mouth, and she responded the way she always did, with an emotion-charged passion that compelled her to give herself to this man body and soul. She loved him so much that it was sheer hell to think about leaving him—and sheer heaven to be in his arms. Logic and common sense would just have to wait.

With Zack in Dallas for the weekend, Liz started packing up her things, preparing to leave Lake Tahoe permanently. She spoke to O'Dwyer every day or two, and was enormously relieved by his progress reports. It turned out that the IRS had been investigating the Crenshaw business interests for years, for possible tax fraud. Once all the appropriate federal agencies pooled their information, they were able to determine that companies controlled by Cren-

shaw also controlled the Diamond Hotel chain. The con
versations on their wiretaps indicated that Crenshaw and the
members of his family, including his goddaughter's hus
band Johnny Hoag, had their fingers in enough illegal pie
to feed a small city. The charges to be filed would run th
gamut from income tax evasion to trafficking in narcotic
to bribery and extortion.

Oddly enough, however, it didn't seem to be money
Crenshaw was after when it came to fixing sporting events
It was power. As close as they could figure it, he was a
megalomaniac who needed to feel he could dominate any
one—or anything—he chose to. Arrests would be made at
seven o'clock Pacific time on Thursday morning, not onl
on the West Coast, but in Texas and several Eastern state
as well.

Liz didn't want to stay in Lake Tahoe a day longer than
she had to. She didn't want to see Whittaker again, either
except in a courtroom. She called his office first thin
Wednesday morning and told him she'd had a panicky cal
from Zack late the night before. She claimed Zack wa
having second thoughts about agreeing to fix Sunday'
game. She thought it would be a good idea to go to Sa
Francisco immediately and get him back on track. Whit
taker immediately agreed.

She loaded up the car, made a final check of the house t
make sure she hadn't left anything behind and drove off. I
was just past ten o'clock. Zack's ring was still in her purse
and she was still as confused as ever about whether to ac
cept it. Somehow, though, none of that seemed to matter
All she felt at that moment was immense relief. The case wa
almost wrapped up, Zack would finally be safe and the trut
would come out.

She switched on the radio for company, changing sta
tions each time the signal would fade on her way west. Firs
she tuned in Placerville, then Sacramento, and finally, Sa
Francisco. She caught the end of a discussion about the lat

est diet books on a network-affiliated all-talk station, and
then the national news came on. She listened with half an
ear. It was the usual mixture of politics, world crises and
natural disasters.

"And now, the local news," the announcer said. "According to a report to be published in this afternoon's San
Francisco *Times*, Gold Rushers' quarterback Zack Delaney
is under investigation by federal authorities for the use of
cocaine and amphetamines. An FBI spokesman in Washington declined comment, as did Rushers head coach Ben
Halliday. Delaney, who was practicing at Moscone Stadium when the news of the story broke, left immediately for
his Pacific Heights home. A spokesman for the team said he
would have no statement to make about the allegations, at
least at the present time." The announcer paused. "That's
quite a shocker, isn't it, Bruce?"

"It sure is, Susan. Of course, the rumors about Delaney
have really been flying lately. It's hard not to believe there
isn't something behind them, especially after last week's loss
to Dallas."

"Right. A lot of people lost money on that one. I've been
hoping it was strictly legitimate, but I have to admit it looks
like it wasn't."

Liz switched off the radio with a savage twist of the dial.
The Dallas defense had been brilliant on Sunday. They'd
stopped the Rushers cold—*all* the Rushers, not just Zack.
She wanted to lynch whoever was responsible for those news
reports. As for "Susan" and "Bruce," lynching was too
good for them.

Her first instinct was to go directly to Zack's home to reassure him, but she knew it would be surrounded by reporters. It made more sense to check in with O'Dwyer first and
find out what was going on. She was breathing fire when she
talked into his office an hour later.

He took one look at her face and stated the obvious. "I
see you've been listening to the news."

"You bet I have," she snapped. "How does garbage like that get on the air?"

"We're not sure. The number of people involved in the case has doubled in the last few weeks. The leak could have come from anywhere. Some clerk somewhere gets a quick look at a memo and spots Zack's name or overhears a phone conversation where he's mentioned, jumps to conclusions and the next thing you know the papers get hold of it." He pointed to a chair. "Come on, sit down and try to relax Zack's okay. I spoke to him half an hour ago. I told him I'd issue a statement tomorrow, as soon as the arrests are announced."

Liz dropped into the chair, heartsick. "But don't you realize how it's going to look? They'll say he only cooperated after the fact, once we'd caught him red-handed with drugs Unless we give the media complete details..." Her voice trailed off. Complete details would destroy her career.

"Obviously you see the problem here," O'Dwyer said "Can I get you a cup of coffee?"

"Please." Liz hoped the caffeine would clear her head She felt stunned, overwhelmed. Maybe she was having a bad dream. When was she going to wake up?

O'Dwyer gave her shoulder a gentle squeeze as he passed by her chair. He didn't sit down behind his desk again after he'd returned with the coffee, but pulled a chair around so he could sit beside her. "I've spent a lot of time turning this over in my mind," he said quietly. "This is how I figure it You've been seen with Zack, and photographed with Zack much too often ever to work this area again. I'd want to see you stay away from the entire West Coast. But you could still go the East or South, especially if you dye your hair and adopt a different look. Everything changes if you go public with the details of your relationship with Zack. It's just too good a story to ignore—love, crime and sports, all in a single package. It will wind up on the network news shows, or magazine covers, you name it. You'll never be able to work undercover again. You'd run too high a risk of being recognized."

"I know that," Liz said. "But what choice do I really have? I can't let Zack live under a shadow for the rest of his life. It wouldn't be fair to him." She paused, then added softly, "Besides, I love him. I don't want to leave him."

O'Dwyer started to smile. "In that case, what's your problem? You're a damn good undercover agent, but if I'm going to lose you in any event, I'd rather have you working a desk job in my office than running around Florida in a red wig."

Liz frowned and picked up her cup of coffee. She didn't understand herself at all. She'd just decided to give up the work she'd always loved, so why wasn't she the least bit upset? Why didn't she resent being pushed into a decision? Why was she actually happy about it?

She felt as though a tremendous weight had been lifted from her shoulders. She found that she was smiling. Had she wanted this all along but been either too stubborn or too set in her ways to recognize it? She sipped her coffee and laughed out loud. The most incredible thoughts were going through her mind—of lazy weekends in bed, during the off-season, of course, and Zack tossing a football to a brown-haired little boy while his big sister played defense, and pets and barbecues and station wagons. She was having a full-blown midlife crisis. She was turning into a bona fide Yuppie.

"I guess there's no problem at all," she said to Jack. "I don't know whether it's love or biology, but marriage and a desk job suddenly sound awfully good."

She started to think out loud. "I'd better stay clear of Zack's house until tomorrow morning. Whittaker would expect me to run for cover after hearing those news reports."

"You can stay at my house tonight," Jack said.

"Thanks." Liz picked up the phone and called Zack up Their conversation was a brief one. She told him to sit tight that she'd be there in the morning with a statement from O'Dwyer as soon as the arrests were completed. She also told him she loved him, then added teasingly that she thought she'd probably stick around San Francisco for the next four or five decades.

She spent the rest of the day at the office, helping with last-minute paperwork and coordination. She and Jack walked into his living room just as his wife was turning on the evening news. Zack Delaney was the lead story. There was film of his dashing into his house through a gauntlet of shouting reporters, and then, in a sudden switch to live coverage, coming outside to talk to them. Liz thought he looked exhausted. She was frustrated she couldn't be with him and angry with the reporters for continuing to harass him.

He held up his hand, silencing the barrage of questions "Why don't you all leave? Nothing's going to happen here."

"Zack, do you expect to be arrested?"

"I have no comment on that."

"Is it true you were granted immunity from prosecution in return for your testimony on drug use in professional football?"

"I have no comment on that, either."

"But the story in this afternoon's *Times* . . ."

"I have no comment on any of it."

"Do you use cocaine?"

"No. Look, if you guys insist on camping here all night do you want me to order you something to eat? Some pizzas or something?"

There was a moment of embarrassed silence at the generosity of the offer, and then the questions started all over again. "How about amphetamines? Have you ever taken amphetamines?"

"No, Charlie. Do you want the pizza or don't you?"

"I want to know about the Dallas game, Zack. Did you take a payoff to engineer a loss?"

At that point Zack simply shook his head. Pain, disgust, fatigue—his face was eloquent with all of them. "You're going to have to excuse me," he said, and went back inside.

Liz was so angry she felt like throwing something at the television set. "Why did he subject himself to that?" she asked. "If it were up to me, I'd be glad to let them starve."

O'Dwyer's wife Nina gave her a smile. "Your future husband has tons of class. Just think how ashamed they're going to be when they find out the truth."

"Not ashamed enough," Liz muttered.

O'Dwyer patted her on the shoulder. "Don't be so hard on them. They're only trying to do their jobs."

"Well, they can take their jobs and shove them! They're all a bunch of bloodsuckers. Reporters, the public, all of them! They make men into heroes and then delight in cutting them down. For over six years now, Zack Delaney has given everything he has to both football and this city. They love him to pieces, but let him have one lousy game and suddenly they're booing. Let him associate with the wrong kind of woman and suddenly he's a suspected criminal. What ever happened to the phrase 'innocent until proven guilty'? It stinks, Jack!"

"Then it's a good thing he has you in his corner, isn't it, sweetheart?" O'Dwyer teased.

Liz's eyes grew moist. "You'd better believe it."

She and Jack were in the office by six the next morning. The arrests began slightly ahead of schedule, the phones ringing constantly with progress reports. Three hours later, it was over. There had been some long drawn-out standoffs and even some exchange of gunfire, but nobody had been killed or injured.

A pair of the biggest cops Liz had ever seen drove her to Zack's house later that morning. They were very pleased when Liz filled them in on Zack's real role in the case and not without a sense of humor about the whole thing. They turned on their siren full blast about half a mile before they reached his house, tore up the hill and screeched to a halt by the curb in front of his door.

Reporters were once again clustered on the sidewalk. Liz, who wondered if they'd spent the whole damn night there, was so fed up with the situation that she took her DEA badge out of her purse and held it high over her head as she got out of the car. The two cops quickly joined her, muscling reporters out of the way as she marched to the door.

"Are you here to arrest Zack Delaney?" a reporter shouted out.

Liz glared at him. "Don't be ridiculous!"

Her knock was answered by Paul Travers. She was glad Paul was there, glad Zack hadn't been alone all this time. "When did you get here?" she asked.

"Late last night, after the mob finally left." He closed the door and kissed her hello. "Zack's upstairs in the bedroom, talking to Jenny."

"How's he doing?"

"He's fine. Relieved it's almost over, naturally. I understand you're staying in San Francisco. Does that mean what we all assume it means?"

Liz nodded, then smiled. "I knew I'd forgotten something. Here, hold these a moment." She handed him the photocopies of O'Dwyer's statement. It was written on behalf of all the participating agencies and thanked Zack for his "invaluable cooperation under very trying circumstances." It also stressed that at no time had he ever committed any illegal acts. Liz wondered if anybody would have believed it, without the corroborating statements she was about to make.

She fished around in her purse until she found the box with Zack's ring in it. "Do you know I've never even tried this on?" She worked it onto her finger. "A little tight, but it'll do."

Zack walked out of the bedroom just in time to see Liz holding up her hand to the light, admiring the way the ring looked on her finger. Now that the ring was finally where it belonged, he admitted that he wasn't nearly so confident about her marrying him as he'd kept telling himself he was. The past day and a half had been hell, but they would have been a lot worse if she hadn't told him she was staying in San Francisco. Still, he didn't want her to marry him out of a sense of guilt or obligation.

When Liz saw him standing in the upstairs hallway, she took off toward the staircase at top speed, dashed up the steps two at a time and flung herself into his arms. For a long couple of moments they were content just to hold each other close. When they finally drew apart, she smiled at him and teased, "I'm here to rescue you."

He laughed softly. "I'm not about to turn you down. By the way, that's a nice ring you've got on. When's the wedding?"

"The wedding? Oh, you mean *our* wedding. Whenever." She kissed him and then giggled, blissfully happy. "I'm going to be a San Francisco matron. A rich man's wife. I'll probably get fat working behind a desk, so we should have those kids you mentioned very soon, so I can keep in shape chasing them around."

He didn't pick up on her lighthearted mood. "You're sure that's what you want? You're not going public with this and giving up your job because you think you owe it to me for helping you?"

She linked her arm through his and started down the steps. "What can I say, Delaney? It's the least I can do for you."

"That's not a straight answer," Zack pointed out.

"Of course it is," Jenny Travers called from the top of the stairs. "Translation—She loves you and she can't live without you."

Liz looked over her shoulder and gave Jenny a wink. "Listen to your best friend's wife," she advised Zack. "We women understand each other perfectly. After all, I'm pushing thirty. It's time to settle down and help populate the world. You've got great genes and tons of money—everything I require in a husband."

"How flattering," Zack muttered.

Liz sobered. "Okay, then. I love you to distraction and I can't live without you. Everything you said last week was true. My work still matters, but other things matter more. You, a home and a family. I don't know why it took me so long to see that. Maybe I was afraid. Maybe too many people have left me, and my work became the only thing I could rely on." She grinned at him, too happy to stay serious. "I'll tell you what, Delaney. If you give up drugs, gambling and shady women, I'll give up playing dumb blondes for a living."

"Sounds like a good deal to me," Paul called out.

"Me too." Zack smiled at her, looking genuinely happy for the first time in much too long. Then he drew her into his arms and kissed her with lazy thoroughness while Paul and Jenny applauded and whistled.

They walked outside arm-in-arm. Liz handed the copies of O'Dwyer's statement to the nearest reporter and told him to pass them out. For a few seconds, everyone was too busy reading to ask questions.

"My full name is Elizabeth Reynolds Pittman," she said. "That's P-I-T-T-M-A-N." She took out her badge and held it up. "As you can see, I'm actually with the DEA. Mr. Delaney has been working very closely with us on this case. As a matter of fact, I happen to be his fiancée, but that's another story. We'll answer your questions as best we can, but I hope you'll understand that there are things we can't discuss, for legal reasons."

"When's the wedding?" a reporter in front called out. "And where?"

Liz gave Zack a smile. "That one's all yours."

"As soon as possible," he answered. "And as for where..." He smiled the smile that had conquered an entire city, not to mention legions of soda drinkers. "Anywhere but Las Vegas."

There was a round of embarrassed laughter. The press was right where Liz liked to see them, eating out of the palm of his hand. The questions would probably get tougher, but that was okay. If any of them went beyond what Zack could legally talk about, Liz would be the one to refuse comment and take the media's heat. The white hat was back on his head where it belonged, and she had no intention of letting anyone knock it off, ever again.

OFFICIAL SWEEPSTAKES INFORMATION

1. **NO PURCHASE NECESSARY.** To enter, complete the official entry/ order form. Be sure to indicate whether or not you wish to take advantage of our subscription offer.

2. Entry blanks have been pre-selected for the prizes offered. Your response will be checked to see if you are a winner. In the event that these are not claimed, a random drawing will be held from all entries received to award not less than $150,000 in prizes. This is in addition to any free, surprise or mystery gifts which might be offered. Versions of this sweepstakes with different prizes will appear in Torstar Ltd. mailings and their affiliates. Winners selected will receive the prize offered in their sweepstakes insert.

3. This promotion is being conducted under the supervision of Marden-Kane, an independent judging organization. By entering the sweepstakes, each entrant accepts and agrees to be bound by these rules and the decisions of the judges which shall be final and binding. Odds of winning in the random drawing are dependent upon the total number of entries received. Taxes, if any, are the sole responsibility of the prize winners. Prizes are non-transferable. All entries must be received by August 31, 1986.

4. This sweepstakes package offers:

1, Grand Prize	: Cruise around the world on the QEII	$100,000 total value
4, First Prizes	: Set of matching pearl necklace and earrings	$ 20,000 total value
10, Second Prizes	: Romantic Weekend in Bermuda	$ 15,000 total value
25, Third Prizes	: Designer Luggage	$ 10,000 total value
200, Fourth Prizes	: $25 Gift Certificate	$ 5,000 total value
		$150,000

Winners may elect to receive the cash equivalent for the prizes offered.

5. This offer is open to residents of the U.S. and Canada, 18 years and older, except employees of Torstar Ltd., its affiliates, subsidiaries, Marden-Kane and all other agencies and persons connected with conducting this sweepstakes. All Federal, State and local laws apply. Void in the province of Quebec and wherever prohibited or restricted by law. Winners will be notified by mail and may be required to execute an affidavit of eligibility and release which must be returned within 14 days after notification. Canadian winners will be required to answer a skill testing question. Winners consent to the use of their names, photograph and/or likeness for advertising and publicity purposes in conjunction with this and similar promotions without additional compensation. One prize per family or household.

6. For a list of our most current prize winners, send a stamped, self-addressed envelope to: WINNERS LIST, c/o Marden-Kane, P.O. Box 10404, Long Island City, New York 11101.

SSR-A-1

COMING NEXT MONTH

NOBODY'S FOOL—Renee Roszel
Cara never minded a little fun and games... but only on her own terms. So when businessman Martin Dante challenged her to a nine-mile race, she feared the results would be "winner take all!"

THE SECURITY MAN—Dixie Browning
Though Valentine had survived both a bad marriage and an accident that had left her widowed, she wasn't quite ready for her new handsome neighbor. Val couldn't risk loving, but with Cody it was all too tempting.

YESTERDAY'S LIES—Lisa Jackson
Iron willed and proud, Tory was not about to be manipulated, especially not by Trask McFadden. The attractive young senator had deceived her in the past—could he convince her that this time his love was real?

AFTER DARK—Elaine Camp
Sebastian was a man haunted by the past. Everly was a woman determined to control her future. Now he was back to reclaim her heart. Could she be convinced of the healing power of love?

MAGIC SEASON—Anne Lacey
Independence was her trademark and Game Warden Laura Marchand kept her image with spit and polish. But sportsman Ryan D'Arco was hunting her territory and was about to capture her heart.

LESSONS LEARNED—Nora Roberts
Juliet could smell success when she was assigned to do the publicity tour for Italy's most famous chef. But Carlo distracted her with his charms, setting his romantic recipes simmering in her heart.

AVAILABLE NOW: